Crow Dark Dawn

Crow Dark Dawn

Tales from the city and far away

David Greygoose

Crow Dark Dawn

Text copyright©2023 David Greygoose
Cover image: Lady of the Harbour by Alice Lenkiewicz

ISBN 978-1-7393239-2-9

British Library Cataloguing in Publication Data.
A catalogue record for this book is available from the British Library.

1 3 5 4 2

First Published in Great Britain
Hawkwood Books 2023

Printed and bound in Great Britain by CPI Group (UK) Ltd.
Croydon CR0 4YY

HB

For
F.A.N.

Acknowledgements

Thanks to Eleanor Rees for listening to all of these tales as they evolved and offering invaluable advice, support and direction; to Jody Ward for his dream of the Night Butcher; and to Ellis Delmonte for unwavering enthusiasm, dedication and understanding.

Cover art: *Lady of the Harbour* by Alice Lenkiewicz.

The Farmer and the Field of Dust first appeared in *Ink Pantry* magazine.

Contents

THE ROOTS OF THE RAIN

Everything moved slowly, sleeping in the dust of decay. The beetle as it crawled to the top of an overgrown wall. The rat as it stirred in its hole. The damp hanging dull as an unopened curtain, muffling the sound from the river.

And the ocean which waited still and silent to spill out its cargo of half-recalled truths. Or lurch back to steal the dreams of the city, though no-one would notice as they stumbled on – the butchers asleep in their killing sheds, blood congealed around their thighs. The lovers aloft near the chimney tops, stifling the breath of their sighs.

And in the streets the slow waiting, the shuffling, the dawdling, the calling of voices with nothing to say until they faded away into the tunnels deep beneath, into the roots of the rain.

THE FARMER and the FIELD OF DUST

There was once a farmer who ploughed a field of dust. Each day as he raked and hoed, the dust billowed all around him until he was the colour of dust, his face, his hands, his clothes.

At night his house was filled with dust. Dust covered his table, the cupboards, the floor. Even his bed was dry with dust. Each morning as he woke, all he had dreamt was dust, fields of dust and hills of dust, barns stacked high with nothing but dust. Then he rose and shook the dust from his pillow, from his sheets, from the curtain which covered the window to block out the dusty sun.

Each night when his work was done, he sat down to eat a bowl of food. But the food was dry. It looked like dust. It tasted of dust. Beside him on the table lay a wooden flute, and when he had finished his meal, the farmer would blow the dust away and then he would sit and play. The tune was fresh and clear, sweet as water running. And the farmer would smile and gaze through the window stained with dust as if he was remembering.

But next morning he returned to the field again. The field of dust, the field where nothing grew. And he would set to ploughing and raking and hoeing and the dust would rise around him all over again.

Then one day he saw the shadow of a traveller approaching through the dust. A stranger in a long grey coat who stopped to ask the way. The farmer pointed on along the road and the traveller thanked him and was about to take his leave. But then he paused.

"Tell me, what do you grow here?" he asked.

"Nothing," said the farmer. "Nothing grows here at all. Every year I plough the dust, I rake it and I hoe. And then I plant the seeds. But nothing ever grows. Nothing at all."

The traveller shook his head and put his hand into his pocket. From the very depths of the lining he brought one red seed.

"I can give you this," he said. "And I promise you it will grow. It will yield the finest crop that you have ever seen."

"Yes, yes," said the farmer, about to grab the seed, but the traveller closed his hand.

"Wait," he said. "First you must give me something in return."

"Anything," said the farmer. "Anything at all."

The traveller scratched his chin.

"This seed is precious to me," he said. "So you must give me something that is precious to you in return. What can you give me?"

The farmer spread his hands in despair.

"I am only a poor farmer. My crops fail year after year. All I have is the clothes that I stand in."

The traveller gazed at him with piercing eyes.

"Nothing at all?" He put his hand back in his pocket. "Then I will keep the seed."

The traveller was about to make his way down the road when the farmer stopped him.

"Wait!" he said. "There is something."

The traveller turned.

"Tell me more."

"I have a flute..." The farmer's words came tumbling out. "I have a flute, it sounds so clear, sweet as the wind in springtime."

"This flute I would like to see," said the traveller.

And so the farmer took the traveller to his house and there he showed him the flute. Then the traveller smiled and gave him the seed, tucked the flute into his bag and soon was on his way.

Next day the farmer dug a hole in the ground right in the very middle of his field, just as the traveller had told him. And then he planted the bright red seed. Covered it over with dry grey dust and sprinkled it with what little water he had. And then he waited. He waited and he waited, day after day in the dust and the sun. But nothing happened. Nothing happened at all. At night he would sit and eat his meal which tasted of dust and slept in his sheets which felt like dust and dreamt of his flute which sounded so clear, sweet as the wind in springtime. The flute which he could play no more.

Next day and next he returned to the field, but still nothing had happened. Nothing happened at all. All was grey dust, just as before. But then one day, a shoot. A tiny green shoot peeking up from the ground. The farmer was overjoyed. He rushed to his house to fetch water and when he returned the shoot had grown even more. When he saw this, the farmer danced all about the tender shoot and sang the song he once played on his flute so that the air blew sweet and cool.

Day by day the shoot grew and grew until it was a firm green stem, and then a bud sprouted at its top. One morning the farmer left his house and tramped across the field until there in the middle he saw that the bud had become a flower, the brightest flower he had ever seen! The farmer sprinkled water on its petals that glowed so red and golden. He watched as the sun rose higher in the sky and spread its rays across the field of flat grey dust. But at the moment when the sun struck the petals of the flower, to the farmer's astonishment it burst into flames. He tried to douse them with the last of the water in his can, but to no avail. The flames licked higher, brighter and hotter so that the farmer had to move away.

And then from the centre of the fire stepped a woman. The most beautiful woman he had ever seen. She wore a robe the colour of flame, red and golden as the flower's petals, though the flower lay burnt and blackened now on the flat grey dust as the woman followed the farmer all the way back to his house.

They sat together at his table and the farmer asked the woman many questions, but each time she answered only with a smile, and spoke slowly in a language of another land that he did not understand. And then she sang to him, humming the tune that he had played on his harp, the tune he sang to the flower. And the woman laughed, and the farmer laughed too and every day they worked together to clean the house and tend the fields, though some nights the farmer wished he still had his flute so that he could play for her.

But then he shook his head and remembered that if the traveller had not taken the flute, then he would not have the seed. And without the seed there would have been no flower and without the flower the woman would never be here at all.

And if the woman had not been here, the seeds which they planted in the fields would never have begun to grow. For grow they did. They grew to give fine crops of corn which the farmer took to sell in the market. Every night when he returned, a sumptuous supper was set on the table and the house which once had been grey with dust now stood sparkling and clean.

But one day when the farmer came home, the woman was lying in the bed. There was no supper on the table and dust had already gathered on the shelves and across the floor.

Each day the woman grew more listless, her tired face pale against the bright red and gold of her robe. Even though the crops in the fields still grew higher, the farmer was sad. The woman no longer smiled at him, they no longer laughed together and she did not sing the song to the tune he had once played on his flute.

One morning he left her lying in bed and went down to the field to tend the crop. He hoed a little, picking out stones, but his heart was not in his task. He straightened his back and peered down the road. In the distance he saw a shadow, a figure coming closer. Not many passed this way and so the farmer waited to see who it was.

It was the traveller. The farmer greeted him.

"I see you still have the flute," he said, for it was sticking out from the traveller's bag.

The traveller hauled it out.

"I still have the flute," he nodded, "but it is useless now. The wood is cracked and no notes will come. I could never learn even one tune. But I see your fields have yielded a great crop. My seed has done its work!"

The farmer agreed. "The seed has brought me all that I

5

wished for."

"Then why look so sad?" the traveller exclaimed.

The farmer paused.

"I wish I had the flute again. It is no good to you, now that it is cracked. Let me take it back."

The traveller looked at the flute and considered.

"I will give you the flute if you return the woman to me."

The farmer dropped his hoe in surprise.

"How do you know of the woman?"

"It was I who gave you the seed, remember? And the seed has done its work..."

The farmer scratched his chin and looked at the flute, looked at his crops, then looked at the flute again.

"The woman is sick," he said at last. "She cannot sing."

"You should have told me," the traveller cried. "Take me to her straight away."

The traveller followed the farmer across the field all the way back to the house. There the woman lay in bed. She scarce raised her head when they walked in. The traveller took her hand and began to talk to her in the language the farmer did not understand. She tried to smile, but as the traveller stared into her eyes, her hands turned to fine grey dust and then her face and soon her body too.

The traveller shook his head and walked away, leaving the broken flute lying on the table. As soon as he stepped through the door, the crops in the fields all withered and died and soon the soil returned to dust.

The house filled with dust. Dust covered the tables, the cupboards, the floor. Each night the farmer slept in a bed of dust, though he knew that once the dust had been woman, had been flame, had been flower, had been seed. But now all was gone and the dust had returned and the farmer sat each day in his flat grey fields and coaxed the tune from his broken flute that once he had sung together with the woman he would always remember. The woman he could never forget.

GROB

They came there as the sky was darkening, as thin snow began to fall, and piled their few possessions in the dim-lit entrance hall. Lummenmilk peered into the gloom, while Skintle fumbled in his pockets, then she frowned and narrowed her eyes.

"Don't tell me you've lost the key."

Skintle bit his lip and shuffled his feet then stuck his hand inside his coat and drew it out. The key sat rusted and cold on the flat of his hand. Lummenmilk pulled her shawl about her shoulders.

"If only I had a coat," she said.

Skintle slowly gathered up their bags.

"In time," he said, "in time. The last shillen that we had, we paid to Gruenskilly for this room."

Lummenmilk bit her tongue and picked up the rest of the bags and set off to follow him up the stairs. They paused at each landing, each one more dimly lit, each one thick with dust which seemed to have lain for years. Behind closed doors they heard mutterings and wailings, beatings and screaming, laughter and blows. Lummenmilk stopped and shook her head, but Skintle just shrugged and shouldered the bags.

"Better than that basement," he muttered.

They hauled their belongings to the top landing. Lummenmilk paused and peered down at the dim outline of the city, a clutter of rooftops and half-lit streets. Skintle fumbled with the key again then turned it with a flourish in the door, which he pushed slowly open.

The small room harboured a smell which lingered of old cooking and the dank mist which pressed against the windows, smothering everything with its moist damp chill.

They heaved their bags inside, then hugged one another.

Next night they returned, tired and worn. Lummenmilk

worked all day in the laundry, washing other people's clothes, though she scarce had any of her own. Skintle swept the pickings down by the docks and then cleaned the windows of folk who had something to look out on. They met on the stairs and tramped up together from the last landing through the shadowy dusk, ready to fall into each other's arms and sleep awhile and forget to eat or forget there was no food to be eaten.

Skintle slipped his key into the door, but to his surprise found it already open. Lummenmilk let out a gasp as they saw a small hunched man sitting on a stool before the fire which he had already stoked high.

"Who are you?" they cried, "and what are you doing here?"

"I live here," the old man replied. "Always lived here."

"But Gruenskilly told us the room was empty. Gave us the key. We gave her money we worked hard to save."

"I live here," the man repeated. "Always lived here. People come and people go. But I still live here. No-one minds."

"Does Gruenskilly know?" Lummenmilk demanded.

The old man shrugged and smiled.

"Would you like some tea?" he asked.

Lummenmilk glanced over and saw he had a pot already brewing on the hob. Skintle loosened his boots and removed his cap. He took a slurp of the tea.

"It's good," he said, grudgingly.

The old man nodded and Lummenmilk nodded too, letting the shawl fall loose from her shoulders as she warmed herself in the glow of the fire. Then there was a pause. They all looked at each other.

"What's your name?" Lummenmilk asked.

"I'm Grob," the man said.

"And what do you do?"

He looked at them squint-eyed.

"I'm a rat-catcher," he said and suddenly sprang from his stool to pounce on a shadow that scurried from the corner. He held it aloft, its tail still snaking. And then he broke its neck.

Lummenmilk stared at Grob as he slipped the twitching

rodent into the bowels of his sack.

Next day and next, Gob would be there. Each night when Lummenmilk and Skintle returned he would be sitting on the stool, in front of a fire already lit, with a pot of tea brewing on the hob.

The young couple muttered darkly in the corner of the kitchen.

"He cannot stay here..."

"But he comes and goes..."

"He must have a key..."

"He listens to our lummen..."

"No - he sleeps soundly..."

"He cannot stay here..."

"Where would he go?..."

"You'll have to tell him..."

"Not me..."

"Not me..."

"He says that Gruenskilly has said he can stay here..."

"He has a key..."

"... I would miss his tea."

Both of them nodded.

"We'd both miss his tea..."

Some nights there would be more than tea. A jug of milk, some onions for the pot. Bundles of twigs to build up the fire. And coal. Dark dusty nuggets of coal.

"Where do you get them?" Lummenmilk asked.

Grob said nothing.

Grob just smiled.

"How can you afford it?"

Grob shrugged.

"Do you filch them?" Skintle demanded.

Grob shook his head.

Lummenmilk was cold. Always cold. Shivering in her shawl

despite the fire which Grob lit. But then one night Skintle watched her climbing the stairs. In the flickering light he could see that she wore the shawl no more. About her shoulders she clutched a long heavy coat. She smiled at her husband and kissed him quickly on the cheek as she pushed past into the light and warmth of the room. She slipped off the coat and hung it from a hook behind the door.

Skintle would not look at her. He stood and stared at the coat. Then he turned.

"Where did you get this?"

Lummenmilk gazed down at her rain-sodden shoes. And then she looked up.

"Bullmass owns the laundry. He gave it to me."

"We cannot afford it."

"It was a gift," she replied. "No-one has asked you to pay. It's not new..."

She pointed to where the sleeve was worn.

"Somebody left it. Bullmass had seen how cold I was, wearing only the shawl. He said I could have it..."

Skintle scowled and refused the cup of tea which Grob held out to him, then stamped off down the stairs.

Grob shrugged.

"He's forgotten his own coat," Lummenmilk remarked, settling down beside the fire.

Some nights Lummenmilk would scamper home, quickly as she could, to be sure to be there before Skintle. She would pull open the door of the chamber in the corner, no bigger than a cupboard with just enough space to fit one double bed. Grob could not see her there as she slid a ring from her finger or a bracelet from her wrist, scarcely stopping to admire it before slipping it into a box. And slipping the box beneath the floorboards in the shadows under the bed. And sitting quickly on the stool beside the fire while Grob winked at her and held out a cup of steaming tea.

Then Skintle would come home and Lummenmilk would kiss him and fuss over him and he would not even look at the coat which he mentioned no more, hanging on the back of the door.

But one night she came home and stamped the snow from a new pair of boots and headed straight past Grob and closed the bedchamber door. She scrabbled quickly in the dust and the shadows to lift up the floorboard and pull out the box. And open the lid. She was about to slip a new necklace inside when she stopped to count all the rings she'd collected.

"One... two... three... four... five....."

One for each finger, yes. But there should be one more.

She counted again. One of the rings was missing. She shoved the necklace into the box and hastily shut it away. She opened the door and stared at Grob as he sat by the fire, prodding at the glowing coals.

"Grob...?" she said slowly.

But said nothing and just at that moment Skintle walked through the door. Lummenmilk paused, glaring at Grob, then rushed over to greet her husband and brush the snow from his coat. Grob turned his back on them both and warmed his knees by the fire.

Then came a knocking at the door. Lummenmilk and Skintle stopped and looked at each other. Grob did not move. The knocking came again. Then a voice.

"You in there?"

It was Gruenskilly.

Skintle turned pale.

Gruenskilly knocked again, harder this time, like it was her shoe hammering against the flimsy slats of the door.

"I know you're in there," she screeched. "I can hear you... Open the door!"

Skintle paused a moment and looked at Lummenmilk, then crossed the room and turned the key.

Gruenskilly stood there, filling the frame.

"Where is the rent?"

She stepped inside.

"The rent is late."

She rapped massive knuckles on the tabletop.

"The rent is late," she said again.

Lummenmilk looked at Skintle.

"You told me you'd paid it," she hissed.

"I... I..." Skintle began to stutter.

Grob slipped another lump of coal on the fire and slurped at his tea.

"You... said we needed pillows," Skintle mumbled.

Lummenmilk shook her head.

"Need lots of things," she whispered.

"I need my rent," Gruenskilly thundered. "You're three days late. If you don't pay me come this time tomorrow, you're out − both of you."

Lummenmilk and Skintle glanced over at Grob. Grob remained silent and turned back again to stare at the fire.

The door slammed.

Gruenskilly had gone.

"This time tomorrow..."

Her words still hung in the room.

Next night Skintle was the first to come home. He sat by the fire, his face pale, his hands shaking.

"What can we do?" he asked Grob, who passed him a cracked cup of stewed tea. "I tried everyone, I asked them. Said I'd clean their windows twice over and more. They all shook their heads. No-one said anything. Loudest sound in the world is the shaking of a head..."

Grob stoked the coals. He did not reply.

Skintle sat up quickly. He heard footsteps on the stairs.

"It's her..." he whispered.

But not Gruenskilly. It was Lummenmilk who opened the door. It was Lummenmilk who slowly took off her coat, then plunged her hand into the pocket and tipped a pile of coin onto the table.

Skintle stared.

"Count it," she said.

Skintle sifted the coins with trembling fingers.

"It is the rent..." he breathed slowly.

Lummenmilk nodded.

"It is the rent," she said. "Not food. Not coal. It is the rent..."

"How...?" Skintle asked.

Lummenmilk said nothing, slipped into the bedchamber and closed the door behind her. Grob hunched his shoulders and poked at the fire, just as Gruenskilly rapped loud on the door.

Next night Lummenmilk rushed quickly up the stairs, her hands deep in her pockets, pushing past Grob who did not even look at her as she closed the bedchamber door. She crouched down and lifted the board beneath the bed. She drew out the box then prized open the lid before tipping in a pendant carved in the shape of a bull. Before counting the rings again.

"One... two..."

Now only three.

She closed the door and took her seat before the fire. Grob sat opposite her, staring into the flames. She shuffled her feet. She coughed softly, then louder.

"Grob..." she said at last.

Grob turned.

"I'm sorry," he said. "Would you like a cup of tea?"

"No," said Lummenmilk firmly. "I want..."

The door opened.

Skintle stood shivering, shaking the rain from his coat.

Lummenmilk smiled quickly, then turned to Grob.

"Yes, of course," she said, "of course I want a cup of tea. And one for Skintle too. Poor man, he looks like a drowned rat."

Grob nodded, tilting the pot.

"Drowned a whole bucketful of rats today," he said. "Tipped them in the cut."

Skintle sniffed, clutching his tea and the three of them sat in silence, staring into the flames.

Under the sink. At the back of an ancient clock which told no time at all. Inside a crack in the wainscot. In the dull shadow of dust on top of the dresser. She tried them all, squeezing the secret of her trinkets into the darkest corners she could find. But someone else found them too. Next day they were gone, same as before. And she couldn't ask Grob, for what would he say? What would he ask her about how she came by all of this finery? And wouldn't Skintle want to know too?

So Lummenmilk said nothing. Didn't even ask when Grob brought home a cut of meat, a loaf of bread, a fist of tatties. Sacks of coal.

"How does he pay for it?" Skintle pondered.

Lummenmilk just shrugged.

"Don't ask him," she said. "Must pay well, catching rats."

Skintle frowned and nodded.

"They're everywhere," he said. "There's rats everywhere you look."

Lummenmilk came home early one afternoon, straining slowly up every stair, one hand on the small of her back as the other gripped the rail. As she opened the door she heard a scurry from the bedchamber. She caught her breath and clutched her skirt, but then Grob scuttled out.

"Thought there was a rat," he said. "Thought there was a rat under the floorboard..."

But Lummenmilk did not respond. Just slumped into the chair. Her face was pale, her forehead sweating. Grob scurried about her.

"Are you sick?" he asked. "Are you ill? Would you like tea...?"

Lummenmilk waved him away.

"Worse than that," she muttered. "Bullmass says I am a stupid girl. Says that I am foolish. Says I'm not to come back to the laundry no more..."

Grob handed her a slop of his tepid brew.

"Why would he say this? What could you have done? You work so hard. He treats you well..."

Grob glanced towards the bedchamber's open door, the

floorboard still askew.

"Nothing I have done," she said. "Nothing at all..."

The cup slipped from her shaking fingers and she placed one hand upon her swollen waist.

Every morning Lummenmilk spat a thin gruel of sick into a chipped bowl. Every night Skintle came home and there was no cut of meat, no loaf, no tatties. No coal for the fire.

He glared at Grob.

"Don't know what good there is you being here if you don't bring nothing like you used to do."

Grob glanced at Lummenmilk. Lummenmilk turned away, clutching at her back as her eyes flitted about the room, staring under the sink, then at the clock and the crack in the wainscot before gazing up at the top of the dresser.

Grob shrugged.

"No rats round here no more. Must have done my job too good."

"Best you look further then," Skintle muttered. "Best you go look up by the laundry."

He glowered at Lummenmilk.

"*She* always told us there was plenty of rats up there."

But Lummenmilk pulled the shawl around her shoulders and stared into the empty grate.

In the ache of the evenings and the long cold nights, Lummenmilk paced. And Skintle paced too, one step behind her, turn and turn about. Up and down the room while Grob squatted on a stool in the corner, peering out at the lone white cup of the moon.

"Soon come," he muttered. "Come soon."

But Lummenmilk wailed and gritted her teeth and paced again, walking the darkness away.

"Twill come this night," Grob comforted

"Said that the night before." Lummenmilk squeezed out the words.

"And if it does not come this night, why then will come on the morrow," Grob declared and turned away to stare at the stars, like as if they were the eyes of rats, all waiting to be caught.

Lummenmilk paced out the dog-end of that night and into a cold bleak morn. Sudden her waters broke and she leant on Skintle's shoulder as they hobbled to the bed. There she lay, breathing heavily, biting back her screaming, gripping her husband's arm as he swabbed her forehead while Grob squatted hunched at the end of the bed, bidding her to pant, to push, to raise her knees, till the cry came at last and the blood and the cord to be cut and the afterbirth.

Then Skintle and Grob sat side by side and looked at the child who wailed and clutched as Lummenmilk held him soft to her breast.

"Morrow," she said as she cradled the child and pushed strands of sweat-matted hair from her eyes. "He did not come at night, for now is the morning... and so his name is Morrow."

MORROW

Grob hobbled quickly through the shadowy back streets with young Morrow scampering alongside.

"Where are we going?" asked the boy.

Grob shot him a wearied glance.

"Rats," he muttered. "We got to find rats."

"Why rats?" Morrow complained. "Was rats yesterday. Can't we find something else today? Can't we catch cats or foxes? Can't we find a bear?"

Grob cuffed his ear.

"Ain't no bears here, Morrow. Now hush your mouth and listen."

Morrow stood still.

In the distance was flower-sellers calling and a rattle of barrels rolled down a flight of steps. But close by was a rustle and a scurrying. And Grob's gloved hand shot out to catch a squirming fist of matted fur, then plunged it into his sack.

"Will we go to the canal again?" Morrow asked him.

"Yes - we will, when the bag is full."

"Can I catch the next one?"

"Watch, and I'll learn you."

Morrow watched.

He watched the flicker of a shadow of a dock leaf next to a litter of soil scuffed out about a hole down by the base of a damp brick wall. Watched Grob plant a snivel of broken biscuit close by in the dirt. Watched the dock leaf quiver. Then a pause longer than the hunger which turned in his belly like an unloved stone.

"Now..." Grob instructed, his voice a rasping whisper.

Morrow pounced, just as he had seen Grob do himself.

Then Morrow's shriek as the creature writhed and wriggled between his fingers till Grob caught hold of it and broke its neck with an expert snap. And dropped it into his sack.

"I wanted to do that," Morrow protested. "I wanted to put it into the sack."

"Caught it, didn't you?" Grob gave him a grudging wink. "Near as quick as me."

"It were squirming."

"But you held it."

"Can I put the next one in the sack?"

Grob nodded, distracted, his own sharp nose sniffing about, his rheumy eyes peering this way and that.

Morrow tugged at him again.

"Can I put the sack in the cut?"

Grob ignored him.

"Don't talk when I'm working."

"But I like the way it goes splash!"

"I'll put *you* in the cut if you don't stop your jabbering."

But then the old man ruffled young Morrow's hair and they walked on together between the tall gaunt walls of the warehouse buildings, down towards the canal.

They sat together under the bridge and watched ripples slowly eddying outwards from where Morrow had flung the sack into the flat dull water.

"Gone now," Grob grunted, about to get up.

"Where do they go?" asked Morrow.

"Down to the bottom."

"Do they ever come back?"

Grob shook his head.

"Nothing comes back," he said.

Morrow frowned for a moment as the sun caught his eyes.

"Not even the man and the woman?"

Grob spat slowly into the water.

"What man and woman?"

"The man and the woman you told me of," Morrow replied. "The man and the woman who used to live in our room."

Grob said nothing, staring into the water as if he was gazing into a fire.

"They're gone," he said at last.

"Where did they go?"

Grob shrugged.

"I don't know. They just went out one morning to work. Her to the laundry. Him to pick up scrats down by the docks. Left me to mind you, same as I always did. Sat there come evening, listening out for the sound of them traipsing up the stairs. That was when I'd always tell you, 'Listen you can hear them coming...' And you'd sit there and clap your hands till they walked through the door. But that night they didn't..."

"Where did they go?" Morrow asked again.

Grob shook his head.

"Don't know... I don't know."

They walked back slowly, Morrow waiting dutifully as Grob stopped for people who would call him over and speak to him urgently, give him directions and point and nod.

"Everyone knows you," said Morrow, taking the old man's hand again.

"They got to know me," Grob replied. "I'm important."

"What's 'important'?" Morrow frowned.

"They need me," said Grob.

"What for?"

"I catch rats," Grob reminded him. "Everyone got rats. That's why they need me. Fast as I catch'em they always come back. Hundreds of 'em. Thousands. Every hole in the ground got a rat in it."

Grob paused. Stooped down suddenly to a gap in the wall and slipped his hand inside, then turned to Morrow and winked.

"Twenty or more."

"Won't they bite you?" Morrow asked.

Grob withdrew his hand.

"No," he said and shook his head. "Never bite you when there's that many. Too busy trying to bite each other. When there's just one – that one'll be dangerous, caught in a hole. That one'll bite your hand!"

He pulled off one glove and pressed his fingers suddenly against the boy's face. Morrow saw again that the old man had one finger shorter at the tip. He looked at his own fingers, and wriggled them carefully.

"Will I have fingers like that?" he asked.

Grob ruffled his hair again.

"One day you will, lad."

"Will that make me 'portant like you?"

Grob paused and gazed towards the setting sun which was sinking slowly behind the harbour.

"We'll see, Morrow, we'll see..."

The sky was darkening. The air smelt of a rain that wanted to fall yet would not. Grob took Morrow by the shoulder, leading him on through the twisted streets.

"Where we going now?" Morrow demanded.

Grob pursed his lips.

"Mayhap find more rats."

"Thought you said we were finished. Thought you said we were going home."

They turned another corner and stopped beside a doorway. From inside came the heavy smell of wet linen and yellow soap. Then came the sound of voices raised from an alleyway that sloped down the side of the building. A man's voice deep and baleful. Roaring. A young woman pitiful, pleading. Then she ran out, a flurry of dishevelled petticoats. Morrow stared at her face, the eyes bewildered, tears scalding. Then the man. A massive man built stocky and stubborn. He bellowed after the young woman as she fled. Grob pulled Morrow away.

"Come," he said. "Let us go."

Morrow said nothing for a while. Then he stopped.

"I do not think I like that man," he declared. "I do not think he is good."

Grob shook his head. He paused a while, rummaging in his pocket while Morrow stared at him. Eventually he fished out a thin silver chain which twisted slowly and shivered in the glistening rain which had begun to fall. Morrow reached out to touch it. At the end of the chain hung a pendant, carved in the shape of a bull.

"What is it?" he asked.

Grob shrugged, gathered up the chain and pressed it into Morrow's hand.

"It's for you..."

TAMARIND

Early morning in the city square, just as the sun slanted low, an old woman would come each day and scatter bread around the fountain. Soon as she did so, the birds would come, sparrows and starlings, pigeons and crows, swooping and squabbling, fluttering and squawking, picking and pecking for every last crumb.

Some mornings children would be there too, waiting for the woman to come scurrying along, then they'd tug at her coat, begging for the bread before the birds could even arrive. And she would smile and break the crusts and share them out between the clamouring hands. But the birds would come all the same, pouncing for the crumbs till the children chased them, flapping their arms like they were birds themselves, then leaping into the fountain, laughing and shrieking as the tumbling water soaked through their raggedy clothes.

When they were gone and the birds were gone and the old woman had tottered away, pulling her shawl around her shoulders, then the silence would return. And through the silence the doctor would come with his heavy black bag. The doctor would come and slip his hand absent-mindedly into his pocket and pull out a coin, always shiny. And he would leave it there on the wall round the edge of the fountain, which was still slippery with water from where the children had played.

And then he would walk away. Sometimes a child would return and grab the coin, and sometimes a shadowy figure scurrying from the alleyway. But most times a jackdaw would swoop down and pluck it up and carry it to a window high in the corner of the square.

Tamarind sat at the window each day, watching the street below, watching the woman who left the bread, watching the children come and go. Watching the birds which swooped and swirled. Waiting for the jackdaw to land on her ledge and drop one bright coin into her outstretched hand. And then she would turn back into the shadows of the room and place the coin in a jar on the table.

After a moment she would return to her board, propped up in the corner. All day long she painted pictures of dancers in a village wearing bright robes streaked with scarlet and saffron, their faces hidden by masks shaped like owls. As each picture was finished she hung it on the wall till the room itself seemed to be dancing. And then Tamarind lay on her bed and watched the colours swirl and imagined that she was back in the village again, just as she had been when she was a girl.

But she never went out. Never left the room. She grew flowers in her window box and filled vases with the blooms and would sit there on her bed and watch the bees come and go, bringing the pollen, seeking out the sweet nectar

As Tamarind drifted and dreamed, there came a knock at the door. She gathered her robe around herself and rose to let in a tall man, the doctor carrying his heavy black bag which he placed on the table and opened.

Tamarind smiled as he brought out a bowl of food which he set before her, and watched in silence while she ate. Then he moved carefully about the room, lighting scented candles which filled the air with a sweet heavy smoke. He produced a bottle of tincture and slipped one silver spoonful into Tamarind's waiting mouth.

They sat a while, looking at each other and then not looking at all as Tamarind slipped from her robe and lay down upon the bed. The doctor slowly took off his clothes and lay still beside her. They did not touch but lay side by side and watched the purple smoke drift about the room. Tamarind stared at her paintings and imagined again she was dancing, back in the village which had been home.

Shadows slid across the windowsill as the sound of muffled voices drifted up from the street below. A single bee floated into the room and touched the petals of an orchid. Then Tamarind sat up and the doctor too.

"Did you find the doll to bring me?" she asked.

The doctor shook his head.

Tamarind turned away.

"Every day I am weary. My body has no strength. I sit on my bed with no will to go out and when dusk falls my limbs shiver and ache. I will not be well until I find the doll," she whispered.

The doctor was buttoning his shirt.

"Tell me again, what does this doll look like?" he asked politely.

"I have told you," said Tamarind, slipping on her robe. "It looks like this." She gestured towards her paintings. "It is a wooden doll wearing long striped robes and the mask of an owl."

The doctor smiled.

"I have not seen it," he said. "It is the medicine that will make you well, not a doll. I will come again."

He moved towards the door.

"Wait," said Tamarind, "I have not paid you."

And she took one coin from the jar on the table. The doctor slipped it into his pocket, picked up his bag and left.

The doctor did not come on his appointed day. Another day passed and another day more. Tamarind watched for him from her window. She watched the old woman feeding the birds. She watched the children fighting for crusts. She waited for the jackdaw who brought her coins from the fountain, but he did not come. And there was no sign of the doctor at all.

Tamarind whispered to the birds on the ledge:

"Bring me food. I am hungry. See what you can find for me..."

But all they ever brought was crumbs and Tamarind was more hungry than she ever knew. And still the doctor did not come. At dusk her limbs began to shake and she ached for the balm of his medicine. She imagined she could still smell the incense he would bring, wafting around the room. She even cast her robe aside and lay down on the bed, just as she would do when he was here. But it was not the same.

She fell to staring at her pictures which hung all about the walls. The garish colours, the dark jagged lines, swirling round and around. And the doll. She painted pictures of the doll she had lost. Its long bright robe, its twisted owl mask. The doll which slept with her every night when she was a child. The doll which shared her every dream. She dreamt of it now as she lay on the bed.

At first she cradled it like a baby. But then it took her hand and led her away to a clear flowing stream where they dipped their toes in the water. Then along a path through the forest. And then they came to a cave. Tamarind shivered but the doll led her inside. And there in the shadows stood a man.

The man was the doctor. Tamarind sat up with a start. Dusk had fallen. She looked all about as she pulled her robe around her shoulders. But there was nobody there.

Still the doctor had not come. She had no food. She had no medicine, though she could taste it in her mouth. Cantaloupe, jezebel and comfrey. It made her body feel alive. But the doctor had not come.

She was hungry. She was cold. She pulled her robe close about her and gathered up a fistful of coins from the jar then quietly opened the door. The well of the stairway swam darkly below her. She touched her toe to each step in turn as she clutched the banister rail.

In the street the colours seemed brighter than she remembered. The screeching of children chasing a ball. The baying of a dog in the alleyway. The clatter of market traders closing up their stalls.

Tamarind rushed from one to another, her hands outstretched.

"Food..." she implored.

They turned away, thinking she was a beggar come out at dusk. She thrust a hand in the pocket of her flowing green robe and produced the bright shining coins. One man looked at her kindly as he stacked his empty baskets.

"I have nothing left," he said. Then peered closer at the coins she was offering.

He shook his head.

"I could not take these anyway. Nobody will take them."

Tamarind stared at the glinting coins.

"They are not of this region," the man explained.

Tamarind looked puzzled.

"But they are from *my* region," she said.

"Where did you get them?" the man asked, tossing a broken basket onto his cart.

Tamarind looked all around, suddenly frightened. And hungrier still.

"A jackdaw brought them," she said at last, then turned and ran with her head down till she lost herself in the shadows.

She came to a house filled with candles at the end of a long silent street. She stood outside, peering through the open windows. Light spilled out all around and she could see the guests wearing long robes streaked with scarlet and saffron, their faces covered with owl masks. They danced slowly, without speaking, swaying to gentle music played on long bamboo pipes.

Tamarind was drawn towards the music. It was *her* music, the music she remembered from the village long ago. She climbed the steps and slipped inside, mingling with the dancers who took no notice of her, even though she wore no mask. She edged her way into the main room where the musicians squatted in the corner. On low tables, bowls of rice were set next to the flickering candles.

Tamarind's body curved to the rhythms and she slipped back and forth between the dancers, her eyes closed now, remembering how she danced like this at dusk back in the village. But not like this, she realised as she bumped into one graceful dancer then another, stumbling between them, knocking into a vase. Not like this at all, she realised. It had been so many years. She had forgotten the steps.

The musicians glanced at each other, then began to play

faster. Tamarind spun around, trying to keep up. But then slow again, and slower still. Two dancers moved in on her, gesturing. Suddenly everyone could see that she wore no mask, that her robe was green not brightly streaked.

They made a lunge at her as the music played on, faster now and louder. But Tamarind slipped past them, dodging their outstretched hands. And seized up a bowl of rice as she went, scurrying out of the door. And away. Back down the silent grey street. After a while she slowed and turned around. Nobody followed. At the end of the street the house stood tall, the candles blazing brighter than ever before. The music swirling louder. And laughter now and cheering. But nobody came. And Tamarind continued on her way, carefully clutching the bowl of white rice so as not to spill a single grain.

She climbed the narrow stairs to her attic room. When she reached the top she saw that the door stood open. She thought nothing of it, remembering that she had left in such a hurry, and walked inside to place the bowl on the table.

And then she saw, sitting in her chair, a woman who looked much like her. Hair long and dark, spilling over a flowing green robe. In her lap, the doll. The doll wearing an owl mask and dressed in cloth streaked saffron and scarlet. The doll that Tamarind lost when she was a child.

The woman looked up.

Tamarind stared at her.

"Ulula," she said at last. "You are Ulula."

The woman smiled.

"You remember me," she replied. "We played together in the village. We hid in the trees and made pies in the mud then threw them all at the boys..."

But Tamarind was staring at the doll.

Ulula smiled.

"Yes," she said, "it was me who took it. The night you made eyes at my brother and twined flowers in his hair. He led you away, I remember, to the cave by the waterfall. I thought you had found what you wanted. I thought you were done with dolls."

Tamarind looked at her and her eyes filled with sadness.

"Your brother was soon done with me," she said. "We walked hand-in-hand down the path to the cave. But then when we got there, my own sister was waiting, with her pretty mouth and her pretty fingers which pulled him away from me. He told me to go home then. So I walked back alone, all along the path by the light of the sorrowing moon. I knew I had lost your brother, but when I got home... I found that my doll was gone too."

The two women stared at each other.

Ulula held out the doll.

"But now I have brought it back," she said gently.

Tamarind leapt forward and snatched it from her.

"Now I can be well again!" she shrieked as she ran from the room and away down the stairs. "Now I must find the doctor and tell him. I won't need his medicine anymore. Now I will be cured!"

Ulula shrugged. The room was filled with shadows. She settled down in Tamarind's chair and began to pick at the rice in the bowl. She peered through the window, sitting with her back to the door. She watched the masked dancers pass by in their robes, beating drums and tambourines, ringing high-pitched bells and scattering petals as they went.

Then Ulula slept where she was in the chair. She did not see the doctor standing at the open door. She did not see him pause, then slowly enter the room. She did not wake as he moved about, placing a tincture bottle on the table, lighting the candles which he always lit and filling the room with the fragrance of incense and a haze of purple smoke.

Then she woke and turned. The doctor was standing, watching her. His face was puzzled, staring at her face as if it was not the face he expected to see. And yet the same as ever before, as she sat in her long green robe in her chair by the window.

The doctor sat down on the bed and slowly removed his clothes, folding them neatly on the floor. He stretched out quietly on the sheets, beckoning her to join him.

Ulula smiled and cast off her robe then lay there beside him, barely touching. She watched for a moment as the purple smoke drifted about the room. And then she reached out and touched his thigh and pulled him slowly to her. She was strong and supple and the candlelight whispered about the walls as a warm breeze kissed the shadows. Then they lay side by side again.

The doctor smiled and spoke softly:

"I have waited so long for this to happen. Now I know that you are cured. You did not need the doll."

Ulula sat up and looked confused.

"But the doll was never mine," she said as the doctor quickly dressed again.

"It is the medicine that has worked," he continued, as he placed the bottle back in his bag and walked out through the door.

Outside in the street he stopped and looked back at the open window. The woman stood there waving. The doctor waved back then strolled away, leaving a coin by the fountain. Dawn was just breaking and Ulula watched as the old woman returned, sweeping away the petals that the dancers had strewn. She paused by the fountain to pick up the coin and tucked it into her apron. Then she threw the last handful of bread as the birds they came flocking, at first sparrows and starlings, then pigeons and crows.

Ulula stepped away from the window, back into the room. She straightened the rumpled sheets on the bed then turned to stare at the pictures which Tamarind had hung on the walls. One by one she took them down and stacked them in the corner. Then she lay back on the bed. The walls were bare now, painted green.

She gazed at the sunlight as it shifted across the ceiling and did not see that outside Tamarind came to the fountain with the jackdaw perched on her shoulder. She trailed her hand in the water, looked up once at the window then slowly walked away.

Ulula rose and stretched. She picked at a little of the rice that was left at the bottom of the bowl before going again to the window. She looked down at the fountain and there she saw one of the children reaching over to try to catch the doll with its robe of saffron and scarlet which was floating, just out of reach, face down in the water.

BLOODWELL

"I seen him again," said Morrow.

Grob wasn't listening. He was counting small sweetmeats laid out on the table. Morrow rushed around and grabbed one, cramming it into his mouth.

"These are good," he said. "Where'd you get them?"

Grob slapped the boy's hand away before he could take another.

"Got them from some woman for fuming out her house."

"Didn't she pay you shillen?"

Grob grunted.

"No lad. This was all she had till next week." He gestured towards the sweetmeats then cuffed Morrow's ear as the boy grabbed one more.

"So who did you see?"

"Thought you weren't listening."

"I always listen... Never know what you'll hear. Never know what you'll catch..."

"I seen him," Morrow said again. "Bloodwell, I call him. Stands at the top of the steps along by the wall. Stands there staring out towards the sea. Wears a long black coat and a low black hat. But his face is pale. Pale as ash. All grey and black he is, cept for one red flower in his buttonhole. Rose, I think."

Grob grunted again.

"What of him?"

"He just stands there. Never moves. Always staring, like I said. Out to sea. But his eyes look dead, like he's not looking at all."

"Does he see you?"

Morrow shook his head.

"He takes no notice. Reckon I could jump up and twitch his nose and he still wouldn't see me."

"Should try it," Grob muttered. "See what he does. Feel in his pockets while you're at it. See what he's got."

Morrow shuddered and shook his head, eyeing the sweetmeats again.

"No…" he said.

"Why not?" Grob challenged.

Morrow turned away.

"Don't want to, that's all."

Grob shoved one of the sweetmeats across the table towards the boy.

"Sure you really saw him? Sure you're not just imagining? Reckon it's nothing, just one of the Mizzle Wrecks."

"What's Mizzle Wrecks?" Morrow demanded.

"You've seen them," Grob replied, "when the mizzle mist seeps through the city. That brings them out. The Mizzle Wrecks – holding out their hands like begging bowls and telling tales such as you've never heard before – like a shiver slipping out from their lips.

"Them tales get into your blood," Grob continued, his own voice husky and low. "And the tales are strong potions - be careful how you use them or they will take your dreams and twist them all about and soon they will slip away to be lost in the Mizzle itself. When the grey light comes at dusk, nothing is real…"

Morrow leapt up.

"You come then," he challenged. "You come and see!"

Grob coughed and shuffled, then pulled on his coat. They both filled their pockets with sweetmeats then closed the door and tramped their way down the dimly-lit stairs. Out on the street, the mist was swirling.

"Mizzle-Wrecks…" Grob cursed as he hobbled on after Morrow who was running ahead towards the step which led down towards the alleyways that cut through to the docks.

"He's gone," Morrow declared when Grob caught up.

"See - what did I tell you?" Grob grunted. "Mizzle-Wreck all along…"

Another day he was there, just as before, staring towards the harbour. His coat black, his face ashen. Only the red rose in his buttonhole, burning bright as an ember in the mist. Morrow remembered what Grob had said, 'Twitch his nose... filtch his pockets...' and bunched up his fists, running towards the man, who just stood rigid, unblinking.

The man's name rattled in Morrow's throat as he ran towards him.

"Bloodwell..." he called. "Bloodwell..."

But the words were snatched away in the wind as the man turned, his rain-hardened face glowering at Morrow as he ran on, ran past, ran all the way back to the tenement, ran up the stairs and through the door where Grob sat waiting, staring deep into the fire.

"Seen him again!" Morrow panted.

"Seen who?"

"Seen Bloodwell..."

"Seen Mizzle-Wreck," Grob spat.

"Come and see!" Morrow clutched at him.

Grob shook his head.

"Be nothing there, same as before. Be nothing there at all."

There was nothing there. There was nothing ever there. At the top of the steps – when Morrow passed by with the other lads, shouting and laughing and calling out names. There was nothing there when Morrow passed by on a misty morning with Grob by his side.

But when he passed alone, when dusk singed the edges of the shadows and dark birds flew to settle under the eaves of the tall gaunt houses, there Bloodwell stood, same as ever before – his black hat pulled low, a rose red and vivid pinned to his lapel. And he never spoke. Never turned. And Morrow never spoke to him. Morrow ran, as he always ran, all the way up the steps and along the narrow back lane till he reached the tenement door.

Then one night, Morrow came racing in.

"I seen him again. Seen Bloodwell."

Grob sighed, scarce shifting on his stool.

"Same as ever," he muttered, "… down by the steps, gazing out to sea."

Morrow shook his head.

"No – I seen him this morning, plain as you like, down by the market."

Grob hunched his shoulders.

"Mizzle-Wrecks…" he grumbled.

"Not Mizzlers at all," Morrow insisted. "I seen him plain as day, standing by the stalls."

"That all he does?" Grob grunted. "Just stands… stands by the steps, stands in the market. What was he doing there? What'd he do next?"

Morrow paused, trying to remember.

"…he wasn't there!" he exclaimed at last.

"Well, if he wasn't there, how'd you see him?"

"Seen him first off – he was there. In the crowd. But soon as I went towards him… he was gone!"

"You're dreaming it, boy. Most like he was never there in the first place."

Morrow said nothing, just flopped down in the chair.

"What's to eat?" he asked.

Another day and another, all about the city, Morrow saw the dark roses. They grew in the gardens of those who had gardens. He saw one again, dropped in an alleyway. He bent down to look at it, wondering that something so soft, so frail, was lying in the dirt in the gutter. As he stooped to pick it up, he saw that ants were crawling all about each petal – and so he hurried on his way as the rain began to fall. Out on the street he saw the dark shape of a figure, ashen faced and huddled, wearing a low black hat.

"Bloodwell…" he called, but the person took no notice, and when Morrow drew closer he was not the man at all but a woman, and before her sat a bucket filled with red roses. She held one out to entice the passing crowds to buy, but they were wrapped deep in their coats, scurrying from the rain.

"How much for a rose?" Morrow asked, for he fancied that

if he had one, he would find Bloodwell again.

The woman turned slowly and stared at him with eyes that seemed to have been watching the sea.

"Tuppence," she said.

Morrow stood on one leg and gouged his fists into his pockets, searching about until he pulled out a penny bright.

"Got a penny," he said.

The old woman sniffed.

"Penny ain't no good."

Morrow stared at the roses, damp with rain and wilting.

"You ain't going to sell them anyway," he argued. "I only got a penny. I'll take any you want to give me."

The old woman looked at him long and hard. She seemed to be listening to something he could not hear.

"A penny," he said, holding it out. "A penny for a rose."

"Be off with you, boy," the woman spat. "I'll *give* you a penny just to go away!"

Morrow didn't wait to take up her offer, but scampered away smartly through the quickening rain.

A woman stood in a doorway. Her lips were bold vermillion and her cheeks all streaked with rouge. Her fingers nipped into crimson gloves while her scarlet dress hung in flowing folds and a bright red ribbon decked her hair. She reached out her hand as Morrow scurried past and gripped him by the shoulder.

"I know you, you are Grob's boy," she said, twisting up his chin. Morrow stood still and shrugged.

"Come, you must help me," she insisted, pushing open the door.

She led him then to a shadowy room, draped in curtains dark as blood.

"I have a rat that is trapped here," she said, sitting down in a large oaken chair. "It will not leave me. It comes to me each night. I hear it scratching in the walls and then it comes scurrying into the room."

She tweaked Morrow's cheek and ruffled his hair.

"I know that Grob has trained you," she continued. "I know you will know what to do."

Morrow wrinkled up his nose and squinted all about.

"Where is it?" he asked. "Show me this rat."

The woman nodded.

"He lives in that hole there, behind the wainscot."

Morrow stared at the darkened gash chewed into the woodwork. And then a scuttle. And then a flash. And the rat was out. It darted past him and leapt into the woman's lap. Morrow stood and waited, not sure what she wanted him to do - for rather than scream or throw her skirts in the air, she just sat there smiling with the rat on her lap, stroking the arch of its back as it nuzzled deep into the dip between her thighs.

"Here it is," she said. "You are Grob's boy. You know what to do. I must be rid of this creature."

Morrow closed his eyes. The dark-curtained room was heavy with musk. He leapt suddenly forward, hands outstretched, but the rat jerked away, its yellow teeth sinking deep through his skin. Blood welled. Morrow stopped and looked down. The crimson blotches on his shirt bloomed vivid as the red rose which he sought.

"Stay!" begged the woman, her arms reaching out as the rat shot from her lap and Morrow fled from the room.

As he ran down the street, the blood still dripped from his hand, planting flowers in the darkening dust, quenched by the thirst of the rain. Morrow sucked at the wound to try and stem the flow. The taste was iron, salt and rust, raw as the sea's breath which shivered on the wind. Dark as the dredge of the sewers which riddled this city's depths.

Morrow ran on, craving the balm of Grob's home-made lotion, mixed from ground rat-droppings, saliva and linseed oil – but knowing he would find none until he reached home.

And his head span as he ran, and his mind ran till the darkness sang, till it seemed as though he was Bloodwell himself, standing alone on the steps with his long black coat and his face pale as ash, wearing that one red rose. It was as if he could see what Bloodwell could see as he gazed out towards the ocean: a belly of grey, heaving and rolling beneath him and around him, under and over until he tossed in the white spume as the gulls circled, wailing.

A sea of salt tears, calling and yearning, turning him round and around till there was nowhere to go but down, though he refused to drown, standing at the top of the steps and waiting, waiting for the tide to turn, waiting for the wind to drop. Waiting for the ship to appear on the horizon which would bring his memories back from the sea.

Morrow staggered queasily up the tenement stairs like as if he was a sea-sick sailor. Rattled the handle on the door and fell into the room. There sat Grob, same as ever before, hunched on his stool by the fire. But all about there were roses, strewn across the floor, set in vases, bottles, jars. The smell of them was heavy, choking. The touch of their petals was soft as flesh.

Grob looked up and smiled.

Morrow reeled, not sure where to turn. The roses covered the table, the cupboard, the shelves. The hearth all around Grob's fire. Even roses in the bedchamber, on the pillows and all across the sheets.

"Where did they come from?"

Grob said nothing for a while, then – "Thought you'd like them," he replied.

Morrow scowled.

"What for?"

"Thought you might like to give one to Bloodwell," Grob grinned mischievously.

Morrow shrugged, then reached out to pluck up one of the flowers. Soon as he did, a thorn bit into his finger. He flinched back, sucking again on the fresh blood. Grob laughed. Morrow gritted his teeth, then reached again for another one. Again he was bitten. He flung it back. Tried another. Each time the thorns pierced his skin.

"I'm going to bed," he yelled and slammed the chamber

door.

Inside the tiny room he raked the blanket of roses from the sheets and lay down to sleep. In his dreams, Bloodwell chased him all down the steps to the harbour and then up the gangway onto a deck and then deep down into the hold of the ship. He could not find him there, Morrow knew. No-one could find him, not Grob, not the woman in red. But all around him were roses more and they gored him and they gashed him and then a white bird came, huge and silent. It hauled up Morrow in its claws and then it spoke in a low rasping voice that was Bloodwell's voice, he knew.

"Do not go to sea," it said. "I have lost all at sea."

Morrow woke to find himself there in the room again and all he could hear was the drip of a tap from the kitchen next door. And the rustle of a rat somewhere in the wall. And Grob snoring.

Morrow turned over but he could not sleep. His arms were raked with the tracts of the thorns and the wound which still ached where the rat had bitten him. And so he got up and pressed open the door. Grob was still snoring. He peered about the room for the roses.

They were gone, he thought. But no, when he looked again, Morrow could see that they still covered the floor, but all of them were withered now. Withered and dead. Shrivelled and blown. He gathered them up by the handful and strewed them all about, even covering Grob with the dull faded petals. But Grob snored on, his fingers twitching, dreaming of rats he had yet to catch.

Next day Bloodwell was there again at the top of the steps, staring out towards the sea. Morrow clenched his fists and gritted his teeth and marched up to stand behind him.

Bloodwell did not turn, but –

"I know you're there," he said.

Morrow took a deep breath.

"What did you lose at sea?" he demanded.

Bloodwell turned then slow, as a gull flapped squawking low above them.

"I know you," he said. "You are Grob's boy."

Then he turned away again, gazing across to the harbour.

"Tell Grob I lost all that I ever longed for. But what I longed for I never had. So truth is I lost nothing at all…"

He paused again.

"Tell Grob that."

Morrow stood a moment, shuffling.

Bloodwell looked back and stared at him with grey piercing eyes. Then croaked in a low rasping voice, as the circling gull swooped down –

"Do not go to sea, boy. Do not go to sea."

Morrow ran. Away from the steps and along the cobbles towards the tenement which loomed against the sky. Just before he reached the door he turned and peered back. The steps were empty. Bloodwell had gone.

Morrow raced up the stairs and stumbled through the door into the room. Grob was sitting there, whittling a piece of wood. He had swept the remains of the dead petals into a heap in the corner.

"Grob – what will happen if I go to sea?" Morrow gasped, catching his breath. "What would I find? What would I lose?"

Grob shook his head.

"I can't tell you, lad. I've never been to sea."

There came a knocking then, loud as a thunderclap. Grob hunched his shoulders. Morrow turned the handle and there in the doorway stood Bloodwell, his shoulders drenched with rain. He did not come in, but stood filling the door frame, his eyes roaming around the room. And then he spoke:

"Once when I was a young seaman, we birthed in a port far away – and there we went ashore. We went, as young seamen did, to a tavern on the waterfront. In the corner sat a girl. Her hair was long, near to her waist, and when she spoke it was like as if the words were singing. She took my hand, her skin was soft, but I saw at once that she was blind.

"She pulled me in close and whispered. 'Come to my house,' she said. I rose up at that instant but she said, 'No, sit –

39

not yet. I will leave now, but do not follow. Come to the house at the end of the wharf when the sun is set. Then my father will be gone. Then you can come.'

"I smiled and kissed her on the cheek and she pulled me closer and said, 'Wait, take this rose.' And she picked it from her hair and slipped it in my buttonhole, neat as you like.

" – 'Wear this,' she said, 'for then when my mother opens the door, she will know I have asked you to come. And when you climb the stairs to my room, I will know you have found me well.'"

"So that's why you always wear a rose!" exclaimed Morrow, " – to remember the girl who kissed you."

Bloodwell shook his head. He still stood rigid in the doorway, but his eyes gazed far away.

"I sat in that bar and waited. I waited for sunset to come. I had a drink and another drink more and then another seaman joined me. He sat beside me on a stool.

" – 'Which ship are you from?' he asked me – and I told him. 'And why do you wear that rose?' And I told him that too. I told him about the girl who had twisted it into my buttonhole. I told him I was waiting till sunset to go to her house.

"He peered through the window at the sky and said, 'Still some time to go.' Then he offered me a drink and another drink more. And he asked me where this girl lived – and I told him that as well.

"As the sun sank lower over the harbour and the sky grew red as my rose, he got up quick and embraced me. Said he wished me well, then hurried out the door. I finished my drink, I buttoned my coat. I smiled a moment as I touched my cheek and remembered the kiss of the girl who I was about to meet. Then I reached to my buttonhole to touch the rose as well – but it was gone. And now I knew why the sailor left so quick. I raced through the door and all down the harbour-front as a drizzle of mist blew in from the sea. But I could still hear the girl's voice whispering to me as I ran. I came at last to the end of the wharf and found the house I was looking for. I knocked and knocked upon the door until her mother opened it.

" – 'I have come to see your daughter,' I said.

"She looked me slowly up and down.

" – 'She told me she waited for a sailor who wore a red rose. He is already here. You have no rose. You must go.'

"She closed the door and I stood in the street and watched the sun slip into the belly of the ocean…"

Bloodwell tugged the red rose from his buttonhole and gazed at it a moment.

"You cannot lose what you never had, but I lost her all the same… I still hear her voice in the rain."

Then he turned and closed the door.

Morrow never saw him again.

"Where do you think he went?" he asked Grob.

"Same as I told you – he was never there at all. Nothing but Mizzle Wreck all along."

VERENA'S DANCE

As she danced, Verena followed the call of the flute, flitting from tree to tree, from archway to alley in every town or village where they played. She would glide and swoon, her arms outstretched, her fingers quivering. All the while the flute's sweet voice led her on, and no-one ever saw Maya, the pale young man who played it, as he slipped between the shadows.

The melody faded and she sank to the ground as if exhausted, then rose to bow to the applause. But when the audience was gone, the nights were cold. They slept each night beneath their handcarts, a ragged troupe of tumblers and tricksters, huddled together for warmth. All except Maya, who would lie by himself out under a tree and play to the stars and the dark scudding clouds.

Some nights Verena went to sit beside him and watch his slender fingers as he played.

"See, the chase is over," she whispered. "I have found you now. Come to me..."

But Maya turned away and played on, slowly and intently, and Verena got to her feet again and left him there as she made her way back towards the cluster of handcarts. When he thought that she was gone, Maya rose to his feet, still playing, and walked out into the moonlight to follow its shimmering trail away from the lights of the town, out to embrace the darkness. But Verena trailed after him to see where he went. Sometimes down to a river, sometimes the edge of a stream. Sometimes deep into a woodland copse, playing on as if the lilting notes were his dream.

One night she danced to his melody as if they were performing still. But there was no applause, only the cold of the night and an owl's call as Maya's wandering steps led her on to a great gaunt house which stood at the edge of the town.

It was empty, she could tell. There had been a fire. The memory of smoke still clung to the timbers as Maya walked inside and she followed. The corridors were strewn with broken glass, fallen wall hangings and the rotting rags of abandoned clothes. Maya continued, sure-footed, almost as if he was dancing himself, on through the maze of passageways, in and out of rooms stacked with splintered furniture. Verena stopped and froze as she thought he might have glimpsed her reflection in a shattered mirror which still clung to the wall. But he turned and walked straight past her and up the stairs.

Boards were broken and steps were missing as she picked her way carefully after him, the notes of the flute rising up and away between the rafters and through the broken roof, out to the open sky.

Then they stopped. Verena held her breath. Where was Maya? She did not know which room he was in, here at the top of the house. She waited to see if the music would start again. But there was no sound except the creaking of the floorboards and the dark wind that blew through the walls. She looked first in one room and then in another, but Maya was not there. She could not tell if he was hiding or if he had crept past her in the dark and made his way down the stairs.

Then it started to rain, leaking down through the roof, bringing with it the dust and the grime. She ran from the house and away, all the way back to the huddle of handcarts, out on the edge of the town. No-one had missed her. No-one knew she was gone. But Maya was gone. They never saw him again. She told them about the house and they searched by light of day but found nothing there.

Jalup the old juggler shrugged.

"Maya will come back," he said. "He'll find us. We have to move on."

But Maya did not come back. He never returned, though Verena's dance continued. There were different men who hid in the shadows for her to follow. But no notes from a flute, instead they whistled or called to her in low urgent voices. And she would find them easily enough after the show, somewhere in the darkness, away from the handcarts and the fire that burned low. Their bodies were swift and their bodies were rough. But she still dreamed of Maya with his long slender fingers, and how tender he would have been.

Now she lay, a ragged shadow on a narrow bed. No starlight here and no moon, only the emptiness of night and the unspoken silence of the room.

She listened to the voices drifting up from the basement below. A dimly-lit cellar with an uneven floor always wet with sweat and liquor. Tattooed dancers slid and slithered through a tired routine to the drone of the accordion player in the corner, the melody slurring from his calloused fingers while the rhythm of his broken boot beat in perfect time.

The sailor-boys all washed up here, the pick-pockets and pimps, the gamblers flush with winnings and the ones who'd lost it all. The stench of desperation trickled down the walls while Jalup, the old juggler, watched with a clouded eye as he swabbed down the bar and poured short measures into murky glasses with a shaky hand. He'd set up this cellar bar after one of his own juggling clubs had slipped and put out his eye.

Verena had danced here once when she tired of trailing the handcarts from town to village, from village to town. When her bones were too weary to sleep out on the heath and she longed for the touch of a feather pillow and the warmth of an eiderdown.

But even those days did not last long. She could not high-step with a slip-shod troupe who could barely keep rhythm or time. Verena's dance had always been her own, out under the stars, following the flute's beckoning call. She did not belong in a cellar bar, trapped by suffocating walls. But Jalup let her stay on and sleep in the attic room.

The shadows lay thick in the gulley between the wall and the hard starless night. Tansy pulled them around her, as if they were blankets, as if they were dreams. But in her dream she could hear her sister's voice again, chiding – "Keep up, keep up. Why do you always drag your legs?"

But Tansy's legs always ached. Her legs always shook and

when she woke, her sister was gone. Gone to dance with the young men in the taverns and bars. Gone to chase their flashing smiles and fall into their arms.

Tansy looked around. There was no sound, but then the tap of a child's ball, fallen from a window. The ball seemed silver in the darkness and as it rolled slowly past her, Tansy dragged herself to her feet. Her legs trembled and tottered as she gripped the wall and watched the ball trickle away. One step then another, then another step more and the ball seemed to hesitate, lodged by a drain before slipping on again towards the street. One step then another, then another step more, Tansy followed on down the hill. Then the ball stopped, stuck in the gutter at the bottom, trapped in a sluice of garbage washed down by yesterday's rain. Tansy bent to fish in out, but then she stopped and looked up.

Verena danced past her. She danced as if she was in a trance. Her lips breathed Maya's name over and over again. She seemed to see him through flickering eyes and turned away suddenly, away down an alleyway, over a wall.

Tansy stood and watched, still clutching the ball. But then she let it fall back into the gutter as she followed, her stuttering feet leading her on till she stood by the wall where Verena had been. Her hands reached up and just for a moment she felt herself strong. She spun slowly round, around and around, then fell to the ground. But when she sat up, her eyes were ablaze, a smile on her face, her hair tangled wild as the clouds raced away and the stars lit the sky.

Verena danced on, out through the streets, under the moon. She danced through silent squares as furtive couples lurked in the shadows. She danced in the public gardens as if they were a silent ballroom. She danced on through the fountains, though not one drop of water seemed to touch her skin.

She danced with the sound of the flute in her head, still following where it led. But not one flute: she could hear the sound from every alley, from upper windows, from overhanging balconies. It rose to a crescendo as she twirled this way and that, gliding and swooning, pirouetting and curtseying, her face upturned to the stars.

Tansy followed, but Jalup followed too, proclaiming to all who saw the dance – "Her name is Verena. It's like watching a dream come to life! So peaceful it can heal you..."

And word soon spread. Night after night, those with shivers and shakes and agues would cluster on corners, hoping to catch sight of her. And those that did all said that they could sleep at night with the dream of her. They could wake refreshed with no shadows in their heads, no voices spinning round and round. They were truly cured.

Tansy heard what they said. She always looked out for Verena, hoping one night she might see her dancing past again – and then she would dance too. She knew that she could because she had before. She had turned around and around before she fell to the ground. This time Verena would take her hand and draw her up again and they would spin together, all across the city. And she would find her sister and dance with her in the taverns and the bars.

She saw Verena coming towards her. Tansy's eyes lit up, but then she saw Verena was stumbling, her hair was tangled, her eyes dull and confused. She stopped and stared at Tansy, then sat down beside her. Verena's lips were bleeding, her arms dirt-streaked and bruised.

The street was silent. A huddle of people who had been watching from a doorway slipped quickly away. Tansy took Verena's hand. The knuckles were grazed and sore. She stroked them a moment.

"What's happened to you?" she asked, then pointed to her own twisted limbs. "My hand is crabbed, my foot is crook'd... but you can dance like a feather on the wind. Why are you broken?"

Verena peered at Tansy as if she could not see her, as if she did not know she was there.

"Maya," she said at last.

Tansy stared at her.

"Who is Maya?" she asked.

Verena raised Tansy's hand and touched it to her swollen lips. A trickle of blood smeared her fingers. Verena gazed distractedly about, her eyes searching this way and that. She covered her ears for a moment and then shook her head.

"Can't you hear his flute?" she whispered.

Tansy listened, but she could hear nothing.

"I know where he is," said Verena. "I know the house. I dance for him every night."

Tansy nodded.

"I know," she murmured. "I have seen you."

Verena grabbed her hand.

"Come," she said. "I will show you."

Verena led Tansy along the shadowy streets, past the gardens and the taverns where people still came out to watch. Tansy stumbled by Verena's side, trying to keep up as best she could. Verena stopped and smiled, then gathered her up into her arms and carried her on till they came to the ruin of a house, standing in the darkness.

Verena put Tansy down and began to dance again, graceful and light as she had always danced before. Her bloodied lips smiled once more and her eyes lit bright. Her arms reached out as if she was craving an audience's delight. She beckoned Tansy to follow.

They entered the house. The corridors were dark and Tansy picked her way carefully across the rubble-strewn floors. Milky moonlight spilt through the rafters where the roof had fallen. Verena climbed the stairs, her head held high, her eyes alert, still following the music that Tansy could not hear. Until they came to the final room at the end of the corridor. The floorboards were scorched by fire and the walls blackened with soot.

Verena danced faster now, whirling and swirling, her feet a blur, until she flung herself against the wall – beating at the stone with her pale bruised arms, kissing the bricks with her raw bleeding lips. Thrusting her body as if tossed by a storm. Letting out one wild cry. And then she fell to the floor.

Tansy pulled herself across to look at her. Verena's eyes were bright, her breath was quick, her lips were fresh with blood.

"Maya…" she called once and then lay still.

Tansy stared at her. Reached out to take her hand, but then quickly drew back.

"She is dead," she whispered to herself.

Tansy dragged herself away across the dusty splintered floorboards of the room. She clambered down the stairs and out into the overgrown garden. A bat flitted close past her face, nearly snagging her hair. Her legs ached and her stomach churned as she stumbled on under a watery moon.

The streets were empty, windows blind. Who could she tell? Who could she tell? Then a clatter of feet. Tansy shrank into a doorway. She curled into a ball, but then froze as a boot prodded at her ribs. A hand grabbed her chin, lifted her face up to the light. It was Jalup who squinted close at her with his one good eye.

"I seen you before," he said. "I seen you with her."

Tansy shook her head and tried to turn away.

"You know who I mean – Verena, the dancer. Someone said they seen you with her, hand in hand. But Verena didn't look well, she didn't look right. She hasn't for days now. But you were with her. Where did you go?"

Tansy shook her head again, then peered up at Jalup staring down at her. Then pointed. Jalup dragged her to her feet.

"No good pointing," he said. "You'll have to take me."

He wiped Tansy's face.

"It's alright," he said. "I won't hurt you. Just want you to show me where Verena has gone."

"She's…" Tansy stuttered, but then said nothing. Wracked her legs slowly and painfully all the way back to the house.

They climbed the stairs. They came to the room. They opened the door. Verena was still lying there on the floor. Tansy gasped and turned away, afraid of what Jalup would say. But then Verena sat up. She opened her eyes.

Jalup crouched beside her.

"What are you doing here?" he asked.

Verena stared around, her eyes still dazed, as if she was caught in a dream. Then she pointed to the wall.

"Maya," she said. "He is in there. He is trapped."

Jalup shook his head.

"Maya left long ago."

"I heard him play... I heard the flute... There behind the wall."

She pointed again.

Jalup looked at the bricks. They were old, they were crumbling, blackened by fire. He struck at the wall with his boot and one piece gave way.

"He is there, he is there," Verena repeated. "I heard him play..."

Jalup found a fallen timber in the corner of the room and swung it. More bricks gave way. He kicked again. The wall loosened brick by brick. And then a crash as more came down. The room was filled with a swirl of dust and mortar. They all stepped back, choking. Then Jalup edged slowly forward.

"Is he there?... Is he there ?" Verena cried. "Tell him to come to me. I have waited so long."

Jalup prodded in the darkness with the length of timber. A large cavity behind the wall. But no Maya. No rags that might be the remains of clothes. No bones. Only mouse droppings and a damp forgotten smell.

Tansy scuttled closer, her fingers picking through the dust.

"What's this?" she said.

Verena covered her eyes.

Out of the debris, Tansy pulled a flute. She held it up and gently shook it. The metal was rusted, the holes choked with dust. She shook it again. Pale moonlight flooded the room. A spider skittered across the floor. Tansy held the flute to her lips. Her fingers felt for the keys. She blew. Jalup held his breath and watched. Verena uncovered her eyes. Tansy blew again.

And then the tune. The tune Maya always played, though

49

Tansy had never heard it before. Slow at first, and halting. But then quickly, smoothly. Verena rose. Her legs firm and sure. Her arms curved in the air. And she danced, there in that blackened room. Danced as she had always danced before, to Maya's tune.

Jalup took her in his arms and kissed her once, then led her away. But Tansy sat still in the midst of the broken bricks and continued to play, her lips pursed, her fingers moving nimbly, turning the tune around and around. The dust settled slowly as the first light of dawn crept in through the windows and the birds began to sing in time with the tune.

LOCHERY and DOCHERY

The two men walked as if they were shackled, though not a chain nor a manacle could be seen. Their legs moved in rhythm. When Lochery turned, so Dochery turned too, though one might lead and then the other. They were thin and bedraggled, their long shabby coats appeared to be covered in strands of river weed, dried to dull husks flapping loose in the wind. They stalked back alleys, padding up softly behind unsuspecting strangers, sifting quickly through their pockets before slipping away, silent as shadows.

"What do you have?" Lochery whispered hoarsely.

They were sitting on a bench, pouring over their latest haul. Dochery turned the object in his grimy hands.

"Tis a key," he replied.

"I can see that," said Lochery, snatching it up, "but what will it unlock?"

Dochery grabbed it back again, squinting at the emblem embossed at the end of its shaft.

"Tis a harp," he said at last. "This is the key to Fricksome's house!"

"No, so!" Lochery exclaimed. "How do you know?"

"Everyone know," replied Dochery scornfully. "Harp is his symbol. He has one on his ring to press into the wax when he wants to make his seal. I seen it before. Many do his bidding…"

Lochery snatched the key back again, peering at it closely.

"We don't want it then. What would we do with it? No-one's going to trade it. If Fricksome is a powerful man, none would want to cross him."

"True, so."

"So true."

"What can we do?"

"Leave it where we found it. Fricksome must have dropped it. He'll come back and look."

Dochery shook his head.

"Wasn't no finding from the dust. This key I filched from a lady's purse."

Lochery frowned.

"What would a lady do with Fricksome's key? Best we give it back."

"But then she'll know I took it," Dochery sighed.

"Better she have it than we be caught with Fricksome's key. What did she look like, this lady whose purse you pilfered?"

Dochery scratched his neck.

"Think she wore a purple dress, or red, or maybe blue…"

"What about the purse?"

"Ah, now the purse was stitched with silver!"

Lispen climbed the steps of the house. She opened up her purse, stitched all about with sliver, and dipped in her fingers to pick up the key.

There was no key.

She peered inside.

She shook out the rest of the contents. A mirror, a comb, a bottle of scented water. Hairpins and ribbons – but still there was no key.

She turned around and walked back into town.

Inside the house, Fricksome paced up and down the carpeted floor. His long ringlets hung damply about his face which was twisted like a toad.

"Where is Lispen?" he demanded.

His brow was sweating.

Jepstow looked at him and said nothing, but idly ran her fingers across the strings of a small harp which she had carried with her into the room.

"Don't touch that!" Fricksome snapped. "You know you must not play until Lispen is here."

He continued to pace the room.

"Where is she? She has a key. She can enter without any fuss. Nobody will see."

The room was laid out with food on the table and in the corner a day-bed set with velvet cushions. Fricksome stroked them impatiently with his stubby fingers. His nails were dirty and in need of trimming. He turned suddenly and gestured to Jepstow.

"Play!" he said. "Play!"

Jepstow shrugged.

"You told me not to play," she reminded him. "You told me to wait until Lispen is here."

"She is always here by now. Play! Play!"

"How should I play?" Jepstow asked mischievously. "Sometimes when she is here the tune is long and languorous, sometimes short and swift. Sometimes it is finished almost before it has started and sometimes it lasts until dawn…"

Fricksome covered his ears.

"I don't care," he said. "Just play!"

He lay down on the day-bed and closed his eyes. Jepstow played slowly, sinuously. Fricksome raised his arms, his own fingers mimicking the melody which Jepstow built even more elaborately. Then she paused and began again – a quicker rhythm in a different key.

Fricksome leapt up.

"Stop!" he said. "You are mocking me. You are playing the tune I cannot play. You are playing the tune my mother played and my father, and their mothers and fathers before."

Jepstow stopped and looked at him.

"I am playing the tune that I always play when Lispen is here."

Fricksome stamped his foot.

"When Lispen is here, then you are in the next room. The tune is muffled through the velvet. My hands play their own games here on these cushions with Lispen beside me…"

He stamped his foot again and paced to the window to peer up and down the street.

"…but Lispen *is not here*!"

Jepstow turned away and continued to stroke the strings idly, remembering how she was once the one who stroked

Fricksome, without any need for a tune, on long afternoons draped across those same velvet cushions where he sat now, running frustrated fingers through his greasy hair.

"Lispen will come," she said gently. "She has a key..."

Lochery and Dochery sat outside the tavern, passing the key backwards and forwards from one to the other.

"Couldn't find her then?" Lochery complained.

"Told you before. I never look at ladies' faces, only at their purses. And most times they keep them tucked from view..." Dochery replied.

"What we going to do?"

Dochery shook his head.

"Hide it where she can find it."

"If we hide it, how will she find it?"

"Just leave it here then," he said.

Lochery picked it up quickly.

"If we just leave it here, any rogue could take it."

"No rogue's going to take it," said Dochery. "Any rogue will know that this is Fricksome's key and none will dare to touch it. Remember what I said. He has many who do his bidding..."

And so they scurried off, side by side, leaving the key in full view on the table outside the tavern.

The shadowy figure of a younger girl slid between the tables. She saw the key and snatched it up so quickly, no-one else could see. No-one saw her slip through the streets till she came to Fricksome's door. No-one saw her slide the key in the lock. No-one saw her turn it.

The door swung open, as she knew it would. Soon as she'd seen the harp embossed, she knew there was only one house in this city that the key would fit.

In the hallway, Jepstow was standing. She looked the young girl up and down. She looked at the key in her hand.

"You are not Lispen," she said.

"No, I am not Lispen. I am Binnory. But I have the key."

Jepstow shrugged.

"If you have the key, then Fricksome is waiting. Be quick, for you are late. Go to the room at the top of the stairs. The key fits that lock too."

Binnory stood in the room. No-one was here. She looked around and shivered nervously, excitedly. She had never been in a room such as this. The deep carpet, the ornate furniture, the heavy curtains which hung at the high windows. Binnory gazed out at the city, the streets she roamed every day.

"You see a chance, you take it," her mother would always say.

She saw the key. She took it. Now she was here. Binnory walked slowly across the room, gazing up at the pattern of light reflected from the chandelier onto the dark hues of the painted portraits which watched her from the walls. She sat down anxiously on the edge of the day-bed, then sprang up quickly as the door opened. It was Jepstow, bearing a tray of sweetmeats which she placed on a small side table. Binnory stared at them hungrily. Jepstow turned at the door and looked back at her.

"Fricksome will be here soon. Sit back down and wait."

Binnory perched herself awkwardly on the edge of the bed. She could hear voices calling in the street outside and suddenly wished she was back out there, flitting where she pleased. This room seemed dark and heavy and hot and she found it hard to breathe.

The door opened. It was Fricksome.

He looked at her.

"You are not Lispen," he said.

Binnory shook her head quickly. Her hands were trembling as she showed him the key.

"Ah – Lispen gave this to you," Fricksome nodded. "I understand."

Binnory was about to tell him that she did not know Lispen, but she swallowed the words as she felt Fricksome slide one hand around her waist. She stared straight ahead at the sweetmeats on the table. Fricksome followed her gaze.

"Later we eat," he said.

As Lochery and Dochery scurried away from the tavern, they near collided with Lispen who walked along slow, peering down into the gutter. Dochery grabbed Lochery's elbow.

"Stop!" he said. "That's her. She's carrying a purse stitched all with silver."

"You said you never saw her face."

"I saw her purse. Don't remember faces. Always remember purses."

"So she will find the key."

"We left it in plain sight."

"Come, let's go and see."

They tiptoed back around the corner. Lispen was outside the tavern, picking among the pots on the table. Lochery and Dochery clapped their hands and capered across, beaming at Lispen.

"The table is empty!" Lochery exclaimed.

"We see that you've found it," Dochery explained.

Lispen stared at them.

"What have I found?"

"You have found the key. We left it for you…"

Lispen frowned.

"I have *lost* the key."

Lochery and Dochery looked bewildered.

"But we left it here on the table for you – and now it is gone."

Lispen glared at him.

"How did you have it? How did you have my key?"

Lochery and Dochery shuffled bashfully.

"You stole my key…!"

"We did not mean to. We left it here for you to find…"

"Somebody else has found it now," Lispen retorted.

She shook her head in disbelief.

"You stole my key," she said again. "Now how will I eat? That key unlocked Fricksome's door. Every day I would go to him and he would give me food."

Lochery and Dochery looked crestfallen. They touched their cheeks as if tears fell from their eyes in a mime of sorrow and regret. Lispen continued to glare at them, then shook her head.

"But I did not want to give what he took from me," she said. "All the while I searched for the key, I knew I did not want to find it – for if I found it I would have to go back… and I do not want to go back!"

Lochery and Dochery clapped their hands and circled their arms about her.

"But how will I eat?" Lispen sobbed.

Lochery and Dochery stepped to one side. Lochery tapped the side of his nose and Dochery gave a great wink.

"Stay here," they said.

Lispen stayed there, staring at the empty pots on the table. Staring at the people ambling by, their shadows lengthening across the cobbles. Then they came back, Lochery and Dochery, bearing a pie. They watched in silence as Lispen sat and ate every crumb. Then she smiled at them.

"But I still do not have the key," she said wistfully.

"Thought you didn't want to go back?" Dochery looked puzzled.

"I want to *eat*," Lispen wailed.

"Come here tomorrow," Lochery smiled. "We will bring you another pie."

The next day Lispen sat in the sun outside the tavern, eating the last piece of a succulent pie, savouring every morsel. She looked up, realising a young woman was standing there, staring at the ring Lispen wore on her forefinger, embossed with the emblem of Fricksome's harp.

Lispen sat back in her chair, smoothing the folds of her satin dress. She looked the young woman up and down. Her clothes were dowdy, her hair bedraggled. Lispen finished the last of the pie and wiped the crumbs from her lips.

"Who are you?" she asked at last.

"I am Binnory," said the young woman.

She shuffled a moment and thrust her hand in her pocket, then produced Fricksome's key.

"I found this here," she said. "It was lying on the table."

Lispen looked at her, but said nothing at first.

Binnory continued. "I took it to Fricksome's house. I recognised the crest."

Lispen nodded.

"Yes, I know it," she said.

"I took it to his room," said Binnory. "He gave me food and drink."

Lispen nodded again.

"Yes, he is a generous man, I have heard."

Binnory paused, turning the key over and over between her fingers.

"And then he used me badly," she whispered, looking away from Lispen's gaze.

"Yes – I have heard that as well," Lispen replied.

"Whatever shall I do?" Binnory began to cry.

Lispen held her a moment, then she clapped her hands. Lochery and Dochery came scurrying round the corner.

"Have you finished the pie?" Lochery asked.

"Was all to your satisfaction?" Dochery echoed.

"Yes, yes," said Lispen, beckoning them closer.

She whispered something in Lochery's ear. Dochery nodded and leered, then they scuttled away.

"Who were they?" Binnory asked.

"You do not need to know their names," Lispen replied. "In fact, I do not know them myself. They will be back soon. Here – come and sit by me and tell me more about Fricksome."

Lochery and Dochery returned a while later and slid a small phial of sallow liquid into Lispen's hand. She whispered to them again and they grinned and nodded, then scurried away.

"Come," said Lispen to Binnory. "Bring your key."

Binnory followed and they threaded their way through the streets to Fricksome's door. The key unlocked it as it had before and they slipped inside. In the hallway stood Jepstow, her arms folded, looking them up and down. She was surprised to see both women together. But Lispen bustled past, leading Binnory by the hand. She unlocked the door at the top of the stairs. Fricksome was already sitting on the day bed. A grin of pleasure spread across his face.

"My, my!" he cried, patting the cushions. "Come you both and sit beside me."

The two women smiled at each other and winked, then arranged themselves on the day bed and set to stroking Fricksome's hands and fondling his fingers.

"What's this?" he chortled with delight as Lispen opened her silver-stitched purse and produced the phial of liquid which Lochery and Dochery had brought her. She held it up to the light and it glinted with an amber gleam.

"This will help your appetite," she explained. "Now that you have two of us, your energy must be sustained…"

At that moment Jepstow knocked on the door and let herself in. She eyed the two women suspiciously.

"Is everything well?" she asked Fricksome. "Do you have all that you need?"

Fricksome waved her away impatiently.

"Yes, yes. You can see I have all that I need and more. I must not be disturbed. You can go…"

"But the music? What would you have me play?"

Fricksome slipped his arms around Lispen and Binnory and squeezed so that they giggled in feigned delight.

"We have music here enough," he told her. "You may go now – take the night off!"

Jepstow frowned, eyeing the two women dubiously, but Fricksome glared at her.

"Go, go!" he said.

Soon as Jepstow had closed the door, Fricksome kissed Binnory full on the lips, then turned to Lispen, but she pulled away.

"The phial..." she reminded him, as she removed the stopper and emptied the contents into a glass of wine from the tray on the table.

"Oh *yes!*" Fricksome exclaimed and drained every drop.

He lay back against the cushions. Lispen and Binnory pressed themselves against him, kissing his cheeks and stroking his forehead and watching as his eyes turned from sparkling to dull, until his lids closed and then he fell deep into sleep.

Lispen peered at him closely.

"Wait," she said, raising a finger to her lips.

They both sat still without moving until Fricksome began to snore and then they peeled themselves quickly away and hurried from the room. They ran through the house, checking to make sure that Jepstow had truly gone. They paused a moment in the entrance hall, then unlocked the front door.

There stood Lochery and Dochery, waiting. Lispen beckoned them inside. They stood a moment, blinking. Dochery eyed the candlesticks, the gilt-framed mirrors, the jewelry boxes – but Lispen stayed his hand.

"One thing," she said, "and one thing only. Remember what we agreed."

She led the way, tiptoeing up the stairs to the ante-room next to where Fricksome was sleeping. There stood the harp which Jepstow played for his rapture and delight. Lispen gestured to it. Lochery and Dochery nodded, wrapped the instrument in a sack and bore it away down the stairs.

Lispen and Binnory could hardly suppress their mirth as they crept back in to the room where Fricksome lay.

"What shall we do with the key?" whispered Binnory, holding it up. "We have no need of it now."

Lispen smiled and took it from her.

"Then we should give it back."

"Where shall we leave it?"

"Leave it where he is sure to find it."

She tiptoed forward, opened up the front of Fricksome's britches and slipped the key inside.

DEZRUN and the GEESE

At dusk, Dezrun gazed from her window as she always did, to watch the day fade away across the rooftops of the city. She looked up to see one dark goose, its wings beating slowly, neck outstretched. And its call, aching like a memory lost, echoing down through the empty streets. Then another goose followed, and another more; drove upon drove heading in from the marshland by the estuary's shore.

Dezrun stood on tiptoe, bewildered and excited, to watch as the flocks landed in the empty squares and alleyways, the gardens by the fountain, the boulevards and backyards. They scrabbled across rooftops, squabbling for food. The noise grew louder than a thunderstorm and the sky was dark with their wings.

Dezrun watched as people hurried to stand in their doorways to stare at the geese arriving, before quickly stepping back inside. Bolts were drawn and shutters lowered. As the moon rose, the geese fell silent, except for the shuffling of their feet and the rattle of settling wings.

In the morning she woke and opened her window to see other windows opening up and down the street and bleary eyes peering out, hoping it had all been a dream: the flocks of geese arriving – a nightmare that would fade with the day. But the geese still swarmed over the cobbles, rapping at locked doors with their hard sharp beaks, wings rising suddenly and beating at closed shutters.

No-one could go out. No-one could fetch food. What they had in their larders was all they had to eat. The geese pressed shoulder to shoulder and would let nobody past.

A day went by and another day more. Dezrun went down to her door, hoping that if she sang to the geese they might let her pick her way through. But there on the step lay one young goose, gazing up at her. She bent to touch it, to see why it did not move and saw that one of its wings was broken.

The other geese moved away, turning their backs as Dezrun gathered the young bird into her arms and carried it carefully up the stairs to her room. She could feel its heart beat quickly next to hers, as she opened the door and laid it on her bed. The goose peered up at her with a frightened look in its eyes, but Dezrun spoke to him quietly and hummed a soothing tune. She fed him what little food she could find and bandaged up his wing.

"Poor thing," she said. "The other geese must have crushed you as they pushed against the door."

All that day she sang to him and he listened, his head relaxed upon her pillow as they watched the rain that fell slowly outside her tiny window. That night Dezrun lay down beside him and they both slept on the narrow bed. She dreamed that he was a goose no more but had turned into a boy.

"Are you glad to be here?" she asked, stroking the down of his hair.

The boy smiled and replied, "My name is Huilst and my home is in the hills, far away across the estuary. I live there near the forest, where Marberry looks after me."

"Who is Marberry?" Dezrun asked.

Huilst smiled. His eyes seemed to gaze beyond the tiny room, beyond the street, beyond the city, out across the marshes.

"She is the goose girl," he told her. "She was driven out from her village because they had no food. Now she walks the roads with a gaggle of birds of her own."

"But you are here now," Dezrun reminded him.

She stroked his hair again.

"Are you glad to be here?" she asked once more.

Huilst turned away.

Dezrun thought he might be crying.

She touched him gently on the shoulder.

"Tell me, why did you come?"

Huilst sat up and looked at her.

"I woke up one morning and Marberry was gone and the other birds as well. I flew around, around and around, calling out her name. And I could hear her calling to me in the woods. But then a great flight of geese gathered me up and took me with them. All the time I called for Marberry but I knew she could not hear me..."

Dezrun took Huilst in her arms.

"Hush," she said. "You are here now. Marberry is gone. If I heal you, will you stay with me? I will sing to you every day."

Huilst turned to her and nodded.

"Yes," he said. "I will stay."

But his eyes looked far away.

All though the days, Dezrun tended to the goose with the broken wing. She fed him what scraps she had in the cupboard and sang the hours away. And all through the nights she dreamt that she lay with the boy and held him in her arms. But some nights she would wake and hear him whispering, 'Marberry', and she would shake him gently till he opened his eyes and looked at her.

"Huilst," she would say, "you are dreaming. Marberry has gone. You are safe here with me..."

Then the day came when she could see that his wing was mended. He raised it high as he stood in the room.

Outside in the street the flocks of geese still paraded up and down. But they grew restless now, rising up and flying in circles as if they could hear someone calling from far away. But then they turned around and landed again, pecking at the dirt between the cobblestones.

Dezrun shook her head.

"All their food is gone."

She caught glimpses of her neighbours, gaunt and hungry behind shuttered windows, still waiting for the geese to leave.

"Come," she said to Huilst. "The geese are ready to fly. Come and say farewell to them and then you can stay here with me."

Huilst followed her down the stairs and she flung open the front door. He walked slowly out into the middle of the flock of geese and then he gave a great cry. He raised his wings and brought them down with one sweeping beat. Dezrun clapped her hands, pleased that she had healed him. But then watched in dismay as he lifted away.

"Come back!" she cried.

But she could hear his voice, calling out for Marberry again and again, calling for the goose girl who lived far away. Then Dezrun saw that the other geese were following after him. Street by street they lifted off and up and away until every square was empty, every garden and every alleyway.

One by one, doors were flung open and people tumbled out into the daylight, to watch the dark flock soar away across the estuary. Then everyone raced towards Dezrun.

"The geese have gone!" they cried. "The goose you trained has led them away."

They clustered about her, crowding as close as the geese had done, filling the street around her door.

"You have saved us!" they said, showering her with kisses.

She looked at them all, their tired hungry faces so happy now that they could leave their homes.

A clamour of voices near deafened her.

"How can we repay you?"

"Soon as we can find flour, I will bake you bread..."

"I will mend your pots and pans..."

"I will stitch you a fine new dress, any colour you choose..."

Dezrun nodded, wiping away tears.

"But all I ever wanted was to be with Huilst and sing to him. He promised he would stay..."

She looked up to the sky again.

"...but now he has flown away."

She turned back to the shadow of her house and opened the door, just as she felt a first fluttering stir softly in her belly.

SNAKE BOY

Binnory found Arrak down by the market. His straggling garments were such a patchwork of rags that it was hard to fathom where his jacket ended and his britches began. His dark eyes darted sharp as hornets, his pick-lock fingers twitching. They sat together, watching scraps of litter drift along the gutter.

Binnory pulled a bag of acajou nuts from her pocket and offered one to Arrak. At first he shook his head, but then he smiled and took one and cracked it between his teeth.

"Acajou nuts are sweet," he said. "Let me tell you... once there was a boy they called the Snake Boy. He was only a little'un and he lived in the village. Out in the woods he would find the snakes, in the shadows under the bamboos. And bring them back with him – though the girls all ran off screaming as the snakes twisted round his wrists and up his arms and across his shoulders to coil around his neck.

"They didn't bite him. None of them touched him. He sang them an old song, like it was with him since he was born. And he played with the snakes soon as he could crawl. And soon as he could crawl, the snakes were all he had. His mother and father died in a fire when he was only small.

"No-one knew how it happened. They kept to themselves in their own hut, out on the edge of the village. People said they weren't man and woman at all. They were children of the Narrogs.

"Narrogs lived out in the woods, in the swamps, between the trees which hung low, down into the water. At night they rose up, swarthy skin all coated in scales and stinking breath reeking with smoke and flame. You could their cries all round the forest while fires glowed through the undergrowth where they went moaning and lumbering.

"When they heard the sound, the villagers clapped their hands over their ears and ran to hide in their huts. But Snake Boy didn't care... the more the Narrogs roared, the more he danced between the huts, laughing all the time with the snakes clutched over his head, so that they could hear it too.

"One day Mandra, one of the girls, went out by herself to the wood to pick up Acajou nuts that the villagers loved to eat. When sunset came, her friends looked around. 'Where is Mandra?' they asked. 'Soon it will be dark, soon the Narrogs will come.' They started to tremble, but then they heard a sound and looked around. There came Mandra, stumbling out of the forest, weeping and wailing. Her arms were covered in great red bites and the strands of her hair were all scorched.

"'Tell us what happened,' her friends begged as they gathered round.

"'A Narrog came,' Mandra told them as she sank to the ground. 'I went deep into the forest to the Acajou tree, where the sweetest nuts all grow. When I came there, the tree was nearly bare, but a trail of nuts led away. I followed the trail, gathering up nuts to put in my pocket, until I came down to the edge of the swamp. There I sat to rest awhile and chew on a nut or two. I saw something lying in the water and thought it was a fallen tree. But as it floated close to me, suddenly it rose up and gave a great roar. It reached out and gripped me to its body. Then it set to try and bite me, all the while its hot breath filled my nostrils and my throat.

"'One half-chewed nut still sat in my mouth. I flung back my head and spat it out. The Narrog let loose a roar of surprise, then dropped me right there at the edge of the swamp and lumbered away, howling and moaning and thrashing the water. Then I ran and tripped and stumbled and got up and kept running again.

"'Now I am safe,' she moaned as she lay there trembling while one of the women fetched her a drink and another wrapped a blanket around her.

"But then people started their muttering. 'The Narrogs are back... Why have they come?... Who has brought them here?'

"'It is Snake Boy,' Mandra told them. 'Who else could it be? He brings the snakes to the village and so the Narrogs will follow.'

"'But Snake Boy is a child,' they said. 'He does no harm, just plays with the snakes. He would not bring the Narrogs here.'

"No-one spoke to Mandra after that. Even though the Narrog had attacked her, seemed it was all her fault. Then one of the boys, Curran, came back from the forest with his clothes all burnt. He said the same as Mandra, he saw a Narrog rise up from a pool of deep water. But no-one wanted to know. No-one wanted the Narrogs to come back.

"They said, could have been anyone that burnt Mandra and Curran. Could have been a hunter. Could have been each other. Could have been that they used to go and meet out in the woods. That's what the women said. They'd meet in the woods for their kissing games and then they burnt each other so no-one would know and blamed it on the Narrog.

"Mandra and Curran didn't know what to do. No-one spoke to them after they got burnt. Spite of what the women said, they didn't rightly know each other at all. But no-one else would speak to them. Even their own parents didn't want them - and they wandered all around till the only people they could speak to was each other. They both needed shelter so they set up home in one of the empty huts out on the edge of the village, same as Snake Boy's mother and father.

"Maybe that's why Snake Boy always played outside their hut. He'd bring the snakes there every day and wait till Mandra came out and then he'd show her. At first she was scared and ran back inside, but then she could see Snake Boy meant no harm. He held out the snakes for her to see. They were beautiful, gold and scarlet and green, the way they twisted and danced.

"Then one day she stretched out her hand. 'Let me touch one,' she said. And Snake Boy let her hold the snake, cradle it in her arms, let it twist and twine round her neck till she did not want to give it back. She kept the snake in her hut from then on and every day Snake Boy would bring her another one, till the whole hut was filled with writhing snakes and Mandra and Curran would lie among them and then they would start to writhe themselves and play the very kissing games that the women always said they did.

"They stopped going out into the woods, and soon as they stopped, no-one saw or heard the Narrogs no more. 'Snake Boy did this,' said the villagers. Mandra and Curran never came out. Spent all their time in the hut, lying on the floor, writhing round with the snakes. One day the women were down by the well, chatting and gossiping, when they turned to see someone else amongst them. It was Mandra, and they stood and stared, not so much at the mark of the fire across her face or the scorched rags which were her clothes, but for the way her belly swelled. They watched her slowly walk away, bearing a pitcher of water. And then they began to whisper, 'Who has done this?... Must be Curran... they spend all their time together in the hut...'

"And some said it was only nature, and some said it was shameful and some said it was the fault of the Narrogs for driving them together. But the oldest of the women, she led them all away to take the news to Mandra's mother.

"'I told her no good would come of this,' the mother wept. 'I begged her to come home. But she never wanted to show her face because of the burns from the Narrog.'

"They set off to the hut where Mandra and Curran lived, out on the edge of the village. Slowly Curran opened the door and stood blinking in the darkness.

"'What have you done to my daughter?' Mandra's mother yelled. The boy just stared at her. 'Can't you see the way her belly is swelled?'

Curran nodded and kept his eyes on the ground.

"'Seen it sure enough,' he said. 'It is the hunger that gnaws at us both. We did not want to leave this hut until our scars were healed.'

"Then he turned and showed the way his own face was burned. But Mandra's mother looked him straight in the eye.

"'It's not hunger that swells her belly, but a child that's growing there. You have lain with her and played the kissing game.'

"'She will not kiss me,' Curran declared. 'She scarcely even speaks. And the only creature she lays with is this mass of writhing snakes.'

"He opened the door wider to show them the slithering shadows crawling over the floor. The women crowded forward but then fell back as the snakes' tongues flickered and hissed.

"'If she has a child, then it is the snakes' child,' Curran told them, '– for she likes them more than anything.'

"The women stood, staring into the hut. Then they turned and walked away, slowly at first but then as quickly as they could.

"Next day Snake Boy came to the hut and sat on the ground outside. Before Mandra and Curran had woken he began to sing a song in his high-pitched voice. One by one the snakes crawled out, slithering under the door. And one by one they followed him, away from the hut and away, all through the village, past the well and out along the dusty track down to the forest. Soon enough all the village knew that the snakes were gone.

"'And the Narrogs do not come no more,' they said. 'All is as it was before...' 'Snake Boy has saved us. See how he plays now with the other children. He doesn't bother with the snakes no more.'

"But Snake Boy did not like playing with the other children. He did not like their games with sticks and stones and catapults. He would rather feel the cool hard scales of the snakes between his fingers. And though the women did not see, the other children taunted him when he would not join their games, when he stood alone just watching them, gazing back to the forest.

"He stopped even trying to join in the games. He would sit each day at the edge of the forest, twisting strands of grass in his hands and listening to the call of the bright-coloured birds. Then he would wander to the hut where Mandra and Curran lived, but they had no time for him now. Mandra was sickly and pale while Curran sat and watched her and fetched water from the well and what little food he could find. Snake Boy did not bring them snakes. He did not bring them anything but just sat outside the hut.

"Mandra took to a fever. Her fists were clenched, her body was sweating. She gritted her teeth as her limbs thrashed and she cried and ripped at her swollen belly as if she could tear it away. Curran mopped her brow and tried to take her hand but she would not have him near her. She cried with pain until the pain was the cry and the cry was the pain and Curran ran out from the hut, out past Snake Boy who still stood and watched, out through the village to wake the midwife, but she was awake already for she had heard the cries.

"'Her time is come,' she told Curran as she hurried with him back to Mandra's side and a cluster of mothers came from their huts to follow on behind.

"The midwife took Mandra's hand and slowly her cries grew quiet and slowly she slipped into a fitful sleep and lay there through the night while Curran paced up and down outside and Snake Boy sat and watched wide-eyed, all the while singing his song.

"But then just before dawn came one great cry and all the villagers were awoken and they lay in their beds, listening and waiting and hardly daring to breathe.

"In the dull light of the hut, Mandra pushed and sweated. She swallowed in the pain and then she spat it out again as she gripped the midwife's hand and the midwife coaxed and cursed her with kindness till Mandra's body arched back and shuddered and out from her belly it came, a bloodied egg the size of a head.

"The midwife passed it to Curran and he took it in his hands. He rushed outside to where the villagers were waiting and held it up to the last star's light.

"As dawn broke, the egg cracked open. The shell fell away and in Curran's hands lay a baby Narrog. Its teeth were sharp and its skin was scaly and a thin plume of smoke breathed from its nostrils.

"The villagers gathered round and then stood back in silence as Snake Boy began to sing again. As he sang, the baby Narrog seemed to smile and nestled in Curran's arms.

"Snake Boy's song grew louder and as he sang the people turned and saw the snakes come slithering back out of the forest. They came right up to the door of the hut and then slid off to either side until it was surrounded. Mandra stood in the doorway and Curran gave her the baby Narrog to hold.

"She took the tiny creature and kissed it and gazed into its eyes, but as she did it threw back its head and breathed a tongue of fire.

"Mandra screamed and flung the Narrog to the ground, as it let out a high-pitched howl and flames shot from its mouth. The thatched roof of the hut was soon ablaze and the walls came crashing down. Mandra and Curran were trapped. No-one tried to save them. They all ran away and left them to burn along with their Narrog child.

"No-one spoke to Snake Boy ever again, for he had brought the snakes back and people feared the Narrogs would come too, and so they drove him away. He wandered here, he wandered there, over mountains and across deserts. Until he came to the city."

Binnory eyed Arrak curiously, as she pulled an acajou nut from her bag and tossed it into the air. She tried to catch it between her teeth, but it dropped into the gutter.

"And what did they call him when he came to the city? There are no snakes for him here."

Arrak paused and looked at her.

"Here they gave him a new name," he said. "Here they call him *Arrak*."

THE LIGHT ON THE WATER

Ghresselle sat next to the lake where the grey geese pecked for scraps. In the distance she could hear children calling, as she gazed down at her reflection. Then she realised that it was not her own face she saw, but the face of Scar Dog, long dead.

She laughed at him.

"Are you there, tricking me again, just like you always did?"

She heard another voice laughing close behind her, and turned around. Scar Dog was standing there. They both laughed then, and he kissed her.

"Come with me," he said, a twinkle in his eye.

Ghresselle laughed again.

"Is this another of your tricks?" she asked, but Scar Dog shook his head.

"No – come with me," he said. "There's something I want to show you."

She followed him quickly away from the lake and out into the crowded streets of the city. The lamplighter saw her scurrying along and called after her:

"Where are you going in such a hurry?"

Ghresselle just smiled and pointed at Scar Dog, but the lamplighter frowned and looked puzzled, and then she realised he could see no-one at all.

"Come on," said Scar Dog. "Keep up!"

Ghresselle quickened her step behind him, turning back to wave at the lamplighter.

Scar Dog led her on to a narrow street where the sun had forgotten to shine. He opened the door of an empty house. Shadows and cobwebs clung all around. They brushed the dust from a wooden bench and sat down. Ghresselle peered into the gloom.

"We used to live here," said Scar Dog.

Ghresselle nodded.

"Yes, I know."

They sat in silence for a while, leaning against each other, listening to the wind in the chimney. Then from a room upstairs they heard the sound of children's laughter.

"Our children," said Scar Dog. "They remember us."

Ghresselle shook her head and smiled.

"We never had any children," she reminded him.

Scar Dog paused and listened again before he replied:

"Then who is it we hear laughing?"

Ghresselle sat for a moment, listening. The voices came from the chimney breast, from the attic, from the walls.

"It is the house that has the children," she said. "They are everywhere. They have eyes like dead roses, hands like sparrows' claws."

Scar Dog coughed.

She turned to embrace him, but he was not there.

"Dead again," she said. "Always dead."

She rose to her feet. The floor slipped and swayed beneath her. It seemed to be covered in sand, as if she was on a beach and the tide was coming in. Outside she heard a commotion of gulls. She opened the door. The lamplighter was standing there.

"Have you been following me?" Ghresselle asked.

The lamplighter scratched his chin.

"I came to see if you were safe," he said.

"Of course I am safe," she told him. "Scar Dog is here."

She closed the door and sat down on the bench. The lamplighter knocked again. Ghresselle sighed and got up. She walked slowly across the shifting floor and opened the door.

The lamplighter peered around the room.

"I cannot see Scar Dog," he said.

"Of course not," Ghresselle replied. "He is dead."

Laughter came again, from underneath the floor. The lamplighter held out his hand.

"Come with me," he said. "It is not safe."

Ghresselle looked around the empty room, then took his hand. She waved to the children, calling each of them by name as he led her through the door.

Ghresselle stood in the street. The lamplighter had gone. She listened out for the gulls she had heard before, but there was only a sparrow, hopping about her feet. And a crow. Its dark wings flapped raggedly as it pecked at a scrap of paper. Ghresselle stepped closer. A scrawled charcoal eye stared back at her. The crow plunged its beak through the centre, then let it drop. As Ghresselle picked it up, she saw there were more. Torn shreds fluttered or lay damply in the gutter. She chased about, gathering them. Another eye. A nose. An ear. Strands of hair scribbled angry and black.

She placed them together on the pavement, until they made a face, all except one piece. The centre of the forehead was missing. Ghresselle felt her own head fill with the sound of gulls, as if they were inside her skull, flapping and harrying. And the sparrows, the starlings. And the crow. It squawked, rasping hoarsely, as the dusk came rolling in. Dark clouds of mist.

Ghresselle sank to the pavement and pressed her head against the face which lay there. Pressed her forehead to the gap in its brow. She lay there a moment, letting the cold dampness pass through her as she trembled and shook. Then she sat up. Someone was touching her shoulder.

She turned to see another face, a young woman peering down. Ghresselle pointed at the torn scraps of eyes, the ears, the nose, all stuck to the pavement by the damp of the mist. She smiled at the woman behind her.

"Look – it's me!"

The young woman shook her head, gathering up the pieces.

"No – it is me," she said. "The lamplighter draws me, every day as he waits for darkness to fall."

Ghresselle glanced up at her, then back at the picture again. The young woman laughed.

"It is me, true. I am Binnory."

Every day the lamplighter shuffled down the steps to take his place by the river. He nailed a tattered piece of paper to a board and propped it up to sketch the same scene. He squinted at the light on the water and the trees along the bank. Sometimes there were birds, sometimes there were not. Sometimes a young woman came, sometimes she did not.

Sometimes she spoke to him. She told him she liked to swim there. She told him she liked to dive under the water.

"What do you see there?" the lamplighter asked her.

The young woman smiled.

"The river is full of drowned children," she said. "Their arms are waving, their eyes are staring."

The lamplighter looked up at the young woman. The sun was shining directly behind her and he could scarcely make out her face.

"Why don't you draw them?" she asked.

The lamplighter shook his head.

"I have not seen them," he said. "I would rather draw *you*."

The young woman laughed and walked away. Sometimes he saw her again and sometimes he did not. Sometimes she stopped to speak with him and sometimes she walked straight past. One hot afternoon she followed him and climbed the stairs to his room.

"I am Binnory," she told him, and sat while he poured her wine. They ate fresh bread and slices of cheese and talked long into the evening.

Then dusk came, and he left her while he went to walk the streets, lighting all the lamps. When he returned, Binnory was waiting. She slipped off her dress.

"Now will you draw me?" she asked.

The lamplighter smiled as they sat and said nothing, watching the shadows lengthen. He set up his board and fastened a scrap of paper. Then he took a stump of charcoal and began to sketch the lines of her.

Ghresselle looked up at Binnory. The sun was shining directly behind her and she could scarcely make out her face.

"Every night I go to him," Binnory explained, "after he has

lit all the lamps. Every night I sit with him and sometimes he sketches and sometimes he does not. Sometimes we just talk. I tell him again of the children who drowned. Then he shakes his head and takes up his charcoal. But the picture is not finished. Every night he rips it into pieces and next day he starts again. He tells me I am harder to draw than the river. Though I am still, my body is shifting, as if I am water..."

Ghresselle grabbed her wrist.

"Are you drowned?" she asked.

Binnory shook her head and said nothing.

Ghresselle watched as she walked away, towards the river. When she got there, she slipped off her dress, turned and smiled again. She took the steps down into the water and disappeared. Ghresselle waited, but she did not come back to the surface. She turned and saw the lamplighter set up his board and begin to sketch the light on the surface of the water, the trees along the bank and the birds. Then she heard the sound of children's laughter all around, coming from deep in the river and echoing on behind her, inside the empty house.

LANTERN OF DARKNESS

A tall woman walked the frozen field, where all about dark flowers grew. The clouds hung low to spill their curses as from the ditch a dead wind blew. Dusk clung to trees and hedgerows while she moved slow across the rutted ground. Her feet slithered in the icy furrows as she bent to pick each flower, then turned towards the sinking sun, her face a mask of bone. She raised her arms and beat them down and so she flew, beyond the marshy river flats and on without a sound.

She pitched down into a city street at dawn. Nobody saw her as she pulled the frozen flowers from the depths of her pocket and began to pace the cobbles. She placed the flowers on ledges, propped against still-sleeping doors, scattered on along the walkways, their petals dripping icy water. Still nobody saw her, except for Arrak who had woken early to scurry down to the market.

Arrak watched, puzzled by the purple hue of the petals. He bent to touch one, but it seemed to shrink and melt, and so he stepped away to sit and wait. The woman had gone, but soon the streets were peopled with the bustle of the day, And there the flowers lay. First one was plucked up and then another, but soon as they were gathered, each was a flower no more – but a coin, a letter, a ring, a page torn from a forgotten book.

Whoever found them cried with delight. Some slipped the object into their pocket. Others rushed to show it off to their friends. But Arrak watched and saw that their joy was short-lived. Soon they fell to coughing, doubled up and retching, as if the flowers carried a fever which quickly spread from one to another. He hurried away, following the trail of purple flowers which lay bedraggled in the gutter, waiting for the touch of a hand to turn them into glittering trinkets.

Arrak raced on. Soon the scatter of flowers stopped. He looked around, wondering if he would see the woman, so strangely tall with her mask of bone.

There was no-one here in this place. This was an empty yard where nobody came, where broken barrels and the splintered remains of packing cases were scattered all around, where leaves and rubbish blew in on the wind, where lost gloves and the stray bones of unwanted dogs lay among pools of fetid water. Arrak prodded at a rumpled pile of rags, a coat spread out like fallen wings. The woman was beneath it, her mask staring silent to the sky, the last of the flowers clutched between lifeless fingers. Arrak shook her, but the woman did not stir. There was nothing in her pockets, Arrak quickly checked. Nothing to be had but the mask of bone.

Arrak picked at the fraying thread which held the mask in place. He tugged as it slowly came away. Beneath he saw a jutting beak, a matted mass of feathers and cold black eyes which stared at the sky.

He seized up the mask and ran, clutching the bowl of bone to his own face, staring out through the bore hole of the eyes. He did not look back and see the figure rise up in the coat of black. He did not see that now the face was crow no more, but a young girl in an ashen dress, who threw back her tresses and walked away, out onto the dusky streets.

Faces loomed closer as Arrak moved towards them, fancying that none would know him now as he filched, as he picked at unsuspecting pockets, as he fingered purses and twisted rings from ungloved hands. Flowers glowed brighter, oranges on a street-side stall shone radiant as the sun. He grabbed one, stuffed it in his pocket, then ran, as he always did, zig-zagging away.

But then he heard voices calling after him.

"Arrak!" they shouted, as if they knew him. But how could they know? He wore the mask now – nobody knew who he was. But the voices came louder as he ran.

He hauled himself nimbly onto a balcony and looked down. People passing in the street took no notice of him. Arrak leaned forward and peered through the window into a room where shadowy figures danced like wisps of smoke. He could hear them talking, muttering and murmuring through lips that never seemed to move. A gentle echo of tambourines and zithers accompanied their shuffling steps. In the corner, a girl in a long dress the colour of ash was standing by herself. Each time the music stopped, the dancers bowed and changed partners. The girl waited silently, her wide eyes begging someone to ask her to dance, but every time the music started again, she was left to stand alone.

As it grew darker, the dancers continued their slow promenade. Suddenly the girl in the corner got up and began to light the lamps which were positioned around the room. Now Arrak could see that the dancers' robes were shimmering turquoise, scarlet and saffron.

He watched as the girl came to the window and seemed to stare straight through him as she pushed it open. A moth flew in, attracted by the lights, and flitted about the room, its wings nearly scorched by the glowing lamps. It darted to land on the girl's ashen dress, for a moment its wings merging with the dull hue of the cloth, until in an instant the garment glowed and shimmered brightly.

Arrak blinked and watched as the dancing couples parted, leaving space for the girl to flit gracefully to the centre of the room to pirouette and twirl. But then she stopped, half smiling, and stared around, bowing to a ripple of applause, before circling the room again to extinguish each of the lamps one by one.

The dancers danced on, but their garments were colourless again, turning back to smoke and shadows. The girl's own dress faded to ashen grey as she slipped through them all and hurried away down the stairs. Arrak turned to see her a moment later as she stepped out onto the street. He dropped down from the balcony and followed close behind her, almost a shadow himself.

The girl turned.

"Why are you following me?" she asked abruptly.

Arrak shrugged.

"Come," she said. "Walk beside me."

Arrak stepped forward into the light.

"Why are you wearing that mask?" she demanded.

"So no-one will know me," he replied.

"But I know you," she said. "You are Arrak. Your face is carved plainly in the bone."

Arrak stopped.

"How do you know me?"

"I am Fenya," she said. "Don't you remember? I lived in the village… you brought the snakes. I'm Mandra's sister. She was lost in the fire."

Arrak stared at Fenya as she held out her hand.

"Come," she said again. "Follow me."

Dusk had slipped into darkness now as they dodged through the rutted puddles at the end of the stagnant canal. They clambered up the embankment to be met by a high wall slippery with lichen.

Arrak dropped to one knee and motioned Fenya to place her foot in the cup of his hands. She steadied herself and caught her breath as Arrak threw her upward. Her legs grazed the wall before she landed with a stumble on the other side. In a moment, Arrak was beside her and they stood, gazing all around. Purple flowers glowered beneath dark bushes as they crossed a mossy lawn towards a grey stone house shrouded in ivy. Fenya pushed her way through over-grown poppies and snagging brambles with Arrak close behind. His fingers probed the window latches, but none would give. He pressed against the heavy doors, but each was tightly bolted.

Then he heard Fenya whistle softly. He followed around to the side of the house and there a door hung half-open. They slipped inside to a passageway lined with tarnished mirrors, and slithered quickly through the shadows to stumble into a darkened room hung with velvet curtains. A clutter of baubles and bones, pressed flowers and polished stones lay strewn along a high dusty shelf.

Arrak heard Fenya laughing and turned, but couldn't see her through the gloom. She laughed again, but seemed further away now, somewhere out in the corridor. He called her name, but there was no reply and so he fumbled for the handle of the door. It was locked. Arrak stood still and listened, but all he could hear was the flutter of moths' wings all about him. Then a shuffling, from somewhere out along the corridor.

"Fenya!" he called again.

A key rattled in the lock and the door creaked open. There stood the tall woman in the long black coat, her arms raised as if they were wings. Arrak peered up at her. The woman's face was beak and feathers. In one hand she carried a lantern which she set down on the table. Arrak watched as she lit it and a warm glow spread slowly through the room, drawing all the moths from the curtains, from the shelves, down from the picture rails. They fluttered and massed, circling the lantern, until the flurry of their wings extinguished the light and a darkness spread, darker than Arrak had ever known before. He was trapped in a casket of darkness, without air, without touch, without sight.

He felt the woman's hands about his face, picking at the cord which held the mask in place. Then she lifted it away. Arrak blinked. Gradually, he could see again. Light filled the room as if it was dawn. The woman stood before him, wearing the mask.

"Where is Fenya?" Arrak demanded, but the woman said nothing as the moths swarmed around her, smothering her face, covering her body until she stumbled and fell, and then lay silent.

Arrak hurried away, out through the door which now stood open, out into the corridor, calling Fenya's name. Out into the garden which was strewn all about with the purple flowers. Arrak ran, still calling for Fenya, then stopped and looked back at the house which stood grey and huddled, seeming smaller now as dawn began to break. He peered at the doors and windows, and called again, "Fenya, where are you?"

He could hear her laughing.

"Arrak, I am here."

She stepped through the door, her ashen dress spattered with moths' wings. On her face she wore the mask of bone, but its features were her own. In her hand she carried the lantern, still seeping glimmers of darkness.

As she drew closer, Arrak saw that the features of the mask began to change. The nose and the chin grew longer, the cheekbones high, until she looked as if she was the tall woman, striding towards him. She stood in front of him and Arrak grasped the thread which attached the bowl of bone to her face. He ripped it away, and there was Fenya again, laughing as he hung the mask from the low-hanging branch of a tree.

A swarm of moths flew from her mouth and hovered about the mask. Arrak grabbed her hand then, and they ran, away through a meadow of purple flowers which wilted and faded beneath their feet. They caught their breath, then turned to see a crow sitting on the bough of the tree. It stared at them with piercing eyes, raised its wings and flew slowly, back towards the house.

A CHILD OF THE RAIN

At the crook of the long narrow alley, Lintel had built a shelter, a stretch of old sheet from wall to wall to keep out the wind and the rain. She had a bed on a pallet there, a three-legged table and flowers in vases set on the shelves of an old broken cupboard.

Each day Lintel brought more flowers: bindweed, dogwort, roses, dandelions, gathered at dawn from the mist-shrouded wasteground. In winter when all was cold and grey, she painted blossoms on the wall, great swirling shapes in every hue.

With ink and needle she tattooed more, pricking out petals, stems and thorns, twining about her arms, her hands, her legs. Others came – ferry-men, stevedores, urchins and ne'er-do-wells, all to have Lintel's flowers inked into their skin as if they might take root there, burrowing for blood.

At night before she slept, Lintel stooped beside a low table and arranged a collection of yellowing skulls under the light of the moon. Rats' skulls, mice and pigeons. A sheep's skull she got from the trough at the back of the Night Butcher's basement. A monkey's skull a sailor brought and one that some said was the skull of a man, though Lintel would never tell if that was true, nor whose it was and how she came by it. But she had painted it all over with blood red roses and thorns which snaked from its eyes.

One night as Lintel slept, something shifted, something shivered. Thin fingers reached to touch the skulls, to feel the certainty of bone. And then faded, back to darkness, back to silence. It was Mellit who came. She was a child of the rain. Rain swept through her body, caressed her skin, possessed her very veins. Though she sheltered in the gunnels, shuddered in dark doorways, the rain was always with her. Even when the sun shone brooding and bright, she shivered, her fingers trembling, a skein of rain dripping moist through her hair.

Lintel woke with a start to see the skulls shifting on the table where she placed them. She shot out a hand to clutch at what felt to be an arm, though in the dark it seemed as though no-one was there. Then she saw Mellit, slowly, like she was a mist of grey water forming in the alleyway. A cringing child, groveling. But eyes sparking, haunting, hunted, wild. The rat's skull dropped onto the table.

"Who are you?" Lintel hissed. "What do you want?"

"Want to touch," Mellit's voice no more than a whisper, seeping into the crumbling mortar of the walls.

Lintel grabbed her, though as she did, it felt as though the child was fading again. Mellit pointed then to the flowers, wilting in their vases.

"Flowers will shrivel," her frail voice murmured. "Flesh will be gone…"

She touched Lintel's arm, staring for a moment at the petals etched there on her skin. She grabbed again at one of the skulls, pressing it to her face.

"… but bones will live on." Lintel prized the skull from Mellit's fingers, though the girl gripped determinedly, then let it fall.

"The bones are dead," Lintel said.

Mellit touched one again.

"If so dead, then why do you keep them?"

Lintel smiled and thought for a moment.

"If so dead, tells me I am alive."

Rain sluiced down from the sodden sheet above them. It seemed to Lintel that the girl was scarcely there at all, just a voice whispering in the darkness.

"Give me one of them," Mellit begged. "Give me one dead bone so I can be alive."

Lintel stroked Mellit's fingers, which trembled in a dance of their own.

"You are live enough, I think," Lintel told her. "Have to find your own bones."

Mellit touched each skull, one by one, and asked Lintel their names. Lintel told her, the rat, the mouse and the pigeon, the sheep and the monkey. All except the largest one.

Mellit paused.

"Who is this?" she said.

Lintel shook her head and smiled.

"Many ask me, but I cannot tell."

Mellit pulled away, then squatted on her haunches.

"Don't you want more?"

Lintel nodded. "Always want more."

"What you want most?"

Lintel considered.

The first stutter of starlings and sparrows shivered in the dark of a dawn that scarce touched the walls of the alley, drowned out by a dull sudden 'craak'.

"Could be a crow," she said at last.

Mellit nodded.

"I can get you a crow."

Jarraque shuffled slow about his shop. Shelves of tallow, candles, wax. Shelves of lamps and twine and hemp. Hanging nets meshed with spider webs. Cabinets filled with nails and tacks. Mallets and hammers, bludgeoning, blunt. Drawers of knives flashing whetted and sharp. Jars of tobacco, carved boxes of snuff. Buttons. Threads. Shelves filled with trinkets that nobody would want.

Jarraque tugged a bale of sailcloth from a top shelf with a bill-hook. Dust billowed and settled. The crow on the perch in the corner let out a tired belch. The doorbell rattled. Jarraque looked up for a moment. The door swung open then closed again. Jarraque lowered the sailcloth onto the floor, glanced over his shoulder and shrugged, cursing the wind. He shook the dust from his calloused hands as the crow ruffled its feathers, clattered its wings and squawked.

Wind from the docks would sweep up the street, carrying the smack of the salt, the lure of the spices, the skirl of the gulls. Customers came and went, bo'suns for ship supplies, painted ladies for tawdry trinkets, urchin children for a twist of licorice. Come and go, fast and slow, Jarraque served them all.

But now the shop was empty. Jarraque sneezed. Wiped his nose with a tattered rag that he hauled from his pocket. He watched the dust settle. Watched as the crow cocked its head, shuffled and squawked along its perch. Jarraque turned away, winding a length of loose ribbon before prodding it back in a drawer.

"Bird's worse than the wind," he muttered. "Always wants you to look at something when something is nothing at all."

The crow raised its wings in a flurry of feathers, beak pecking wildly.

"Hush your racket," Jarraque grumbled. He glared at the crow then seized up a small wooden flute which lay among the clutter of trinkets on the counter. He raised it to his lips and blew. Out came a sound like the trilling of birds. The crow cocked its head, shuffled up and down the perch. Jarraque played on until one final, sudden breath produced a rasping cry, so like the crow's own croaking 'kraaw'. The crow stopped and blinked and settled its wings.

Jarraque smiled, placed the flute back on the counter and stepped forward to stroke the bird's feathers. As he did, the motes of dust hovering in the light which sloped through the door seemed all at once to cling together, till he could see the shape of Mellit standing there.

She made a grab at the crow, but it flew up, screeching, its wings beating the air. Jarraque tried to hold the girl, but she slipped from his grip. Slipped almost through him, through the dust and the glint of the sun from the door till she lighted by the counter, glanced quickly around, seized up the flute and was gone before Jarraque could stop her.

The shop bell jangled. Jarraque scratched his head and watched the dust settle as the crow scuttled up and down its perch, then folded its wings and stared bewildered at the street beyond the door.

Lintcl sat in the dirt of the alley. Sun sloped down the wall, lighting the flowers she had painted, as she traced the outline of a willowherb, creeping between the mortar. All about, the birds sang more loudly than ever. She turned around, sensing Mellit was there, somewhere in the shadows. Mellit smiled, pressed the wooden flute to her lips and played, imitating thrushes, blackbirds, warblers, their voices meshed in song.

Then she stepped forward.

Lintel looked at her.

"Thought you were bringing me a crow," she chided.

Mellit shrugged.

"Crow will come," she said. "Watch."

She blew again. Harder, louder, harsher. The birds in the alley fell silent. Lintel put down her brush. A crow landed beside them. A young one, its feathers still soft, its eyes ablaze. It looked around, then hopped boldly up to Lintel's outstretched hand.

"Welcome," she said, grasping the bird and stroking the feathers of its head.

"Put it down," Mellit instructed.

Lintel just stared, her eyes glazed over as her fingers probed the shape of the crow's young skull.

"Put it down!" said Mellit again, then blew a blast on the flute so it sounded like a great mother crow. The young one squirmed in Lintel's hands, then pecked at her fingers till she opened them and the bird flew away.

Mellit put down the flute.

"He is not ready. Leave him be."

Lintel sighed.

Mellit came and sat on the floor beside her and rested her head on the older woman's knee. She glanced again at the skulls on the table, shifting them about so they caught the sun while Lintel stroked her hair, fingers probing the lines of her scalp.

Mellit jumped up.

"Do something for me!"

Lintel frowned. "You promised a crow and you brought a flute."

Mellit nodded. "Crow will come when I call, you know that."

She held out one arm.

"Make flowers grow there," she pointed, tracing one finger along the lines of dark veins.

Lintel shrugged and reached for her inks and her needle.

"Hold still,' she said. "What flowers do you want?"

Mellit considered, then picked up the skull all painted with roses.

"Same as these," she said.

The sun faded then and they sat in the shadow. Lintel gripped Mellit's arm. She smeared crimson ink with her thumb and then began to prick with her needle. Mellit watched intently until Lintel rubbed the ink away and stared.

"Nothing is there," she exclaimed.

She shook her head and laid the needle aside.

"Ink will not take," she said. "What are you made with, child? Seems to me you are nothing but dust and your veins flow only with rain."

Mellit grinned and shook back her hair. She picked up the flute, blew lightly once and then faded into the shadows.

The doorbell jangled. Jarraque looked up. The crow scuttled awkwardly up and down its perch as a tall woman walked in. She was dressed all in black, grey hair hanging loose about her shoulders. She stared at Jarraque with dark piercing eyes as she placed a battered case on the counter and snapped open the catch. Inside lay a fiddle, covered in dust. Two strings were broken, its body cracked.

"How much?" she said.

Jarraque stared at it a while, rubbing the back of his neck. Then looked up at the woman.

"How much?" she said again, lifting the fiddle from its case, tenderly, as if it was a lost child, and placing it in his hands.

Jarraque held the instrument a moment. Plucked the two remaining strings, both out of tune. The crow croaked in complaint.

"This fiddle," said the woman, "has played many tunes."

She almost smiled, as if remembering, before repeating, "How much?"

Jarraque shook his head, turning the instrument over in his hands.

"What can I say?" he pondered. "Who will buy it? It needs so much work to fix it…"

"So fix it then," said the woman impatiently and turned to glare at the crow who was rasping with displeasure.

"Fix it and then you can play to the bird. See if you can teach it to sing!"

The bird quietened then as the woman turned back to stare straight at Jarraque.

"How much?"

Jarraque shrugged. Named a price. It was low. He expected the woman to haggle for more, but she pushed the fiddle towards him and held out her hand. He paid her quickly, the doorbell rattled and she was gone.

As the days passed, Jarraque fixed the fiddle. He fitted new pegs, he found new strings. He repaired the bridge and kneaded wax into the crack along its back. He re-strung the bow and rosined it. There the instrument lay in its shabby case until one day, just as dusk was falling, he took it out and held it, turning it in his hands. He pressed it against his shoulder and raised the bow to the strings. One long harsh note and then another, as the crow squawked indignantly. Jarraque played on, his fingers slowly finding the tunes that he'd forgotten, there beneath his fingers - melodies from childhood, till the dust in the shop seemed to dance with the joy of it.

Jarraque unlocked the back door and carried the fiddle out into the darkened courtyard. He played for the moon. A sighing song that seemed to sweep and rise and fall again, trembling like a lover's sighs. And then a voice joined in. Jarraque looked up to see if a face had appeared at any of the windows surrounding the courtyard, but they all remained closed. He played on and the voice sang with him. It was the voice of a woman and she seemed to know the tune of this song that he had not played since his childhood days.

Somehow Jarraque fancied this was the voice of the woman who had brought him the fiddle. He tapped his foot and speeded up the rhythm, smiling beguilingly to see if she would appear, to dance with him in this dingy courtyard deep in the city.

But no-one came, though the voice sang on, seeming, if anything, further away. Jarraque made his way back through the shop and out into the street. Hardly anyone was about, only the odd drunkard stumbling home and two lovers sharing the darkness of an unlit doorway.

Jarraque played on, following the voice which seemed to be leading him, teasing him, flitting close by, then far away. His fingers were tiring now, stumbling on the strings, his brain numb from trying to vary the tune, so that he just repeated the one simple melody.

His boots echoed eerily across the empty cobbles as the voice led him down towards the canal. He stood beside the looming water, the notes from the fiddle sounding back from the arching brickwork of the nearby bridge.

Then he stopped. Jarraque realised he could not hear the singing any more. He looked around, but nobody was there. He walked on, a few paces, till his boot stumbled against the carcass of a donkey lying on the towpath. He stared down at the animal's face, one of its eyes still open, as if it was watching him. The night was so still. Only a drip of water from the parapet of the bridge.

Jarraque played again, the tune, very slowly. Very slowly the animal heaved itself onto its legs and hobbled, hesitantly at first, up the path which led back to the streets. The donkey's hooves clattered across the cobbles, leading Jarraque through the darkness till they came to the courtyard again. They passed through the gateway where the carts came and went, then came to a stop. Jarraque stood a moment, catching his breath, when he heard the tune again. This time not the woman singing, but another fiddle, up in one of the attic rooms.

Jarraque smiled, stuck his own fiddle back under his chin, raking his bow, weaving and churning, improvising harmonies, his boot tapping out the rhythm as they played. Then he heard footsteps behind him. He turned around. It was the tall woman, her black coat gaunt against the moonlight. Her eyes seemed not to see him, though he caught the glimmer of a smile.

And then she sang, the notes soaring high, echoing back from the courtyard walls, as the voices of the two fiddles swooped and dived around her like birds in flight. Then she stopped and swung onto the back of the waiting donkey and rode slowly away. Jarraque ceased playing, his fiddle dangling by his side while the other played on. Jarraque stood for a moment and then joined in again, but soon as he did, the other fiddler stopped. Jarraque waited, but he heard nothing more. The night had grown cold. Jarraque shrugged, slipped through the back entrance into his shop and quickly bolted the door.

Mellit ran scrawny fingers over the monkey's skull, the pigeon's, while Lintel slept in the sun. She seized up the biggest skull, the skull painted with roses, and held it to her lips as if she might kiss it.

Lintel opened one eye.

"Put it down!" she said.

Mellit placed the skull carefully back on the table with the others.

"Do not touch them," Lintel grated. "I told you before."

She gripped Mellit's arm.

"You're a strange one. What's the matter? You got no bones of your own? That why you're always picking at mine?"

She rapped Mellit's knuckles.

"Keep your fingers off... or go and take them to filch something else."

Mellit pulled away from her, then smiled.

"What do you want?' she said. "Got you the flute... is that not enough?"

"Course it's not enough," Lintel grunted. "If I had enough,

would I live here?"

She pointed up at the tattered sheet, stretched between the walls of the alley, so thin it scarce kept out the rain and faded bare in the glare of the sun.

In the shadow of the shop, nobody saw her. Customers came and went, picking through Jarraque's trinkets while the crow sat and watched them, silent on its perch. Sometimes Mellit thought that the bird caught her eye, but it just looked sad and lost, staring straight through her. Jarraque seemed long-faced too. When the shop was empty he picked up the fiddle, but the crow gave one 'craak' and he put it down. He ran his thumb lightly across the strings and looked at the bird.

"*She* sang," he said. "You cannot sing. And I cannot blow on the flute anymore to bring you other birds' songs."

He looked up suddenly. The door bell rattled as if someone was leaving. He turned back to the crow with its head hung low.

"Must have been the wind..."

Mellit sat again in the alleyway, underneath Lintel's canopy. Her fingers idly stroked the flute, then she raised it to her lips. As she played, sparrows came hopping, like bobbing gobbets of rain. Then starlings, rattling and tussling before a blackbird silenced them all with his song. Finches and a robin came, a thrush and wagtail too, scurrying through the dust.

Lintel reached out a hand to still Mellit's playing.

"The crow," she said. "Where is the crow? Play a crow for me. You know I want a crow."

Mellit shook her head and pretended the note was too low.

"I cannot reach it anymore," she said.

She looked up at the grey clouds looming in the sky.

"And anyway, the crow that you want is too sad. I saw it yesterday, clinging to its perch. It will not come."

Lintel grunted and threw crumbs to the birds who pecked all around.

"They're a noisy lot. Don't know why you call them here.

And the mess they make... all I wanted was a crow," she complained.

Mellit stopped playing and made to slip the flute into her pocket.

"Mayhap I should take it back."

Lintel stopped her.

"If I take it back," Mellit continued, "mayhap I can bring you the crow you truly want – the one in Jarraque's shop."

Lintel snatched the flute.

"This stays here," she said, tucking it into her apron. "This is for the birds that fly in the sky. Don't need no flute to trap a crow that spends all day sat on a perch."

Mellit scowled and wrapped her arms about her head, rocking to and fro. Lintel turned away.

"Don't know what you hang round here for every day," she muttered.

But when she looked back, Mellit had gone.

The skull had gone too. The skull painted round with twisted thorns and roses. Mellit clutched it to her like it was a baby as she scuttled through the streets.

Jarraque looked up as the doorbell clattered and Mellit placed the skull on the counter.

"What is this?" he asked.

The crow raised its head to stare at the girl who said nothing at all.

Jarraque picked up the skull and turned it in his hands, then he put it down again. It lay on the dusty counter. Nobody said anything. The crow sat silent and watched, then let out an ear-splitting 'craaak!'

The painted flowers on the skull began to fade, but the thorns knotted tighter as the bone started to moulder, rotting like a fruit. Jarraque watched as its skin split open, filling the shop with a damp odour of decay. A seething mass of worms spilled out, writhing about an egg which glistened and then cracked.

Jarraque leaned forward, mesmerized, and did not notice

Mellit as she slipped away. The crow clattered its wings and then flew after her, out through the open door.

The egg hatched an eye, pale and unblinking. Jarraque stared deeply through it until he saw the courtyard outside the back door of the shop. There stood the tall woman in her long black coat. Jarraque listened as she began to sing again, and as she sang, a girl came running out of the shadows. It was Mellit. She ran to the woman and wrapped her arms around her waist. The woman smiled briefly and ruffled Mellit's hair. As she continued with her song, the crow came flying from an open window, circled the courtyard and perched on Mellit's shoulder.

Jarraque could scarce control his tears. He seized up the fiddle from its case and hurried out through the back of the shop to join them. But the courtyard was empty and rain began to fall as roses grew everywhere, blood-red and bloated, their jagged thorns clawing at the walls.

SPARROW IN A CAGE

Ghresselle woke in an attic at the top of the old hotel. The room was strewn with feathers from the birds which landed on the windowsill and the webs of spiders which wove their way from wall to ceiling to floor.

Sometimes Ghresselle wondered if anybody knew she was there. No-one ever bothered her, or came to collect the rent, though sometimes a tray of food would be left outside the door. And sometimes there would be nothing left at all. Sometimes Ghresselle would be hungry, and sometimes she would not. Sometimes she could not remember if she was ever hungry at all.

Sometimes she wondered if perhaps it was her who owned the hotel. She would wander out at night and roam along the corridors and listen to the sounds behind the doors of laughing, drinking, cursing. Of strangers lost in passion. But she would see no-one as she walked and some nights she heard no-one at all, as if the whole building was deserted. Then she opened the doors of the empty rooms to gaze upon the unmade beds, the clothing lying where it had fallen, trinkets strewn across dressing tables and the dregs of bottles spilling onto the floor.

But the people would return. She could hear the chatter, the excitement rising, the echo of music from the floor below. Then Ghresselle swept down the curve of the staircase, her long dress trailing out behind, to dance by herself in the silent ballroom, the chandeliers glistening, wine glasses sparkling. She twirled and swirled and smiled and curtseyed to the shadows and the drift of musk and snuff and the clatter of painted fans, the whispers and sighs which ebbed from another room. A room which she could never find.

She could never find herself, lost in all these rooms. Each day when she woke, Ghresselle did not know who she was or where she was. The insects in the walls, if walls they were at all, rattled louder than the clatter of cartwheels on the street, while the colours in her head blazed bright as burning coals and her tongue tasted bitter as stone. When she wandered out into the streets, some saw her on her flittings and thought she was their mother lost, or sister or lover who had left them. They called out to her, but Ghresselle did not hear, thinking these shadows to be only her own imagining.

In the iron-grey morning, a man wheeled a handcart towards her across the wasteground. It was piled high with rags he had collected, but on top lay a gown she once wore, she knew. She reached out to grab it and begged him to stop, but the man did not turn and the cart trundled on to be lost between the shadows of the warehouses which loomed all around.

Ghresselle walked along another street which seemed both wide and endless. The sky pressed down, her hands were heavy, her arms, her legs. She gazed at the ground where a brown leaf skittered past her. She bent to pick it up, but the leaf was caught in a swirl of wind and danced away. Ghresselle reached out to catch it, but each time she did, the leaf slipped beyond her until it was not a leaf anymore but a small brown sparrow, hopping and chirruping.

The tiny bird led her along the street until she came to a house and there the sparrow flitted inside. Ghresselle followed again and found herself in a paneled hallway. The sparrow flew on, darting up the staircase and along a shadowy corridor until it came to an open door. There it seemed to pause, waiting to make sure that Ghresselle was behind before fluttering inside.

Inside the room, a table was laid for a meal. The food had already been served onto plates, but nobody sat in the chairs. Ghresselle listened, expecting to hear approaching voices, but nobody came. She looked around for the sparrow, just to see it fly out through the heavy door again which then closed suddenly, as if a gust of wind had blown it shut.

Large dark paintings hung on the wall, but each showed the same view, the long wide street which had brought her here, the tall houses seeming to lean inward, blocking out the sky.

Ghresselle peered at each one of them. There were no people in any of the pictures, not at the windows nor down in the street below. Just as there seemed to be no people in this house.

Ghresselle sat down at the table and stared at the plates of food: baked fish and sliced vegetables, covered in a milky sauce. The steam still rose from each portion, as if they had been newly-served. She picked up a fork and prodded, lifted a morsel to her lips. She blew a moment, cautiously, then touched it with her tongue. The food was quite cold, though the steam still rose. And it tasted of dust. Ghresselle pushed the plate away. In the centre of the table sat a bowl of brightly-coloured sweetmeats, a kaleidoscope of orange, turquoise and green.

Ghresselle eyed them curiously, but then turned back to stare at the paintings on the wall. The lines of the streets and the frames themselves rose hard and rigid, as if they were bars. As if this was a cage and not a room at all. The table had gone, the plates, the food. Ghresselle tried to sit, but there were no chairs. She could only beat her wings frantically inside the cage.

A girl came then to feed her. She had picked up the bowl of sweetmeats from the table and also carried a bag of seeds. She smiled and cooed and poked her fingers through the bars, pulling them out quickly as Ghresselle tried to peck. Ghresselle stared intently at the seeds and opened her beak in anticipation. But to her surprise, the girl began to pick at the seeds herself, nibbling them between her teeth. And then she broke off pieces of sweetmeat and fed them through the bars of the cage.

Ghresselle stared at them. The girl cooed again, encouragingly.

"Eat," she said. "Eat…"

Ghresselle picked at the vividly-coloured fragments. They were sweeter than anything she had tasted before. The girl's face loomed closer, her hazel eyes translucent.

Ghresselle beat her wings furiously and retreated into the corner. The girl sat silent now, her eyes muted, still chewing at the bag of seeds as Ghresselle tried to sing to her, but all that came from her stunted beak was a plaintive chirrup. The girl smiled again and tiptoed slowly away. Ghresselle peered up at the looming bars, tucked her head beneath her wing and slept.

As she slept, Ghresselle dreamt, sparrow that she was, that she hopped and pecked through the gunnels of the city. Grit and grain, apple peelings and crusts of bread. She dodged the rats, their sleuth eyes bright, the dogs and cats, the slithering slugs that left their listless silver trails. The walls were dark with water, the sky a baleful grey. Behind her a tall man came, swinging wild on wooden crutches, pursuing her down the alley. He loomed above her, the shadow of his flapping coat swirling about her like a cloud.

Ghresselle squawked. She flapped her wings but the man grabbed sudden, his fingers gripping, his crutches slipping to the ground. He held her then, leaning against the wall. She could smell his breath, rank with bile and garlic. His teeth were broken, his tongue rolled darkly.

And then he smiled.

"You're a pretty one," he said.

His name was Lucksore.

He tucked Ghresselle in his pocket and swung himself back onto his crutches, then made his way along the narrow passage, dodging between barrels and broken boxes and gutter spouts spilling dull rain.

He sat in the doorway of a tall, blackened building and there he taught Ghresselle how to sing. He hummed the notes, but when she tried to repeat them, all she heard was the bark of harsh voices, the tolling of bells and the rattle of chains. Lucksore smiled and sang the notes again.

Ghresselle puffed out her chest and took in a breath, but each time she opened her beak, all that came out was a sad sparrow's squawk. Lucksore laughed and ruffled her feathers. He sat in the doorway with his cap set before him and called out to strangers to toss him loose coins.

Ghresselle hopped down and pecked at the money. The

copper shone brightly, the sweet silver gleamed.

Lucksore laughed again.

"You cannot eat it," he said.

"Then what is it worth?" she pondered as he sang her the tune again and she repeated it but still flat and low until his voice slowed. Ghresselle looked up. Lucksore was asleep.

Soon as he slept, Ghresselle saw into his dreams. He dreamt he was flying high over a mountain, gazing down at the clouds, the forests and streams. He was singing the song he had tried to teach Ghresselle, but now she could hear it as it should be sung and she could sing it too. And she was not a sparrow no more but a beautiful bird with feathers of gold. And the scatter of coins in Lucksore's cap all turned to sweetmeats, bright vivid colours. Then Ghresselle was back in the cage again in the room in the house and the girl whose eyes shone hazel bright was peering at her through the bars.

The girl smiled as she opened the door of Ghresselle's cage and held out her hand. Ghresselle looked up and hopped closer as she beckoned to her, fluttered onto her finger as the girl bent and kissed her.

The girl's tongue was soft as a leaf. Her arms were branches as Ghresselle nestled soft within her and shadows wrapped around them both. Ghresselle stepped forward, raking fingers through her hair, plucking out twigs and spiders as if she was emerging from a forest. She blinked as she stood in the street again, which seemed both wide and long. In her hand she clutched a leaf, brown and shriveled. She opened her fingers to look at it, but the leaf was caught in a swirl of wind and danced away.

Ghresselle smiled as she brushed cobwebs from her dress and continued on along the street. Her hands felt freed now, her arms, her legs. As she watched the brown leaf twist away, it seemed to her it became a sparrow that hopped and chirruped and turned once to look back before it flapped its wings and flew.

Ghresselle kept walking. It was dusk now, the grey light

stirring with a tang of salt and rumours of rain. She rubbed her eyes. In the distance, motes of dust clung to one another, gathering until they became a clutch of bedraggled feathers. The sparrow flying towards her again. Yet as it came closer, was not a bird but the girl walking slowly, her thin coat flapping in the wind.

Ghresselle stood still as the girl approached and stared into her face as the shadow of a memory woke inside her. She reached out and touched the girl's cheek. It was cold. Not the cold of this rain-damp evening but another day long ago.

"I left you in the doorway, daughter," Ghresselle whispered. "I left you in the snow. I could not wait to watch the dark door open. I left you there. I had to go."

But the girl just smiled as she stroked Ghresselle's hand.

"Mother - how could you leave me? You never bore me at all. I was a dream in your eyes. I was a sigh on your lips as my father took you. But you never saw me. You never held me. You never bore me at all..."

Ghresselle let her hand drop. The girl had gone. Now not even a sparrow, not even a leaf. Only the cold wind and the slow gentle kiss of the rain. In the distance, the creaking wheel of a handcart. As it turned the corner, Ghresselle reached out and grabbed the robe which had once been hers, from the top of the pile of rags. She held it to her and began to dance as if she could hear the music from the ballroom of a hotel filled with dust and shadows on the other side of the city. The man pushing the handcart turned back and looked at her, but said nothing as he trundled on, over the cobbles and down towards the harbour.

IN THE SHADOW OF THE FOUNTAIN

Grob was dead, Morrow knew. But when he woke and looked into the room, he saw the old man still sitting there, staring into the fire. But it was only Grob's threadbare coat, hanging over a chair. Yet he still heard his voice:

"I have taught you all I know."

How to move quick and catch the rats twixt his fingers as they scuttled in the shadows. To hold them up, to snap their necks, to cast them in his sack.

Morrow rose and put on the coat, its long black sleeves, the deep dark pockets, and found it fitted him well enough. So then he shuffled out and down the stairs, just as Grob had ever done.

The deserted streets were grey with the dust of dawn. Nothing stirred except one clumsy pigeon, pecking at the trail of grain spilt from a sack on the back of a cart. Morrow's legs set to running, dodging between shadows and puddles. As he ran faster, the streets became busier with huddles of people, threading their way to the packing sheds and the markets. Morrow kept running, slipping between them, closer than the air they breathed, but never so much as touching them. It was as if no-one could see him.

He rounded the corner on the road which led down to the waterfront, crowded with figures all jostling and shoving, heads down without looking. Morrow ran straight into a shipwright with his bag of mallets and chisels. The man's whole body became a mass of flowers of every colour which tumbled to the ground.

As Morrow pressed his way deeper into the crowd, people became pigeons and gulls, spiralling away on the breeze. Then on the quayside, he collided with a sail-maker about to board his ship. The man became a tree, rooted there on the dockside, sprouting leaves and blossom which cascaded down onto the hard paving stones.

Morrow ran on and nobody noticed. Nobody saw the

flowers or the birds. Nobody saw the tree. Morrow kept running until he came to a street all covered in ivy and weeds. The lintels were rotted, the windows gaped empty and the gutters were choked with silt. He did not recognise the door to the tenement where he lived, hanging half open, its lock corroded with rust.

Morrow looked about. It was night again and a thin rain was falling. He shivered inside Grob's dark coat, bunched his fists in the depths of the pockets, and set off towards a square of tall gaunt houses. All was silent. As Morrow approached, he saw a woman standing beside the fountain. Her long hair spilled over a flowing robe sewn from scarlet and gold, which turned to flame – but she did not burn. She held out her hand to him, and in it lay a small red seed. Morrow reached to take it, but the woman was gone. The seed fell to the ground, and from it sprang a pale flower which bloomed in the shadow of the fountain.

As Morrow watched, the flame returned. It crawled the length of the flower's stem and wrapped itself about the petals, which burned and burned. But the flower was not consumed. Morrow drew his hands from his pockets and held them out, hoping they might be warmed.

As the waters of the fountain rose and fell, through their rippling cascade, Morrow heard the sound of a flute playing low. And the woman's voice calling, laughing and crying, then laughing again as he walked away.

*

Tansy shuffled her way slowly towards the square. It was dusk and already people were gathering, spreading blankets by the fountain, opening baskets of fresh bread, cheeses and fine wine. Sometimes they threw morsels to the shadowy figures that lurked around the edges of the crowd. But Tansy was always too slow to catch even a crumb.

She threaded her way through the throng until she sat as close as she could to the flower which blossomed brightly, its petals still open, even though the sun had gone. And around it the

103

flame which seemed to spring from its stem. As the people watched, it burned and burned. But the flower was never consumed.

As the night grew colder and darker, the crowds slowly drifted away, leaving Tansy alone to pick out the crusts of bread which lay in the grass. She gnawed at them hungrily, then sat to watch the flame which wrapped itself around the flower and spread a little warmth to Tansy's trembling hands.

She watched the flickering flame for a while, letting it lull her into a waking sleep in which she saw geese swooping across distant marsh flats and a white horse galloping across a darkened field. Tansy followed the horse which led her to a low stone cottage wreathed with tangled ivy where an old woman sat, swathed in a patchwork shawl. Children were coming, running towards her, as if she was the old woman and these were her grandchildren bringing cakes and cheeses and bread. And then one more girl came slowly, across the shadows of the marsh flats, and presented her with a small carved wooden boat.

Tansy smiled. The boat was packed with spices. She lifted it up to breathe in the rich aroma which she had never smelt before. And then she fell asleep. She was lying now inside the boat as it drifted on along the dark waters of the canal, knocking gently against the walls of passing warehouses, wharfs and locks. High up at every window she could see young girls and old women making lace, the white moonlight catching the pale bones of their bobbins as they shuttled them quickly with long skillful fingers.

The boat stopped. Tansy watched as the cargo of spice was unloaded. The gaunt door of the warehouse opened as the boxes were trundled across the cobbles and set down inside to be exchanged for bales of lace.

The boat moved again slowly, drifting back through the deep black water. Tansy wore a long lace dress as she stood in the bows in the moonlight. The stark high walls and the stunted trees all shimmered with frost. Her limbs were so cold, it was as if the blood in her veins had frozen.

She stared straight ahead, as her body stood rigid, a sculpture of ice. Then cracked. Her hands splintered, her arms, her legs as she toppled down to the bank of the canal, watching the boat slip away.

She lay as the night seeped into her: the stars, the moon, the dew from the grass, the moss which lodged between the cobbles. The lick of a tongue across her face. Tansy looked up. A great black dog stood over her, its eyes like fires in the darkness. She reached out a hand to rub its nose and the dog licked her fingers, her arms, her neck. She hugged it then and held it close until the warmth returned to her veins.

The dog rose and shook itself, then walked away, leaving Tansy alone again. She stared at a bright flower which had thrust its way between the cobble stones. Its petals spread and opened even though darkness still gripped all around. Its petals were pale as the frost and its stem pallid as bone. As Tansy reached out to touch it, the flower burst into flames.

She smiled, cupping her cold fingers around its heat. But the lace of her dress caught the flame and flared up, wrapping her body in a sheath of fire. Tansy stood, her hair blazing in the darkness of the night. She tried to scream, but no sound came as she looked up to the lace-makers' windows, and saw all the shutters were closed.

She burned. She burned but she was not consumed. She burned. She burned but she felt no pain. She burned but the white lace dress still clung to her body. She burned as she walked, a living torch, along the bank of the canal.

She reached out to touch the long stems of rushes, grabbed fistfuls of brambles and weeds, to see if they would burn too. But all remained the same as she walked on, back towards the city, where she slipped between tall buildings, down unlit gullies, slithering cat-like along the gutters as she peered in through open windows at unsuspecting lovers.

But no-one saw her. No-one saw her come and no one saw her go, blazing like a slow comet through the city's night until she returned to the square. There beside the fountain she woke from her sleep to stare into the pale grey eye of the dawn.

She was not burned. She wore her own old clothes, dull as dust, and she was curled close to the flower of flame which still flickered in the early morning light.

Tansy sat up then and looked about. The square was empty. Nobody else was awake. But then across the grass, a tall woman in a long lace dress came walking towards her, a large black dog beside her on a lead. As they came closer, the dog leapt forward and began to lick Tansy's face.

Tansy smiled and flung her arms around his neck. His tongue seemed familiar. She looked up and saw the woman was smiling too.

"You must be hungry," the woman said, and bent down to give Tansy a package wrapped in paper.

Tansy opened it carefully. Inside was a nest of small sweetmeats.

"Eat…" said the woman, as she tugged the dog away.

A soft wind rustled the leaves on the trees which surrounded the square and the flame of the burning flower flickered gently. Tansy pressed one of the sweetmeats to her lips. Touched it with her tongue. It tasted of the spices which had been packed into the small carved boat of her dream. She ate hungrily, reaching down, her fingers sticky, to take another one. Then she turned to ask the woman where she had got these delicious sweetmeats. She looked all about. The square was empty. The woman had gone.

Instead, by her side lay a small carved boat. As Tansy reached out to touch, it crumbled to ashes. A gentle rain began to fall, but beside the fountain's shimmering water, the flame of the flower burned on.

NO SORROW

Fenya walked the streets at dusk trying to find the harbour, each narrow alleyway threading to another, the basements lewd with bawdiness and the gutters sluiced with liquor. Then silent cobbles and no sound of strife or laughter till her eye was drawn to an upper window where sat a young girl weeping.

Fenya hurried on, but before long she saw another, in another house, another window, but as if the same girl sat there in a green flowing dress, calling wordlessly for help till her voice seemed to follow round every shadowy corner. The same girl in the same dress, the same cry from house after house, again and again till Fenya could bear it no longer and she stopped and she knocked upon the door of the dwelling where she could hear the girl above, wailing at the window.

An old woman shuffled down and asked what was wanted.

"That girl upstairs," Fenya explained. "She must be in sorrow, she must be in pain. Can you not help her?"

The old woman glared.

"No sorrow here," she said.

But Fenya pushed past her and stood in the passageway.

"Please take me to her."

The old woman shrugged.

"No sorrow here," she repeated. "Come see."

And she led Fenya up the rickety stairs then pushed open the door to the room at the top. Fenya peered inside. The room was bare, just one narrow bed and a dressing table..

"No sorrow," the old woman repeated.

Fenya turned, but then she heard laughter close by.

"Is there another room?" she asked.

The old woman paused then reluctantly drew back a curtain to reveal a second door. Again there was the sound of laughter inside. The old woman turned the handle and shuffled slowly in.

A young girl sat on a crumpled bed, dressed same as each of the other wailing figures that Fenya had seen before: long flowing hair and a dark green dress. Fenya stepped towards her, holding out a hand. The girl turned and smiled then laughed again, the sound rippling clear and light in the darkening room. Fenya was about to speak to her, but the old woman drew her away.

"See," she said. "No sorrow here."

Fenya was ushered down the stairs and out into the street. She stood a moment puzzling before walking slowly on. Then she turned and looked back at the window again and saw that the young girl stood there, just as she had before, with tears in her eyes and gesturing wordlessly, imploring Fenya not to leave.

But Fenya shook her head and turned away, her footsteps echoing in the silent street. She felt so someone was watching her and when she looked up she saw, as before, the girl standing at yet another upper window, her long flowing hair tumbling over her dark green dress. The face was harrowed and Fenya heard her wailing, but this time ignored the sound and hurried quickly on, heading for the harbour.

She did not stop and turn. She did not look to see that the girl had opened the window and flung a screw of paper to the street below. She did not walk back and open the paper. She did not find that on the paper the girl had drawn a skull.

Fenya turned another corner and another corner more. And then she saw, daubed upon a wall, etched into the mortar in a grume of grime and water, the outline of a skull, same as the skull drawn on the paper. She hurried on, her eyes turned to the floor, not wanting to look back.

She passed through a shadowy passageway out onto another street. Still the silence, still the windows which gazed down as before. And as before, the young girl in a dress of flowing green. Fenya looked up at her, and as she did the window opened and the girl threw down a screw of folded paper. Fenya glanced up at her. The girl gestured urgently that she should catch the paper as it fluttered down in the gathering dusk like a moth with pale grey wings.

Fenya chased along the pavement, reached and caught it

breathlessly then turned to look back at the window. The weeping girl was smiling now and blew Fenya a kiss. Fenya was about to call out to her when the girl drew the curtain. Fenya stared uncertainly, then slowly unfolded the paper. On it, etched in bitter ink, the outline of a skull, same as the one she had seen before, daubed upon the wall.

The darkness was gathering. Though these streets were silent, in the distance Fenya could hear the echo of the riverside, voices calling and raucous laughter. She saw another skull painted on a wall and then another and then another more, each one drawing her on towards the harbour.

Fenya came then to a flight of uneven steps. She stopped a moment, peering into the gloom. She thought she heard the sound of shuffling feet following close behind her and held her breath, but then the silence returned. There was a skull on the wall half-way down. Fenya made her way towards it, slithering on the slippery steps, her fingers gripping to a rickety rail hanging from the wall.

At the bottom she found herself at the edge of a narrow canal. A thin mist swirled about her, but then beneath the shadow of a bridge she saw the figure of the weeping girl, gazing into the water. Fenya approached her, but the girl said nothing, her thin hands clutching at the folds of her long green dress. Fenya stood with her a moment and followed her gaze into the water. There in the murky gloom she saw the refection, not of the weeping girl's face but of the skull she had seen on the walls.

Fenya turned suddenly to look at the girl. Grey pigeons scuttled on a ledge beneath the bridge, their muffled calls mingling with the echo of water dripping into the canal below. But the girl had gone.

Fenya retraced her steps, determined now to find her. She followed the trail of skulls back along the walls and passageways until she came again to the street where she first saw the girl in the green dress, calling from an upper window

The moon came out. A curtain opened. A figure stood there as before and Fenya heard the weeping once again. But when she looked closely at the face of the girl, she saw that it was her own.

RANGORE

Fenya pulled her thin shawl close around her shoulders and shivered. A slow snow was falling, icicles clung to crumbling ledges and the light seemed already failing as the day hung cold and grey. At the end of the street sat an old man huddled in a long musty coat the colour of dust. As she approached he held out his hand.

"Spare any food..." he whimpered.

"I'm looking for food myself," she replied as she stared into his rheumy eyes.

He clutched her sleeve.

"You must help me," he said. His grip was tight though his fingers were shaking. "I must eat soon or my blood will freeze."

Fenya tried to pull herself away, but the old man clung harder. His body seemed to shrink inside his coat as he gazed up at her.

"The only food I can take, the only food which will warm my bones is a soup cooked from the fruit of the Rangore tree. Its skin is dark as night and its flesh glows gold as the sun. The soup is seasoned with cinnamon and marjoram and must be simmered just as dusk is falling."

Fenya's mouth was watering.

"You're making me more hungry than I was before. I'll search for Rangore fruit by the crates in the harbour. I'd like to taste this soup myself."

"So you shall," said the old man. "But go quickly. I cannot wait too long. I feel the cold gnaw at my bones."

Fenya turned and ran, loping swiftly through the shadowy streets until she came to the crowded market. Here the stalls were heaving with sides of meat and a dazzling array of every fruit that you could wish for, brought in fresh from the boats moored up in the docks.

"Be off with you!"

"Get away!"

The stall-keepers berated her, for they knew she would try and filch an orange here, a damson there; though some were more kindly and at the end of the day would let her take her pick of whatever they had left. Fenya grabbed the sleeve of an old woman who sat beside a pile of melons and peaches.

"Do you know of the Rangore fruit?" she inquired.

"Know of it, but ain't got none. Never seen any of them on this market."

Fenya ran on. At the corner she met Arrak.

"Rangore fruit, Rangore fruit," she begged him. "You can get anything, I know that you can. Find me this fruit for I must save the life of an old man."

Arrak shrugged.

"Save his life," he snorted. "Aren't we busy enough saving our own?"

"May be good for us as well," Fenya replied. "For if I find this fruit it will make the most delicious soup... and we can have a taste."

"Want more than a taste of soup to fill my belly," Arrak spat as he eyed a brace of rabbits hanging on a stall. "But let me look and run around and see what I can find..."

Fenya watched him go as the thin wind wrapped itself around her. She closed her eyes and dreamt of the golden soup, but even that did not make her feel any warmer as she shuffled slowly through the frozen streets.

In front of her she spied a woman all wrapped up in a long flowing cloak. Step by step she followed as the woman walked quickly, her high boots clattering across the icy paving stones. But Fenya moved swifter than swift, flitting about – first close at the woman's heels and then in front and then behind, all the while taking care that she could not be seen.

The snow was falling more heavily as they reached the woman's door, a tall house with windows that glowed from the warmth inside. Fenya followed her up the steps, but the woman turned sharply.

"What do you want?" she demanded. "I know you've been

following me."

Her eyes glowered colder than the sky and before Fenya could grab the hem of her cloak and plead for food and shelter, the woman had hauled a silver key from deep in her pockets, opened the door and slipped inside. Fenya was left shivering on the step. But she recalled the old man in the musty coat and knew he must be far colder than her. Then she remembered the soup that he needed and wondered again whether Arrak would find the Rangore fruit.

She tugged her shawl about her arms and then she sneezed. Not with the cold she realised, but with the warm aroma of spices which had floated out from the woman's hallway before she slammed the door.

"Why – if I can't get in the front door, for sure I can get in the back – and that is where the kitchen must be and there this woman must keep every kind of spice – and mayhap the cinnamon and marjoram I need to make the soup."

Fenya sneezed again then scampered quickly down the street and along an alley that led to a wall at the back. She glanced around, took one deep breath and scaled the brickwork. As she sat at the top, she peered down into the shadows of the garden. The sun was already sliding low behind the city's towering tenements, but through the glowing windows of the house she could see the woman moving slowly from room to room, lighting the lamps and warming herself.

In the garden stood a lone tree, its branches bleak and gaunt. One fruit still hung there – and even though it was cold and shrivelled, Fenya knew by its skin, still dark as midnight, that this was the Rangore that the old man needed for his soup. She sprang down from the top of the wall and landed nimbly on her toes, then raced across and pulled herself hand over hand to the top of the tree where she reached out to touch the fruit. She felt its gnarled skin with her fingertips but could not grip it firmly. She stretched out further but then she slipped and came tumbling down. As she crashed through the branches, the whole tree shook and the trembling stem of the fruit finally snapped and it fell to land beside her.

Just as she bent to pick it up, the door of the house swung open and out stepped the woman still wrapped in her long flowing cloak. She spied Fenya immediately.

"Who are you?" she cried before Fenya could spring back over the wall. "What do you want? And why have you stolen my fruit?"

Fenya stood before her trembling, with the Rangore in her hand.

"I haven't come to harm you," she explained. "But today I met an old man shivering in the snow. He was colder than me by far, and far colder than you, for you have a house to keep you warm. But all he has is a musty coat so threadbare that the wind blows through and you can see his. limbs so thin he has only shreds of skin clinging to his bones."

The woman stared at Fenya.

"What has this to do with climbing into my garden and stealing the last fruit from the tree?"

"He asked me to find him food," Fenya continued. "But he said his bones were so cold there was only one thing that he could swallow – and that was a soup made from the fruit of the Rangore tree."

The woman's eyes narrowed. She stared at Fenya long and hard.

"How do you know of this soup?" she asked.

Fenya twisted the fruit in her hand.

"I only know what the old man told me. I only know he said that the soup was made from the Rangore fruit, seasoned with cinnamon and marjoram."

Fenya gazed through the lighted window into the warmth of the woman's kitchen.

"Tell me – do you have marjoram and cinnamon among the jars upon your shelf?"

The woman said nothing and looked away, but then she turned again.

"The fruit you have plucked from the tree is indeed a

Rangore... you'd better come in," she said.

As the grey light of dusk spread through the garden, Fenya followed down the steps to the basement door of the kitchen. Inside all was warm and bright. Copper pans gleamed on the hob and shelves of spice jars lined the walls. Fenya clapped her hands, turning and spinning in delight. At last the woman smiled.

"Come in, child. You must be chilled to the bone. My name is Marrabelle. You are welcome. Come and warm yourself."

Fenya rubbed her hands together before the roaring fire, while Marrabelle brewed a pot of elderflower tea.

"Where is the Rangore?" she asked.

Fenya held out the dark shrivelled fruit. Marrabelle rolled it gently between the palms of her hands. As she did the fruit seemed to glow. Its flesh grew plump, and the wrinkles vanished till at last it was as ripe as ever it would have been before the winter's frost.

"Take up that blade," Marrabelle instructed and Fenya picked up a silver knife that was lying on the table before her.

"Now watch as I peel," she continued and Fenya watched as the knife revealed the golden flesh that nestled inside. Then Marrabelle passed her the knife and the fruit.

"Here," she said. "Now it's your turn."

Slowly and carefully, Fenya sliced the fruit, peeling back the skin until each segment of golden flesh lay on the cutting board. Marrabelle placed each piece in a pot and then reached down the jars of cinnamon and marjoram. She handed them to Fenya to sprinkle over the fruit while she poured in a jug of boiling water which had been simmering on the hob. They sat in silence a moment and watched as the soup bubbled to a gold that was brighter than the sun while outside darkness spread through the garden as dusk stole into night.

"Do you live here all alone?" Fenya asked suddenly.

"Yes, I am all alone. But how did you guess?"

"I could tell by the sadness which turns your eyes as grey as rain."

Marrabelle sighed.

"It was not always like this. Once a young man lived here with me. His name was Lissom. He had long raven hair and pale green eyes. He would spend all day tending the garden and at night he played the harp to me more sweetly than you could ever hear."

"So where is he now?" Fenya was curious.

Marrabelle turned away to stir the soup.

"I do not know. I wish I knew. One day we had a quarrel and then he went away. He has never come back."

"Why did you quarrel?" Fenya asked.

Marrabelle turned from the stove.

"It was at the full moon," she said. "I had a new dress - the one that I am wearing now." She cast aside her cloak to reveal a robe that flowed as dark as the night, patterned all over with stars. "I wanted to go out dancing. I wanted show off my dress to all of my friends. See how it floats and swirls!"

She pirouetted as Fenya clapped in rhythm.

But Marrabelle looked sad again.

"Lissom did not notice. He did not want to go dancing. He wanted to spend the night sitting in the garden out under the Rangore tree, playing his harp to the moon."

"What happened then?" asked Fenya.

"I would not let him," said Marrabelle. "I would not let him play his harp. But he insisted. He continued to play while the moon rose higher in the sky. And so I took this knife."

She seized up the silver blade from the table, which only a few moments earlier had sliced the Rangore fruit. Fenya shuddered and shrank away. Marrabelle's eyes were cold and hard.

"And then I cut the strings so that he could play no more. That night he left and I have never seen him again."

"Did you dance?" asked Fenya, springing up and twirling round. "Did you dance like this and this?"

Marrabelle put down the knife.

"Yes, I danced," she said. "I danced with every man I could find – out in the square and through the streets, around the market and down to the docks. I danced with them all."

"Did they admire your beautiful dress?"

Marrabelle hung her head.

"I don't think they even noticed the dress."

"But at least you were happy – you were dancing just as you wanted."

"I was not happy at all," Marrabelle confessed. "I wanted to be with Lissom. I wanted to dance with *him*. But I had cut the strings of his harp and he had gone... and I have never seen him again."

Fenya grabbed her hand.

"The soup!" she cried.

The golden soup was bubbling to the top of the pan. Marrabelle removed it from the heat, all the time stirring it with a long wooden spoon. She could see Fenya's mouth was watering as she poured the soup into a bowl.

"Here – take a sip."

Fenya closed her eyes as she lifted the spoon to her lips. The taste was dark as the earth and yet as radiant as the sun. As she drank, the warmth spread from her belly, out to the very tips of her fingers.

Then she leapt up.

"I must go!" she exclaimed. "Now I know why the old man loves this soup so much – I must take it to him before his bones freeze with cold!"

She seized up the bowl and covered it with a cloth.

"Thank you," she cried as Marrabelle watched her go – a wistful expression in her pale grey eyes.

Fenya sped from the house, out into the darkness of the streets. Her hands wrapped around the warmth of the bowl, but with each step she took she could feel it growing colder as the snow fell all around.

"I hope I am in time," she muttered, "I hope I find the old man again, before it is too late."

But as she hurried through the snow, each street looked the

same and the faster she walked the harder it was to remember which way she came. She stumbled past deserted market stalls and small darkened shops with shutters at their windows and then found herself breathless in a dingy courtyard. The cobblestones beneath her feet were mired with a slime of rotted fruit while the freezing breath of the wind from the river scoured into every corner. A winch hung like a creaking gibbet from the loading hatch at the top of a towering warehouse as children scratched at the broken doors, begging to be let in. When they smelt the soup which Fenya carried, they tugged at the hem of her shawl.

"Get away!" she cried. "This is not for you. It's not even for me, but for a poor old man who is dying of cold. Have any of you seen him?"

One child pointed this way and another pointed that. A third tried to steal a sip of the golden soup while none of them were looking.

"Get away," cried Fenya again.

Then a hand gripped her shoulder and Fenya screamed, nearly dropping the bowl. The children fled as she screamed again, then the hand shifted swiftly to cover her mouth.

"What have we here?" a croaky voice exclaimed.

Fenya bit into one of the fingers which was wedged against her lips.

"Arrak," she spat. "I know it's you. Get off me."

The dishevelled figure of the boy fell back into the darkness.

"Fenya," he said, "- what are you doing? It isn't safe here."

"It isn't safe when *you're* here," Fenya snorted, pushing him away.

"What you got?" Arrak demanded, jabbing a finger under the cloth which covered the bowl. He felt the soup, still moist and warm, then licked his finger slowly.

"Mmmm..." he exclaimed. "This is good. Give me more," he pleaded as he grabbed at the bowl. But Fenya held fast.

"This is not for you. This is the soup of the Rangore fruit that I had to find to warm the bones of the old man who was curled up in the snow this morning."

Arrak smiled.

"You promised me if you found this soup then I could have a taste and it would keep me warm."

Fenya glowered at him.

"*You* promised me you would search for the fruit to make the soup and I've not seen you again all day."

Arrak shrugged.

"I could not find the Rangore fruit. Not in the markets, not on the docks."

"No," Fenya chided him, "– for it only grows on the tree in Marrabelle's garden."

"And have you tasted this soup yourself?"

Fenya lowered her eyes.

"I have only taken one sip – and I tell you now, it is warm as the sun."

"And I am cold as this snow," Arrak retorted. "Let me take just one mouthful."

As Fenya offered the bowl, Arrak took it to his lips and began to drink.

"Stop! Only one mouthful – the rest is for the old man," Fenya cried as she wrenched the bowl away.

"Where is he?" asked Arrak, the taste of the soup still lingering in his mouth.

"He is where I found him this morning, near where you saw me on the street next to the river bridge. But how to get there I do not know, for I am lost in the snow."

"Come," said Arrak and he led her, past the carcasses of buildings that had long since stopped breathing, whose doorways were so dark there was no memory of dreaming, down past piles of living litter to where the sewers emptied into the belly of the river.

"Here," he said, as he pointed to the bridge. "Now you know where you are."

Before she had time to thank him, Arrak was gone and Fenya was left there all alone, clutching the bowl in her trembling hands. In the swirling snow she traipsed to where she had met the old man in the frail light of morning. At the end of the narrow street leading to the bridge, she peered all around – but there was nobody in sight. And then she saw a bundle of rags, nearly covered over by the drifting snow. She slowly approached, realising that the rags were the colour of the man's musty coat. This was the old man himself curled up, making no sound at all.

"Please wake, please wake," Fenya cried as she shook his shoulder and placed the bowl on the ground beside him. "I have brought you the soup made from Rangore fruit... please wake."

As the fragrance of the spices reached his nostrils, Fenya shook him again and the old man blinked then sat up. Fenya pulled back the cloth which covered the bowl to reveal the soup.

"Here, drink it," she begged.

The old man reached out, took the bowl in his long bony fingers and raised it to his shivering lips. Fenya watched wide-eyed as he drank, as the colour returned to his frozen cheeks, as the wrinkles smoothed on his wizened brow, as his lank white hair became darker and darker until there before her stood a tall young man with raven locks and pale green eyes.

He gazed at Fenya questioningly.

"Tell me," he said, "– where did you find the Rangore fruit to make this soup – and how did you season it so exquisitely with cinnamon and marjoram... and how did you simmer it so perfectly?"

"I have been to the house of Marrabelle," Fenya said quickly. "Just as dusk fell I sprang upon her wall and spied the only Rangore fruit hanging from the tree..."

"I knew it," said the young man. "That tree in the garden is not just the only place in this city, but the only place in this whole region where the Rangore fruit will grow. And only Marrabelle knows how to cook it, which spices to blend to bring out the flavour. And I am the only other person who has dined on the soup that she makes."

Fenya smiled.

"Then Marrabelle knew," she said. "She knew when I asked her for the fruit that she was making this soup for *you*."

The young man laughed.

"Did she give you a message?"

Fenya shook her head.

"No," she said. "But I know your name, for she told me. Your name is Lissom — and this soup is message enough, for she knew that I would bring it to you. She told me how you quarrelled, how she wanted to dance in her new dress dark as night - and you wanted to sit beneath the tree and play your harp to the moon!"

Lissom tossed back his long raven hair and laughed.

"We were foolish," he said. "As soon as I left the house I grew colder and colder as I wandered the streets of this city. Without my harp it was as if I had lost my voice and I could speak to no-one to ask the way. As the snow came I grew colder and colder - and the colder I became the older I grew until I did not know myself and I could eat nothing at all, for all I wanted to taste was Marrabelle's golden soup."

Fenya took his hand.

"I think it is time to go home," she said. "Marrabelle misses you. Since you have been gone her eyes are dull as rain and she is filled with sadness every day."

As they walked side by side the snow stopped falling and the stars shone bright in the sky. By the time they reached Marrabelle's house the full moon had risen high. Marrabelle opened the door as if she had been waiting for them and took Lissom in her arms.

"Will you play your harp for me now, out in the garden where I can dance for you?"

Lissom looked sorrowful.

"How can I play when you have cut the strings?" he asked.

Marrabelle smiled.

"When I gave up roaming the cold streets to find you, I returned and sought out the finest harp maker to repair your strings. It is waiting for you now in the garden – waiting for you to come home and play."

As she took his arm and led him through the house, Fenya

followed like a shadow behind them. In the garden beneath the Rangore tree stood his harp. Lissom sat down and touched the new strings which were lit by the light of the moon. Then his fingers ran faster and faster and the notes flowed like silver rain. As he played, Marrabelle arched her back and raised her arms high in the air. She began to turn slowly, reaching out to the notes of the harp as if she caressed a shimmering waterfall. Lissom played on while Marrabelle turned faster, spinning and gliding until it seemed as if she floated about the garden. Yet all the while her eyes were fixed on Lissom and his were fixed on her supple body as she bent low beneath the Rangore tree.

Fenya held her breath as she watched, for the full moon seemed to hang between the branches where the fruit had been before. She wished she could dance as Marrabelle danced, wished Marrabelle might sweep her up into the folds of her dress until she became one of the silver stars. But Lissom played on and Marrabelle danced on while Fenya hugged herself and spun round and around, as if she was dancing too. Lissom and Marrabelle could not see her now – and she hurried away through the house and out into the street where the night burned strong and clear and the taste of Rangore soup lingered sweet as a kiss on her lips.

BUTTERCUP YELLOW and
A JACKET OF GRASSY GREEN

Jarraque gazed at the fiddle every day as it lay in its dusty case. Sometimes when there were no customers in the shop, he ran his thumb across the strings and listened to the sound. Sometimes he'd pick it up and rest it against his shoulder. Sometimes he'd sigh and finger the bow, then put it down again.

Then, late one dreary afternoon, he sat waiting for the doorbell to ring, his ears plagued by the silence of the ticking clock, the rattle of beetles in the wainscot and the slow shift of the dust. He seized up the fiddle and bolted the door, then hurried out the back way to the courtyard. There the air smelled fresh from that morning's rain as blackbirds sang from the gutters and the roof tops.

Jarraque copied their songs on the fiddle, his fingers feeling out the notes. And the blackbirds sang till a ringing roundelay ran echoing from wall to wall. But no-one else took any notice. People came and went through the doors of the courtyard, going about their business. But no-one stopped to listen. None turned their heads and no-one threw open a window to let in the sound. But Jarraque did not mind, he just played on and on as the tunes kept flowing in the warmth of the afternoon sun.

A small girl sat out on a doorstep, her chin cupped in her hands. She was watching him intently, her freckled brow crumpled in a puzzled frown. Jarraque stopped playing and looked at her.

"Where do the tunes come from?" she asked.

Jarraque shook the rosin from his bow and used it to point to the birds in the gutter who had all started singing again.

"Their songs, not mine," he told her.

The girl frowned again.

"But your tunes sound sad. And the birds all sound happy."

Jarraque frowned now and scratched his head.

"Mayhap I copy them wrong. Or mayhap their singing makes me feel sad."

"Why so?" said the girl. "Why would their singing make anyone sad?"

She walked slowly across the uneven flagstones to the centre of the courtyard and stood looking up at Jarraque.

"Play again," she said. "But this time play faster. This time play happy."

Jarraque smiled, tightened his bow and raised the fiddle to his shoulder again. He played slow at first till the girl stamped her foot but then he played faster and faster till she danced in a whirl all about the courtyard. Then Jarraque stopped sudden and the girl stopped and all the blackbirds stopped singing too. She ran back to stand beside him.

"That was good," she said, quite out of breath. "And it wasn't sad at all."

"Not sad, no," said Jarraque. "But it made me remember…"

He smiled down at the girl, but his eyes seemed far away.

"Remember what?" she asked him.

Jarraque shook his head.

The girl tugged at his coat.

"My name is Gillow," she said. "Come and tell me."

Jarraque sighed, then smiled again. The girl ran back to the step and waited. He followed her slowly and sat down beside her with the fiddle laid across his knees.

"Let me tell you…" he said. "A long time ago in my village there was a boy and a girl. They were a little older than you are now, but one day you will be my age and then you'll know what I'm talking about. They would see each other down by the well and over by the byre. The girl would always smile at the boy, though he would only scowl. But the boy liked the way she smiled and so he carved a button from a knot of wood in the shape of a buttercup. He kept it in his pocket so the other boys wouldn't see. He waited for the moment when they might be alone and then he could press it into her hand. But the girl she had stopped smiling now, and whenever he came close, she always walked away.

"The other girlen knew that really she wanted to talk to him. Mayhap she had whispered it to them, mayhap we'll never know. So one day they sent her to the barn and told her there was a cat trapped there, underneath the straw. The girl loved cats as much as she liked the boy and so she ran there happily, but the other girls quickly shut the door. Then they ran to the boy and said, 'Come quickly, a pigeon is in the barn'. He ran straight there and pulled open the door – and there he found, not a pigeon at all, but the girl sitting on top of a pile of straw.

"'What are you doing here?' he asked. 'You are not a pigeon.'

"'Why would you think I am a pigeon?' said the girl. 'I came here to find a cat, but there is nothing here.' With that she turned her back on him and continued her search through the straw. The boy stood there watching her. 'I have something for you,' he said at last.

"The girl looked up. 'What is it?' she asked. The boy fumbled in his pocket and pulled out the button he had made, shaped like the petals of a buttercup. The girl smoothed down her dress and pulled the straw from her hair. She looked at it quickly, then turned away. 'I don't want a button,' she said. 'I came here to look for a cat' – and carried on rooting in the straw.

"The boy just stood there and watched her, but then she turned around. 'Stop looking at me,' she said and walked out of the barn and shut the door behind her.

"The boy didn't know what to do. He stood there awhile, clutching the button in his hand."

Gillow was still sitting beside Jarraque on the step, her chin cupped in her hands.

"Now that is sad," she said.

Jarraque shook his head.

"I never saw her again. Her grandmother was sick in the next village and her family took her with them to look after her."

Gillow frowned her crinkly frown.

"That's even sadder," she said. But then she stopped. "'I'

you said – *'I never saw her again.'* So the boy was you!"

Old Jarraque nodded. He fumbled in his pocket.

"Here, I still have the button I made."

He held it out in his wrinkled hand. Gillow peered at it closely.

"It's pretty!" she exclaimed.

Jarraque shrugged.

"Mayhap you should keep it. I've no-one else to give it to now."

"Thankyou, thank you," said Gillow. She took the button and tucked it in her pocket. Then she got up and tossed her hair.

"I can hear my mother calling," she said as she ran to the stairs, but then turned back.

"What were they wearing, the girl and the boy, when they met in the barn?"

Jarraque scratched his head.

"I don't know, I don't know. Was a long time ago."

"You *must* remember," said Gillow. "You remembered all the rest of the story."

Jarraque swung his fiddle up to his shoulder and played a snatch of the tune. Gillow hopped impatiently. She could hear her mother calling again. Jarraque stopped playing.

"Now I can see it," he said. "The girl was wearing a yellow dress, same as she always did. Yellow as a buttercup – that's why I made the button."

"And you – what did you wear?"

"A faded green jacket, the colour of the fields."

Gillow tugged at the old man's sleeve.

"Same as you're wearing now?"

Jarraque looked down and smiled. His jacket was so grubby and threadbare, you could scarce tell what colour it was.

"Yes," he replied, " – much like this one… though this is not the jacket the boy wore in the barn."

"The boy was *you*," Gillow reminded him.

Old Jarraque nodded.

"Yes, he was," he said. "Now be off with you – I can hear

your mother calling again!"

That night in her room, and the next night and the next, Gillow made two marionette figures out of bits of wood and scraps of cloth. She plaited wool for hair, and then she made the clothes. A dress as yellow as a buttercup for the girl and a patched green jacket for the boy. Last of all, she sewed on a pocket and reached inside her apron to pull out the button which Jarraque had given her. She slipped it inside the boy doll's pocket and then she patted it down.

She put away her scissors and needle and smiled as she swirled the marionettes around, as if they were dancing, as if they were singing. She made up words for them to say and then she ran down the stairs with them to the courtyard and sat herself on the step to wait for Jarraque to come out with his fiddle and play.

But he did not come. He did not come that evening, nor yet the next day.

"I want him to see them," Gillow told her mother. "I want him to watch as the boy pulls the buttercup button from his pocket. And this time the girl will take it and not run away."

But her mother just smiled faintly, shrugged and turned back to patching a shirt. Gillow ran out through the courtyard, round to the street at the side. Then she looked for Jarraque's shop. She knocked on the door, but there was no reply. She called out his name and held up the marionettes, but then she saw that the shutters were closed.

Gillow hurried back then to her mother.

"Where is Jarraque?" she cried.

Her mother put an arm around her.

"Jarraque was old," she said. "He took sick suddenly while you were busy with your sewing and making, and last night he died."

Gillow sat down then, still holding the marionettes. She slipped her fingers into the boy doll's pocket and pulled out the button shaped like a buttercup. She looked at it a moment, and then carefully put it back.

Sep lived in a narrow room pressed tight against a wall, so close that when he stepped out from his bed he could scarce turn around, scarce stretch his arms to pull on his shirt, scarce bend down to tie up his boots. Scarce button up his patched green jacket the colour of the fields. But fields he had never seen, here under grey city skies.

He shook his head. He had dreamed again of a girl in a yellow dress, She walked across the wastelands, a-picking of the buttercups. He saw her face, her open smile – but only in the dreams. He knew he had never met her as he traipsed across the city, yet every night she came to him, more vivid than before.

Myrelle dreamt of a tousle-haired boy who wore a jacket, grassy green. She dreamt she walked with him down shadowy streets and in and out the houses till they came at last to a leafy meadow sloping down to the river. There they went picking buttercups to match the dress she wore. And he would hold one beneath her chin and then he'd bend to kiss her. She'd spread her arms and purse her lips… and then she'd wake and there'd be no-one. No-one in this dark stooped room that was scarce a room at all but a cupboard beneath the stairs. And she could hear a voice calling her, but not the boy with the tousled hair, but the coarse-mouthed kitchen lad in this house of mildewed velvet who came to ferret her out.

Now Myrelle took to looking for the boy with the jacket of grassy-green when she went about her errands. And Sep too, he looked for the girlen in a buttercup-yellow dress. Day after day they searched through the crowds, and night after night they dreamt again, of a smile, of a laugh, of the touch of a hand.

There was a throng about the fish market one cold and drizzly morning. Myrelle pushed her way through with her basket, seeking out the finest herring to take back to the house where she worked.

Just for a moment she was jostled against a boy, pressed tight against him as she tried to reach the stall. She looked up and saw his hazel eyes, his jaunty face. Just for a moment she thought he smiled. Just for a moment she was swept back to her dreams. But then the crowd pushed them on. And she could not see any grass-green jacket, for this boy wore a top-coat pulled tight against the rain. And she could not tell if his hair was tousled or not, for his cap was pressed down tight to his ears.

And Sep, he had wondered a moment if this might be the girl in the dress of buttercup yellow. But she too was covered, in a long heavy cloak pulled about her shoulders.

So they moved on, running their errands, and neither remembered, though that night they dreamed again, more vivid than before, of a girl in a dress all buttercup yellow and a boy in a jacket of grassy-green. In their dreams they met again and pressed each other close and then they kissed, and then they spoke... and then with a start they woke. Sep lay still in his narrow room and Myrelle sat up in the cold dark cupboard tucked away beneath the stairs.

That night as she slept, Myrelle saw a cat and followed it, shadowy grey as a dream itself, flitting fleet-foot along sagging guttering, leaping then running, belly low to the ground, through backways she had never been before, where only a cat would go. She noticed the cat had only one eye, though its senses were so sharp, seemed more like it had three. It drew her on. She was shivering. She wished the boy was there, to press her close, to keep her warm.

But Sep was dreaming of a pigeon. Grey as the cat and hobble-footed. It hopped and pecked and harried and fluttered. Sep followed after, though it seemed as if the pigeon itself was following a trail he could not see, of grains of corn scattered on through this maze of shadows and drizzling rain. Sep hoped it might lead him to the girl in the yellow dress, that he might take her hand and kiss her lips again.

Myrelle heard a fiddle playing, out of time and slow. Sep

heard it too. They both of them woke then, with a broken tune still sounding in their ears. But Sep was in his narrow room and Myrelle lay in the darkness, shut away under the stairs.

They dreamt on, night after night, until winter was gone. Then on a bright spring morning, Myrelle arose, put on her yellow dress and set off into the streets without need of the heavy cloak, her hair hanging loose in the sun.

Sep closed the door on the lodging where he lived, tugging his green jacket about his shoulders. Just then he saw a pigeon, club-footed and hobbled, just like in his dream. And just like in his dream, he set off and followed to see where it would lead.

It led him to a part of the city he'd never been before. He mapped the streets in his head, to be sure to remember which way he should return. Just then he heard the sound of a fiddle, somewhere over the rooftops, playing slow and out of tune.

That's when he lost the pigeon as it flew off sudden with a flap of its wings, scared away by a dull grey one-eyed cat that came stalking out of an alleyway. Sep shrugged. The pigeon had gone. But the fiddle played on and he followed till he came to the entrance to a courtyard, and stepped inside.

A small girl sat on the step, the fiddle balanced under her chin, her freckled face frowning as she reached for notes which seemed too far away for her fingers. Sep looked around. The grey cat had followed and sloped its way up to the step. And behind the cat came a girlen, in a dress of buttercup yellow. She stared at Sep as if she knew him, as he stood there in his jacket as green as the grass.

Gillow stopped playing and put down the fiddle. She laughed as she looked up at Myrelle and Sep, then reached behind her back and pulled out two marionettes. One was a girl in a yellow dress and the other a boy in a jacket of green.

Myrelle gasped and bent down, seized up the boy doll and kissed it. Sep looked confused, but took the other marionette from Gillow's outstretched hand. He looked at Myrelle. She looked at him.

"Wait," Gillow grinned. She stood up and fished with her fingers in the boy doll's pocket till she pulled out the carved wooden button. She paused a moment, frowning seriously, then she handed it to Sep. He looked at it a moment and then smiled.

"Why, it's shaped like a buttercup," he said, turning to Myrelle. "I think this must be for you – to match your yellow dress."

Myrelle smiled and gazed at Sep standing there, his jacket of green, his hair all tousled in the sun. The grey cat rubbed around her legs and she bent to pick it up, just as the pigeon returned and flew down to land on Sep's shoulder.

Gillow picked up the fiddle again and pressed the bow to the strings, though somehow the notes flowed freely now, as if it was Jarraque playing the tune.

THE NIGHT BUTCHER'S DAUGHTER

A meaty hand gripped Morrow's shoulder as he slipped down the alley. The door of the laundry hung open and a bulk of a man stepped out, blocking his way. Bullmass looked him up and down.

"You're a likely lad," he said. "I want you to run an errand."

Bullmass leaned in closer, pressing harder on Morrow's shoulder.

"Go down to the harbour," he hissed. "There's a ship newly in dock. Find a man called Swallow. He'll give you a package. Say that Bullmass sent you. He'll tell you where to take it…"

Morrow ran to the harbour, fast as any rat, scuttling down alleys and dimly lit gunnels. He picked his way between crates and baskets all along the wharfways till he came to the ship most recently docked. A gang of surly stevedores were already unloading its cargo, hauling heavy barrels from the belly of its hold.

One man watched, perched on a bollard. He seemed younger than Morrow expected, though his face was weathered and his pale grey eyes looked older than the ocean.

"You Swallow?"

The young man glanced behind him.

"Who sent you?"

Morrow lowered his voice.

"Bullmass," he said.

Swallow nodded and spat onto the slimy cobbles, then drew a package from inside his coat.

"Take this to Lummenmilk's shop."

Morrow quickly tucked the package inside his own jacket.

"Who is Lummenmilk?" he asked.

Swallow looked at him.

"You don't know much. Lummenmilk sells perfumes. Thought everyone knew that."

He whispered directions, then walked away.

Morrow stood a moment. Suddenly he felt like every pair of eyes on the dock was watching him. He gripped the package tightly under his jacket and ran.

He found the shop half-way down a side street, tucked between a cobblers and a hatters. As he opened the door, a pungent drift of perfumes surrounded him. Damiana and Cilantro, Patchouli and Tarragon. Rows of tiny bottles lined the dark shelves. A huddle of young women pressed around the counter, simpering and chattering as they tried a clutch of samples. Soon as they saw Morrow, they clustered about him, their dark eyes a-flutter.

"Can we help you?" one asked, lightly touching his forearm.

Another stepped closer, her fingers toying quickly with the pendant which hung about his neck.

"Are you strong as this bull?" she asked.

Morrow's face reddened and he turned away.

"I'm here on an errand," he said. "I have to see Lummenmilk."

"So Lummenmilk is the lucky one!" She feigned a frown, then rang the shop bell which stood on the counter. Lummenmilk stepped out from behind a curtain. As she raised one eyebrow, the young women stood back and pushed Morrow forward.

"He's here on an errand. He has something for you."

"In that case," said Lummenmilk, "you must come this way."

She lifted the counter and drew Morrow through the curtain. As they entered a darkened passage, he could hear peals of smothered laughter rippling round the shop.

"What have you brought?" demanded Lummenmilk.

Her face looked harsher now in the flickering half-light. Morrow slipped his hand inside his jacket and pulled out the packet which he had brought from the harbour. Lummenmilk stared at him curiously.

"Who gave you this?"

"It was a man called Swallow."

"Who sent you to Swallow?"

"Another man... a big man. Bullmass, I think... down by the laundry."

Lummenmilk nodded.

"Good enough," she said, and opened a door behind a velvet curtain.

A pungent odour of darkness that was not dark but awash with shifting colour. A music dredged from another room, a cellar beneath a cellar which reached deep into the drowning pulse of the sea. Morrow blinked. Dull figures lolled against each other like lifeless puppets stitched from human skin. One of them stirred and stared suddenly, as if seeing every rat-riddled nightmare that lodged in Morrow's head, and yet seeing nothing at all.

Lummenmilk took Morrow's arm.

"I make potions more potent than any of the perfumes," she explained. "Follow me."

He followed her into a room strewn with cushions, a low bed in one corner. She lit a candle and then another and another more, each one releasing a different fragrance, until Morrow's head was spinning. Lummenmilk sat on the bed.

"You're a fine looking boy," she whispered. "Now show me what you got."

Morrow handed her the package. Lummenmilk weighed it a moment in her hands, then ripped it open with practiced fingers. She smiled, leaned forward and inhaled.

"This is finest power of Mandrake Root," she told him. "It is in all my perfumes for the ladies, that's why they come. But the gentlemen seek it too."

She took Morrow's hand and pulled him down to sit beside her.

"Will you try some?" she said, her eyes dancing in the flickering candlelight.

Morrow stared as she opened her dress and sprinkled the powder across her chest. Her eyes closed over as she drew him closer and placed his hand on her breast.

"Now breathe," she sighed. "Breathe with me."

She slipped an arm around his waist and unbuttoned his shirt. Her fingers touched the pendant which dangled there. She stroked it a moment delicately, then stopped. She opened her eyes and stared.

"Where did you get this?" she asked.

Morrow rubbed his eyes, confused.

"Man called Grob gave it to me. He found it when I was a little'un, out by the laundry. He put it round my neck. 'It's for you,' he said."

Lummenmilk sat back and looked at him strangely.

"Who is your mother?" she asked.

Morrow shook his head.

"Mother have I none. Only Grob. Grob was all the mother to me – and father too."

Lummenmilk suddenly threw her arms around him. He could feel the warmth and moistness of her skin, the softness of her breathing. Then she pushed him away and buttoned her dress.

"Grob has raised you well," she said. "Now go. Go back to Bullmass. He will pay you."

A sparrow watched from the guttering at the end of the building. Watched as Morrow stepped out from the door of the shop. Watched as he wandered into the street. Watched as a tall girl watched him from the shadow of the alley. Her eyes were dark. Her dress was darker. She watched Morrow as he blinked in the sunlight. Watched as a group of girlen clustered about him. Watched as they laughed with him, their eyelids a-flutter. Watched as one of them touched his hand playfully, stroking his sleeve then opening his shirt to fondle the pendant which hung about his neck.

Watched as this girl took his arm and walked away with him towards the shadow of the alley. She saw that about the girlen's throat dangled a rose red as blood, molded from wax. She did not stop to watch them kiss. She did not stop to see Morrow lead the girlen away, over towards the tenement building which stood at the end of the steps.

She did not stop, but ran off, away past Lummenmilk's shop, away past the knot of other girlen standing there. She did not stop to see the sparrow which had been watching her, spread its wings and flutter up to the chimney top.

She had seen him before, the boy with the pendant shaped like a bull. It wasn't the pendant which caught her eye, but the way that he walked, sturdy and tall. And his eyes always darting, this way and that, keen and alert, with his fingers all a-twitch. She'd seen the way the girlen came to him and talked with him and walked away with him. Always towards the tenement at the top of the steps. But each one always wore a waxen red rose.

She threaded her way between high walls, dodging the overflow from low-hanging gutters, lifting her dark skirt as she stepped through deep puddles. At the end of the alley she came to Lintel's shelter, the sodden sheet stretched across the top scarce keeping out the drizzle, though the flowers painted on the wall blazed brightly, as if their petals were reaching out for the sweet touch of rain.

Lintel sat on a rickety stool, cradling a skull in her hands. She looked up sudden at the dark-haired girl who stood shivering before her.

"Who are you?" she demanded.

"I'm Kavana. I'm the Night Butcher's daughter."

The girl stared at the skull which Lintel let slip into her lap. Stared at the blood red roses painted about its crown and the thorns which snaked from its eyes.

Lintel nodded.

"Does your father know you're here?"

Kavana said nothing, her eyes still fixed on the skull.

"No matter," Lintel grunted. "What do you want?"

She reached for her needles.

"Is it a tattoo you're after, same as the rest?"

Kavana shook her head and bit her lip.

"No," she said. "I hear you make waxen roses. I would like

one to wear around my neck."

Lintel squinted at her.

"What you want with it?"

Kavana looked her in the eye.

"Want to gain a man."

Lintel nodded and smiled.

"You will gain a man and more." She paused. "Sure you're ready? These roses are potent."

"I'm ready," said Kavana. "There is a fine young man…"

Lintel raised her hand.

"No need to tell me. There is always a fine young man."

"So you will make me a rose?"

"Can't just make one," Lintel explained. "Need something from you first."

"I got money," Kavana said quickly, reaching into her pocket for a purse.

Lintel shook her head.

"No, child. Money comes later. I will make you a rose when you're ready. Fetch for me in a thimble one drop of your own sweet blood which trickles down your thigh each moon, and I will shape you a bright red rose that will gain you any man."

She stared deep into Kavana's eyes.

"Are you ready?" she asked again.

Kavana nodded.

Lintel took her hand.

"Come back to me when it is your time…"

Kavana watched the days crawl down the walls. She rode in the empty arms of the night. She shivered in the shadows as Morrow walked in the sun, always with another girl on his arm, always one who wore a waxen rose. And always Kavana knew her own flow was not yet due, not till the full moon had waned and gone, and she knew that she could not wait that long. So she pushed open the heavy rusted door of her father's basement. He did not see her, he was busy at his bench, hacking through flesh and bone. Then he turned.

"What do you want here, daughter?"

"Nothing," she said, slipping a thimble back into her pocket.

"Then nothing you will find," said her father, raising his blade again.

Kavana winced as he brought it down with a crack. She turned away to the carcass of a bull, still oozing dark red blood. And swift she drew her thimble out and swift she caught the flow till she had gathered up enough.

Her father scarcely looked around as she slipped out of the door. And away and away through the gunnels and alleys till she came to where Lintel waited.

She pressed the thimble into Lintel's hand. Lintel gazed at it a moment, sniffed the blood suspiciously, then looked at Kavana askance.

"If this your blood it truly be, then you have power more than me."

Kavana's face paled.

"It is mine," she said quickly. "Please, I need a waxen rose…"

Lintel sighed.

"I'll make you a rose, child. Some roses bloom dark, some roses bloom wild. Leave me this thimble and come see me tomorrow."

In the small bedchamber of a tenement room, Kavana shed her clothes, all except for the waxen rose which she wore about her throat. She lay on top of the crumpled sheets and waited.

"Morrow…?" she called

There was no reply, only the clanking of a coal scuttle and the rattle of a poker thrust deep into the embers. Kavana got up and stepped into the kitchen. Morrow sat with his back to her, staring into the fire, a black coat draped about his shoulders.

Kavana walked slowly about the room. She ran her fingers along the edge of the table, lightly stroked the face of the clock, brushed the dust from a vase filled with withered flowers. She glanced at Morrow's reflection in the broken mirror, then stood close behind him and wound her arms around his shoulders. She touched one finger to the pendant which hung about his neck.

Morrow pushed her away.

"What do you want?" she asked.

Morrow said nothing as he continued to stare into the fire. Kavana moved to stand in front of him and cupped the waxen rose in her hand.

Morrow looked up.

"This room was filled with roses once," he said. "Now it is empty."

"Who used to live here?" Kavana asked.

"A man called Grob," Morrow replied. "He taught me all I know. This is where I grew."

"What of your mother?"

"My mother is gone."

Kavana knelt beside him and wrapped an arm about his knees.

"My mother is gone too," she said. "I never see her. My father is the Night Butcher. His basement stinks of blood. Sometimes he brings me perfume to take away the stench. He says my mother makes it and sells it in her shop."

Morrow looked up.

"What does it smell of?"

"Smells of Mandrake petals," Kavana said, and pressed her slender wrist under Morrow's nose.

Morrow pushed her away again, then reached out and grabbed the rose which hung about her neck. He twisted once until it snapped, and flung it on the fire. They sat in silence and watched. As the waxen petals melted, a shadow crossed the room and their nostrils were filled with the stench of the dark red blood of the bull.

THERE IS A SADNESS SOMETIMES COMES

Skither's long fingers gathered every skein of the webs which hung from the gutters, glistening with dew. From the railings and doorways, the eaves and the shutters and the corners of walls, he picked them. Twisted them and poked them all into a bag, then he stole through the silence, back to his workroom. There the spiders had been spinning through the long darkness and he harvested their labour which hung from the shelves, under the tables and down from the chairs.

He emptied the bag and combed out the fibres, the grey and the white and the fine-spun silver. He twined and he knotted all through the morning till the fabric was made, shimmering and soft, to weave into gossamer cloth.

From the gossamer cloth he stitched long flowing costumes, dresses and shawls which sparkled and shimmered. Then the women came, the old and the young – to be measured, to be fitted, to twirl and to turn in front of his mirror. But their eyes only lingered on their own reflection. None of them spared one glance for Skither, who sat all alone when they hastened away with their dresses wrapped neatly in paper.

Gillow had grown to be taller now. Her hair flowed long and wild to her waist, her eyes flashed bright as sudden lightning. And everywhere she went, she carried Jarraque's fiddle.

She played at dances, she played at parties. She played at weddings, carnivals and parades. She played all night for a handful of pennies, till her shoulders ached and her fingers grew sore. But still she played on and the revelers wanted more as they danced through the night and sang on the table-tops, brawled in the doorways and spewed on the floor.

But when it was over, when the commotion was done and only broken glasses and empty plates remained, nobody spoke to Gillow, no-one came to kiss her. No-one took her in their arms to dance a silent measure. Each had a partner to walk them home and Gillow was left, sitting all alone, to caress the strings of the fiddle, to feel the rhythms that still sang through its body as she clutched it close before laying it down to rest in its case. Then she slackened the bow and snapped shut the lid, before slipping out into the waking dawn.

All alone, Skither walked out each day. All alone with his sadness as he gathered up the gossamer to spin into dresses which the fine women wanted. But sometimes he wished that one of them might want something more than a dress. He wished one might want to stay with him, to talk with him, to fill his room with laughter, songs and happiness.

But the dawn was grey as ever as Skither set out. The cobwebs trailed from his fingers as the dew glistened about his boots. There was no sound but the silence. Skither wondered if even he was here. But he knew that he was, for his nose was cold, and his fingertips and his toes. And a hunger gnawed at his belly as if it might be a dog. And then there *was* a dog. He heard it whine. He heard it whimper. He saw it come limping towards him, slowly out of the fog.

Skither tried to ignore it. He kept on walking, his eyes roaming about to catch the sparkle of cobwebs. But the dog followed on till its nose sniffed at Skither's heels. He turned around and looked down at its eyes large and brown, its fur bedraggled.

"I have nothing to give you," he said. "I am hungry myself."

The dog did not respond, just carried on gazing up at him. Skither shrugged and made a motion as if he was throwing something for the dog to catch. It followed the arc of his arm, but did not move, just turned to stare at Skither, who shrugged again and began to walk slowly away.

The dog walked too, following Skither step for step. Skither tried to lose it, taking sudden turnings, running swiftly across waste ground. But the dog caught up with him, in spite of its limp. The sun had risen. The day was waking. The fog had gone. Dew disappeared from the grass, from the weeds, from the brambles, leaving the pathways damp and expectant.

Skither paused and listened. The first sleepy rattle of pigeons' wings as they scrambled across the rooftops. The voices of boys out running errands, the call of the milk-girl filling up pitchers, the strike of a hammer on an anvil down a back street. The first people came slowly, no more than shadows. Coughing and muttering, their eyes cast down. But as the sun brightened, there were smiles and curt greetings, curses and insults and begrudging laughter.

Skither kept walking, but then somebody called him.

"Fine dog you got there!"

Skither looked around. It was no-one he knew. Just a smile and a wave. He shrugged, but it happened again. Complete strangers spoke to him, praising the dog. And then people he knew only by sight, who he saw in the butchers, the bakers, the chandlers, going about their way. People who normally ignored him, or at best gave a nod – they all stopped and spoke to him, all on account of the dog.

Skither smiled. He looked down at the dog and patted its head. The dog wagged its tail.

"Come on," Skither said. "We're nearly home. Let's find you a bone."

The dog ate bones. The dog ate scraps of meat from the butchers. Skither called the dog Raddle. Sometimes Raddle ate food from Skither's plate as soon as he turned away.

Raddle's limbs grew healthy and strong. Skither liked the company. He knew the dog lay at the foot of his bed all through the long cold nights. He liked the way Raddle walked beside him when he went out collecting gossamer. He threw sticks for Raddle to chase while he gathered the webs from a bush quick as quick before the dog could get back. It came bounding up to him, licking his face and panting, demanding the stick be thrown again. And again. And again. Until Skither spent as much time throwing sticks as he did in gathering cobwebs.

"I need to collect more than this," he would say. But Raddle only wanted to play.

Customers came for their dresses and went away empty-handed.

"You'll have to come back next week," Skither told them. "I need to gather more webs."

The customers frowned and looked annoyed.

"The spiders do not seem to be spinning so fast at this time of year," Skither explained.

When they had gone, Skither glowered at Raddle. "It's all your fault, you won't let me work."

Raddle curled his lip and growled.

Raddle was grown strong now, on the food that Skither fed him. When they were out, Skither noticed that people stopped greeting him, to compliment him on his dog, because Raddle would not let them. Raddle would not let anyone come near Skither. Raddle would not let anyone speak to him. Raddle growled and bared his teeth and they quickly turned away. He would not let anyone close enough to stroke his back and pat his head the way they did before.

"I need the dress by the day after next," one customer told Skither sharply.

She was a good customer, she had bought many dresses from him before.

"You shall have it," Skither promised. "I just need to gather more gauze."

"See that you do," she said and slammed the door of Skither's tiny shop as she hurried away.

Skither returned to his workroom. Raddle sat gazing up at him, waiting to be taken out.

"Not today," said Skither firmly. "Today I must gather more gauze. Today you stay here."

Raddle whined.

"Stay!" Skither commanded, picked up his bag, put on his

coat and set off, firmly locking the door. He hurried down the steps, closing his ears to the dog's howling and whimpering, which he could still hear from the street.

Skither ran quickly. His step was light, his fingers quick as he gathered cobwebs hither and thither, from corners and crevices he had never spied before, along alleys and across wastelands that he had scarce ever noticed. People greeted him wherever he went, came up and spoke to him, clapped him on the back and shook him by the hand now that Raddle was not lurking at his heels. Few even asked about the dog. They seemed as glad as Skither that Raddle was not with him.

He took a bridge across the canal, to a quarter that was new to him. The yellowed bricks of the houses held cobwebs a-many, and he filled his bag rapidly as he hurried along.

He came to a courtyard all filled with shadows. The morning sun creeping across the dull grey paving stones had not yet reached the doorways. He stood a moment, watching. On a step in the corner sat a tall young woman. Her hair hung long and tangled all down to her waist. On her lap lay a fiddle case, frayed and tattered. Her fingers drummed a rhythm across its lid. She looked up a moment when she felt Skither watching her, then she stood suddenly, snatched the case and vanished through the door.

Skither shrugged. He was looking for cobwebs. He could see none here in the damp, in the shadows, and hurried away.

A tune sang in his head as he walked back to his room, though he had no notion where he had heard it. His bag was filled with gossamer, he was ready to begin work. Time was short to make the dress, he knew. As he approached the door, he listened to hear if the dog was still whining. All was silent. He drew out his key and slid it into the lock. Still no sound. When he flung open the door, Raddle did not bound to greet him. The dog was draped all about with cobwebs, sitting in the middle of the room. Every dress that had been hanging along the walls was dragged to the floor and ripped to shreds. Not a stitch of Skither's fine needlework remained. Just tatters and scraps strewn all around.

Raddle's tail wagged uncertainly, but Skither stared in disbelief as he wailed, *"What have you done?"*

The dog lowered its head.

Skither raced about, trying to retrieve any scraps that might still make a dress.

"Tomorrow!" he shouted. *"Tomorrow.* I must have a dress by tomorrow."

He flung his bag to the floor. The gauze he had gathered that morning was only enough for the finishing trims to a dress he had started nights before. Now none of it was left. He would have to start all over again. But he knew there was no time as he seized up a broom and shook it at Raddle, who cowered away into the corner. Skither ignored the dog and began to sweep, till all of his handiwork was just a pile of dust and tangled threads.

Next day Skither sat in his shop. His best customer had been to collect her dress. Her face was thunder when he told her it was not ready. She demanded he return her deposit and told him she would never come to him again. Other customers came and went, asking when their dresses would be ready. Soon the word spread. In the days that followed, no-one came to Skither's shop. No-one placed new orders. Nobody spoke to him as he walked the streets, too weary to bother gathering cobwebs anymore.

The air hung thin and still. Skither walked as if he was sleeping, heavy and slow. He crossed the bridge again, gazing down into the sludge of the water. On the other side there was gossamer a-plenty, clinging to the yellow bricks of the houses. But Skither ignored it. Then from a courtyard there came a tune which seemed to him familiar, though he had never heard it before. He stepped through the entrance-way. The tall young woman was there again, though this time she had taken the fiddle from its case. And then she played. Skither stopped to listen.

She glanced up at him, but then turned away. Skither saw that beside her on the step were two marionettes. One wore a dress of buttercup-yellow, the other a jacket of grassy green. But both were tattered and patched, faded by the sun. As the woman tapped one foot, they danced, jerky and clumsy, hung by rusted wires from a wooden frame.

The woman played on as Skither watched. And then she stopped. Skither clapped. She turned around slowly and smiled, gave a little curtsey as the marionettes bowed their heads. Skither clapped even louder. Then he stepped forward and bent down to look at the figures dressed in yellow and green.

"I made them many years ago," the young woman explained, "when I was a child."

Skither looked up.

"I'm Gillow," she said. "I know they need mending, but I don't make puppets no more. I don't have the time. This fiddle has me playing it, every minute of the day."

Skither nodded.

"You play well," he said. "Do you make the tunes?"

Gillow shook her head.

"The tunes are not mine. They come from the sky, from the birds you see perched all around. They come from deep inside the fiddle. They were there beneath my fingers, soon as I started to play it."

"Would you play for me?" Skither asked.

Gillow looked at him.

"I think I just did."

"Would you play for me more?"

"I play every day. All round the streets. I stand and I play and my marionettes do their jig and people throw me pennies and then they walk away…"

"I won't walk away," Skither said suddenly. "I could listen all the day. Come with me and play to me. I make dresses of gossamer, but lately I have stopped. It is dull and dreary in my workshop. I have no-one to talk to. But if you come and play for me – why then I could start again!"

He looked at Gillow. He could see that she was smiling. The puppets had dropped into a crumpled heap beside her. Skither bent and touched the patches on the buttercup dress.

"I might even fit them both with a new set of clothes!" he said.

Skither pressed the key into the lock. He could hear the dog barking on the other side. He glanced at Gillow nervously.

"That's Raddle," he explained.

Gillow smiled, still clutching the two marionettes and her fiddle case. Skither leaned against the door and slowly pushed it open. Raddle leapt up at him, tail wagging. Skither rubbed the dog's ears.

"Come on, Raddle," Skither exclaimed. "Here's Gillow – she's come to see you."

Gillow stood where she was.

"You didn't tell me you had a dog."

"He won't hurt you," Skither reassured her.

Gillow stepped forward.

Raddle snarled and lay flat to the floor, ears back, hair bristling. Gillow froze. Skither shouted at the dog, ordering it inside. He turned back to Gillow.

"Come in," he said, reaching out to take her arm, but she flinched away.

"He won't hurt you," Skither said again.

He raised his fist to the dog, which slunk into the corner and lay there, cowering but growling.

Gillow stepped inside. The tattered remains of dresses hung around the walls. Scissors and needles were strewn all about. The workbench was covered with half-stitched lengths of gauze.

"Come in, come in," Skither repeated.

Gillow moved forward. Her nose wrinkled. The room smelt damply of dog.

"Sit down, sit down," Skither fussed. "Let me take your coat. Can I make you a drink?"

Gillow glanced uneasily at the dog hairs on the chair and bent to brush them away. She sat down gingerly but Raddle growled as Skither turned away to fill a pan with water. The dog leapt forward, teeth barred, snarling at Gillow. She stood up suddenly.

"Stop that!" Skither barked.

The dog did not listen and jumped up at Gillow, teeth tearing at the edge of the marionette's yellow dress. Gillow raised both puppets high above her head, dropping the fiddle case as she did so. Raddle placed two paws firmly on it, then bounded up at the marionettes. Skither raced forward and grabbed the dog's collar, hauling it back.

Gillow snatched up the fiddle again.

"I think I should go," she said.

"Please stay," Skither begged. "He's not used to visitors. He'll soon get to know you. Please stay. I was going to make a new dress for the girl doll and patch the jacket..."

Gillow stared at the littered workbench.

"I think you have work enough of your own," she said as she walked out of the door.

Skither watched her go, then turned to the dog, whose tail was wagging now.

"Look what you've done," Skither snarled. "I live here all alone. No-one comes to see me. Gillow was going to play for me. I was going to fix her marionettes... now you've driven her away!"

But Raddle's tail was wagging as he gazed up at Skither with large faithful eyes as if he had done nothing at all.

All that day, Skither cursed and railed.

"The only time I bring someone here, you will not let her stay. How will I ever make dresses again if you drive the customers away?"

Skither left the dog's bowl empty.

"And how can I afford to feed you if my customers do not come?"

Raddle lay dejectedly in the corner, watching as his master sat, head down in his chair. All about the room the spiders were crawling and weaving and spinning. Skither could not see this, he could only think of Gillow, her dancing marionettes in their ragged clothes and the wistful tune she played.

Skither did not rise from his chair, he slept there through the night, then woke with a start to find it was morning. Raddle was still watching him, but he paid the dog no mind. He could hear the birds all singing, outside in the street. And above their voices, another tune, played plaintive on a fiddle. He rushed to the window and threw it open.

There below was Gillow. She did not look up, but kept on playing, tapping her foot in time so that the marionettes danced at the end of their strings. Skither tugged on his jacket and rushed down the stairs, not even stopping to brush his hair. Raddle followed him, though Skither hardly cared. He just wanted to hear Gillow play again, to listen to her tune again. As he stood and watched, Raddle came and sat beside him, gazing up at Gillow. This time the dog did not snarl or bare its teeth. Gillow smiled. Skither smiled back, then realised she was not looking at him, but Raddle.

The dog moved closer, to lie beside her, entranced by the music. When Gillow reached the end of her refrain, she stopped, shook out her long hair and bent to stroke the dog's head. Raddle looked up and licked her hand. Gillow smiled all the more, but still said nothing. Skither stood and watched as she picked up the puppets, put the fiddle in its case and walked away, with Raddle trailing on behind her.

Skither was about to call out, to call Raddle back, but instead he turned away and climbed the steps to his workroom. There he began to collect up the scraps from all the dresses that the dog had ripped apart. He spooled the threads and set them neatly in lines. He gathered his needles and scissors and placed them back in their box. He opened his order book to read the list of customers still waiting for their dresses, and wondered which of them would ever return.

Then he went out walking, through streets lit bright with sunshine. He watched the clouds drift by, and the changing colours of the leaves. As evening came, he heard the sound of

Gillow playing again. The tune led him on till he came to the courtyard. There in the corner stood Gillow, same as ever before, her fiddle tucked under her chin, her marionettes dancing at her side. And Raddle. Raddle lay faithfully at her feet, gazing up at her.

Skither called, but the dog took no notice, edging closer to Gillow. Skither came up to them, held out a hand to Raddle, but the dog turned away. Gillow smiled as she continued to play.

"Go home," she said to Skither. "See what you will find."

Skither hesitated, but then walked away. He glanced back once, to see if Raddle was following, but the dog still lay where it had been, close by Gillow's side.

Skither climbed the steps to his workshop and opened the door. The spiders had been busy while he followed Gillow's tune. The room was filled with webs, hanging down beneath the shelves, under the table, dangling from the chair and spilling out across the floor. He had enough gossamer for every name in his order book and more.

DREAMING DEW

The small boat rocked gently as Myrelle let her hand dangle in the water. Sep leaned forward to kiss her on the cheek.

Myrelle smiled.

"No-one can see us here," she said as she gazed out across the lake.

They were moored beneath the trees, where they could watch the troupe of players on the nearby island, making ready for the show. On the shore, crowds were gathering with lanterns already lit in the fading light. Behind them the outline of the city stood dark against the sky.

"Look," said Myrelle as a fisherman appeared and tied up his boat.

Sep nodded.

"That's Drumbold – he's part of the show."

Myrelle gazed out across the surface of the water where the shadows of the trees danced as if they were puppets. She leaned forward and pointed. The shapes were broken by ripples as a soft wind skimmed across the lake, followed by a low flight of birds, flickering and murmuring.

Myrelle clapped her hands.

"Watch!" she cried. "The shadows look like a flower floating on the water – and there, far away, a butterfly..."

Sep laughed and touched her arm as he pointed back to the island.

"Never mind the shadows," he said. "The real play is starting."

There was a rattle of drums and a fanfare of blaring horns from the musicians crouched down in the rushes by the water's edge. The crowds on the bank fell silent as on a wooden platform a young woman in a turquoise dress climbed the stairs to the upper window of a house. She looked out and watched as the hunched figure of her grandmother appeared and shuffled to stand in the doorway.

"Dreaming Dew, are you there?" the old woman called.

"I am here, Nana Broomswitch," came the reply.

"What do you see?"

Dreaming Dew raised her hand to her eyes and peered between the trees which were all decked out with lanterns. Then she gave a little shriek and covered her face with her fan.

"Oh, Nana," she cried. "It is Jinkster. I do not want to see him. Tell him I'm not here! Send him away…"

A young man stepped out from between the trees and strode resolutely towards the house. He raised his hand to knock on the door, but Broomswitch, the grandmother, stopped him.

"I have come to see Dreaming Dew," he declared.

"Dreaming Dew is not here," Broomswitch replied.

Jinkster looked up and pointed.

"She is there at the window."

Dreaming Dew peeked out from behind her fan and then disappeared into the house. Broomswitch shook her head.

"She does not want to see you."

In the boat, Myrelle turned to Sep and ran one finger down his arm.

"Why does she not want to see him?" she asked, arching one eyebrow. "Jinkster is a fine looking man. If I was her, I would let him in!"

"Would you let me in?" Sep asked playfully.

Myrelle frowned and pushed him away.

"Hush," she said. "We are missing the show."

On the island, Jinkster hung his head dejectedly, then held out a flower which he gave to Nana Broomswitch.

"Give this to Dreaming Dew," he said. "Tell her that I brought it."

Broomswitch took the flower and looked at it disdainfully, then went inside and closed the door. One of the musicians struck a small gong and there was a rattling of chimes.

Myrelle leaned forward and pointed again at the shadows on the water.

"There," she said, "– can you see? The butterfly is moving

towards the flower."

Sep laughed and stretched his arms. A small cloud appeared, trailing its shadow across the lake.

"Now a bird is coming!" Myrelle cried. "Don't let her swallow the butterfly!"

She clung to Sep, burying her face in his chest, then looked up again. The boat rocked suddenly as Sep sat back, sending ripples across the water.

"Ah," Myrelle sighed and smiled. "The bird has climbed higher and flown away."

On the island, the musicians stopped playing as Jinkster made his way down to the edge of the water and started talking with the fisherman.

"I told you he was part of the play," said Sep, directing Myrelle's attention back to the island.

They watched as the old fisherman gave Jinkster another gift, an apple this time, which the young man took back to the house and knocked upon the door. Nana Broomswitch opened it and stood glaring at him.

"Dreaming Dew does not want to se you!"

"Then give her this apple, please, from me."

Broomswitch took the apple and quickly closed the door, but plainly through the window, where everyone could see, the old woman ate the fruit.

"Who was at the door?" called Dreaming Dew.

The grandmother wiped her mouth.

"No-one," she said. "Only Jinkster – and you do not want to see him."

"Does he bring me presents?" Dreaming Dew asked.

Broomswitch hid the flower which still stood in a vase behind the door.

"Nothing," she said. "He brings you nothing at all."

"I wish that I could see him," Dreaming Dew said plaintively.

Broomswitch shook her head.

"You cannot change your mind, child. The man is a no-good

rascal. If he comes again, I will still send him away."

"Jinkster does not look like a rascal to me," Myrelle whispered. "If he came knocking at my door, I would open it wide for him!"

She grabbed Sep's hand and pointed across the water.

"The shadows are moving again," she said. "The butterfly is fluttering closer to the flower. She must be careful – it might be full of thorns!"

Sep laughed, but turned away to watch the players on the island. The gong sounded out again, chiming across the water, as Drumbold drew out a necklace which he handed to Jinkster.

Once again, the young man made his way to the house. Once again he knocked upon the door. Once again, Nana Broomswitch opened it and took the necklace which he implored her to give to Dreaming Dew. Once again, Nana Broomswitch closed the door.

"Oh Nana," cried Dreaming Dew. "I thought I heard a knocking. Where is Jinkster? Does he not come anymore?"

But Broomswitch was busy fixing the clasp of the necklace and viewing herself in the mirror.

"There was no-one there," she said idly. "Jinkster does not come. I have not seen him for days."

There were gasps and mutterings from the audience on the shore when they heard Nana Broomswitch's falsehood. One of the musicians stood and blew a baleful blast on his horn. Myrelle scanned the surface of the lake and squeezed Sep's hand.

"See," she said. "The butterfly is near touching the petals of the flower."

Back on the island, Dreaming Dew called, "Nana – come to me!"

She clapped a hand to her forehead.

"What is it?" Broomswitch replied.

"I am sick with a fever…"

Broomswitch hurried up the stairs to look at the girl who had swooned upon the bed.

"What ails you, child?" she cried.

154

Dreaming Dew lifted her head and turned upon her pillow.

"It is Jinkster," Dreaming Dew replied. "I am sick with the lack of him. Tell me, why does he not come?"

Broomswitch bent over her.

"He is nothing but a rascal. You will see him no more."

Dreaming Dew sat up and seized hold of the necklace which her grandmother wore as it dangled before her eyes.

"On Nana," she exclaimed. "What is this? I have never seen it before!..."

Broomswitch tucked the necklace hastily inside her dress.

"It's nothing," she said quickly. "Just something old Drumbold, the fisherman, gave me."

Dreaming Dawn eyed her grandmother suspiciously.

"I have not seen Drumbold since I was a child. Tell me, when did he come here?"

"Why, Dreaming Dew, you look a little better now," Broomswitch said, placing a hand on her grandchild's forehead. "Lie down again and rest," she continued, before hurrying back down the stairs.

Dreaming Dew raised herself up, went to the window and called, a long soft crooning note. She called again and a bluebird came fluttering out of the trees. Dreaming Dew quickly cut a lock from her hair and placed it in the bird's beak.

"Fly quickly," she begged. "Take this token to Jinkster, that he may come again!"

In the boat, Myrelle let her shawl fall from her shoulders and gave a shiver of pleasure.

"Oh let him come soon," she whispered to Sep, her eyes opening wider.

Sep laughed.

"He will come soon enough," he replied, then gazed out at the shadows on the water.

"Why look," he pointed, " – your butterfly has vanished now. Perhaps she has lost her way."

Myrelle seized his hand and frowned.

"I hope she comes to no harm…"

On the island, Jinkster sat dejected when the bluebird landed on his shoulder, dropped the lock of hair into his lap, then quickly flew away.

Jinkster leapt up.

"What is this?" he cried. "I recognise this hair. I know that it is Dreaming Dew's own."

Myrelle clapped her hands and watched as Jinkster began to dance. Then he stopped and smiled and touched the lock of hair to his cheek. He fashioned it into a ring which he tied around his finger before slipping quickly to Drumbold's boat again.

Drumbold nodded and gave him one more gift, a comb which Jinkster seized and bore to Dreaming Dew's door. He knocked loud and hard while the musicians joined in, beating on gongs and drums.

Dreaming Dew leapt up.

"Oh Nana," she called. "What is that noise? Go see, go see. It must be Jinkster come to visit me."

Broomswitch rushed so quick to the door, she forgot to hide the necklace which she still wore. Jinkster stared at it, but said nothing, before placing the comb in the grandmother's hands.

"Take this," he said quietly, "and give it to Dreaming Dew, just as you have all my other gifts."

Broomswitch glared at him and quickly closed the door.

"Oh Nana, was it him?" Dreaming Dew cried.

"No, my child, it was only the wind," Broomswitch lied.

Sep and Myrelle watched as Jinkster returned to Drumbold and whispered in his ear. The old fisherman nodded and reached into his boat to pull out a bottle of potion, which he held aloft before pouring a drop onto a delicious looking cake.

"What is he doing?" Myrelle gasped. "Is that truly poison?"

Sep pressed his finger to her lips.

"Wait and see," he whispered.

Myrelle pulled away.

"If it is poison," she lowered her voice as Jinkster approached the house, "then Dreaming Dew will die."

"Perhaps it is not for Dreaming Dew," Sep replied.

"Remember – the grandmother has kept every other gift for herself."

They watched as Broomswitch took the cake and closed the door.

"Who was that?" Dreaming Dew asked.

"Only that wretched boy," Broomswitch replied.

"What did he say?"

"Said nothing much. Just left you this cake."

"Oh Nana, bring it here. You can share it with me."

But Broomswitch shook her head as she climbed the stair.

"You're welcome to the cake, child. You can eat it all. A cake so sweet will rot my teeth, and I have precious few of them left…."

Myrelle and Sep watched in dismay as Dreaming Dew ate every last morsel, wiped her lips, and then fell fast asleep. Myrelle gasped and clung tightly to Sep.

"She is dead!"

Sep stroked her arm.

"Perhaps not dead," he said. "Look – she is stirring… but Jinkster returns."

Jinkster knocked on the door. He seemed surprised when Broomswitch opened it.

"Where is the cake that I gave you?" he demanded.

"I gave it to Dreaming Dew, just as you asked me," Broomswitch replied.

Jinkster pushed her aside.

"You never gave her any of my other gifts!" he exclaimed as he ran up the stairs to kneel by Dreaming Dew as she slept.

He shook her gently, but she did not stir and so he took the ring of hair from his finger and placed it on hers. As soon as he did, Dreaming Dew sat up, stared for a moment at Jinkster, and then they kissed.

Myrelle squeezed Sep tightly.

"Not poison at all but a sleeping draught," he explained, "meant for the grandmother…"

"What will happen to Broomswitch now?" Myrelle asked.

But Dreaming Dew and Jinkster seemed not to care, they were so happy in each other's arms. The bluebird returned and led Broomswitch away, all down to where Drumbold was waiting at the edge of the lake. He greeted her then like a long-lost friend as she stepped into his boat and they rowed away.

The crowd on the shore broke out in applause while the musicians struck up a tune. Myrelle glanced away to the shadows of the clouds dancing on the surface of the lake.

"Look," she said, touching Sep's hand. "The butterfly has landed on the petals of the flower!"

At that moment, a real butterfly fluttered down from the tree above and lighted on Myrelle's outstretched hand. She raised it to her lips and blew a kiss before it flew away. Sep laughed and picked up the oars. More lanterns were lit all along the shore.

"The show is over," he said.

"Wait," Myrelle smiled. "We don't have to go. No-one can see us here, under trees."

She trailed her fingers in the water, then lay back in the boat and slid the hem of her yellow dress up above her knees.

THE BUTTERFLY MAKER

The room was cluttered with scraps of cloth and bits of twisted wire. An old man scuttled about, his hands fluttering excitedly as he twined and poked, stitched and knotted, creating intricate butterflies which he hung on strings from the ceiling.

Old Nipthimble sang as he worked, in a creaky voice which told of the hills and the bright shining sun far from this gaunt hungered room at the top of a tenement block. Told of the day his mother showed him a butterfly, a bright yellow butterfly that had come to rest on her hand as they sat outside her cottage, while his young brother Chilter ran up and down, whirling his wings as if he could fly.

Now Nipthimble lived here all alone, for childern had he none and his wife was long since gone. But Nipthimble sang on, for he had his butterflies to keep him company, every colour and every hue. He worked through the night, twisting the wire and threading the strips of cloth. He did not sleep and he did not dream, for his dreams they were the butterflies and the butterflies they were his dreams.

In the morning he would take them down to the harbour, to a huddle of street stalls close by the docks. There mothers would buy them, sailors and lovers, and Nipthimble would smile to see their smiles, for it was as if when the butterfly passed from his hand to theirs, why then the sun would return.

The sun it did not shine often in the shadowy streets when the wind blew in from the ocean and the cold crept down from his head to his chilblained toes. Next to him, a woman whose earrings hung dark as silent moons, set out an array of mirrors burnished from frozen tears. Another displayed clay creatures so twisted none had seen the like before and yet each one had been modelled from the tales the sailors told. Some they sold threadbare clothing strewn about on a blanket on the ground as the grey rain blew all around; while all day long an old fiddle player wove mournful melodies that he plucked from the sorrowing wind.

Some days there, as Nipthimble stood beside his line of bright coloured butterflies, he would catch sight of a small boy watching him. At sunset, when the others packed their wares away, Nipthimble would look over and see the boy still waiting as the shadows wrapped around him and the chill of darkness crept in from the sea.

Nipthimble walked towards him, holding out the last butterfly he had brought that day. But soon as he did so the boy was gone, vanished around the corner and away and away into the maze of alleyways. Each time he saw the boy, Nipthimble was struck by how much the lad looked like his own brother when they had been young, playing by their mother's cottage, running and laughing in the heat of the sun.

He called to him sometimes, but the boy gave no mind, only turning away to look longingly at the last golden peaches set out close by him. If Nipthimble came closer he would hide himself quickly behind the last stragglers picking around at the stalls.

Soon Nipthimble came to calling the boy by the name of his very own brother.

"Chilter!" he shouted, but it made no difference. Soon as he ever looked at him, the young lad would be gone. And then Nipthimble would not see him all the next day and all the day after. Sometimes it was not for days on end until Nipthimble would catch sight of him again.

And again, "Chilter!" he would cry. And again the boy would be gone.

"He must be hungry," Nipthimble muttered. "All day he stands there and I never see him eating nothing at all. Just staring at the peaches and the sweetmeats and the pies piled high on the stalls."

Nipthimble took to thinking of Chilter, his brother.

"What was it he liked best to eat? Why yes, I remember, it was sweet cherry pie, such as our mother used to bake."

Next day, when he'd sold his butterflies, Nipthimble wandered about the huddle of wind-blown stalls till he came upon one which sold cakes and loaves, freshly made.

"Give me a pie, the biggest one, the juiciest one," Nipthimble cried, then rushed off to find the boy again by the corner where he always stood.

"Chilter! Chilter!! Chilter!!!" he called long and loud. "I have brought your favourite cherry pie, just the way you always liked it, just the way our mother baked it!"

But Chilter had gone, same as ever before and Nipthimble stood at the corner, clutching the sweet cherry pie.

"Mayhap he will find it, for I know it is his favourite. Mayhap if I leave it for him, he will come back."

So Nipthimble left the pie on a close-by window ledge. And he waited and he watched until the night had fallen, but Chilter did not come. And so Nipthimble went home and returned the next morning soon after dawn, before anyone had pitched their stalls. Nobody was around, but the pie had gone.

"He must have come back," Nipthimble declared as he waited and he watched to see if Chilter would arrive. But the boy did not come.

Next day the same. He could not afford a pie this time, so Nipthimble left a morsel of bread. Next morning when he looked on the ledge, every crumb was gone. Same with his last tasty morsels of cheese. Every day the food would be gone, but never any sign of the boy.

Each evening Nipthimble would return to his room and work on new butterflies through the long waking night, bending and twisting the wires and the ribbons by one candle's flickering light.

Then early one cold misty dawn, Nipthimble folded his butterflies' colourful wings carefully into a bag. He set out as usual through the grey silent streets all down to the corner close by the docks where the lone fiddle player sat twisting the pegs that tuned up his strings and rubbing a lump of hard resin along the length of his bow. But somebody else was there too. There on the corner by the window ledge where Nipthimble had left all the morsels of food, there stood the boy Chilter, waiting and watching the gentle rain which had begun to fall all around.

Nipthimble called, "Chilter!" – but this time the boy did not run. He turned and smiled and opened his mouth as if he was about to speak. Nipthimble hurried towards him, calling his name again. But the boy slipped sudden down an alleyway and Nipthimble quickly followed him as the fiddle player struck up the first notes of his tune.

The boy hurried on, never looking back, leading Nipthimble along the maze of alleyways till they stopped by a set of steps that led down to a basement room. Nipthimble paused and watched as the boy sped down and through the door. A moment later Nipthimble glimpsed him through the dingy window. A woman stood there, who must be Chilter's mother, though Nipthimble was struck by how much she looked like his own mother, way back when they'd lived out on the hills and she had shown him the bright yellow butterfly which glinted in the sun.

Her voice was muffled by the grimy glass, but he could make out plain enough by the way she gestured and shook her fist that Chilter was being scolded.

"What do you mean," she demanded, "by coming back here empty-handed?"

She reached out then to cuff him about the ear, but Chilter was too quick for her and came bounding back up the steps, nearly knocking over Nipthimble in his haste.

Nipthimble gripped the boy by his shoulders.

"What is the matter?" he asked.

"My mother Lundle says I cannot come back till I bring something to give her," he gasped. "But look at the rain..."

He pointed up at the darkening sky.

"Here," said Nipthimble. "Give your mother this."

He reached into his bag and pulled out a butterfly with wings so yellow and bright they shone like the sun.

Chilter smiled. He twisted it and turned it, the shimmer of its colours lighting up his eyes. Then he scrambled quickly down the steps and into the basement room again where his mother Lundle was waiting.

Nipthimble watched as she wrenched the cluster of cloth and wire from Chilter's trembling hands.

"What's this?" she screeched. "Is that all you can find? We cannot eat a butterfly. We need food to fill our bellies!"

Nipthimble picked his way down the steps to the basement and knocked on the door.

"Who's that?" Mother Lundle demanded. "We've got no money – what do you want? If you've come for rent then you're out of luck."

Nipthimble knocked again.

"I've not come for money, but I can help you. Let me in."

The door opened a crack and Mother Lundle peered out. Nipthimble could see Chilter standing behind her smiling, while in the street above a seagull screamed and wheeled as a cart clattered by, loaded with barrels of fish.

In the dank basement room, cobwebs hung from a low peeling ceiling. A mouse scurried brazenly across an empty table, searching out the last remnants of crumbs. The grate was empty, the remains of the ashes raked all away, and a line of burned-down candle stubs dripped their melted wax from the soot-laden mantelpiece.

Lundle opened the door wider and stared him full in the face.

"How can you help us?" she challenged. "Have you brought food? Do you have money?"

Nipthimble shook his head.

"I have given you a butterfly," he said.

Lundle thrust it under his nose, shaking it so its wings nearly fell away.

"What? This thing? What good is this? I cannot boil it to make a stew. I cannot wear it to keep me warm."

Nipthimble looked down at his broken-toed boots.

"You can sell it," he said.

"Who would buy this?" Lundle snapped, near ripping the butterfly in two. "It's no good at all. It cannot even fly."

Nipthimble smiled.

"Many people buy them," he replied. "This is what I do all night. I do not sleep. I make butterflies from my dreams. Then in the morning, down by the harbour, I go to sell them. People pay good money..."

"People got more money than sense," Lundle spat. "Mayhap they should give some to me."

"Well *you* got a butterfly now," Nipthimble paused and smiled. "Ask any price you like. People tell me they hang them above the bed as they sleep to bring them the sweetest dreams. Dreams of sunshine on faraway hills. They do not know that these are *my* dreams, the dreams that would have come to me while I sat all night twisting and stitching. But I do not need them anymore. I have dreamt a lifetime of dreams."

Lundle snorted.

"All I dream of is a table filled with food."

She reached for a broom as Chilter shrank into the corner of the room and then she advanced on Nipthimble as if she might sweep him out of the door. Nipthimble stood for a moment and bowed his head.

"You have the butterfly," he said. "There is nothing more I can give."

As Lundle slammed the door in his face he turned away, although as he walked slowly down the street he felt sure he heard Chilter's voice calling after him. Then the crack of the broom. Then silence.

That night in the corner of the basement room, Chilter slept huddled under his coat and dreamt that Mother Lundle was a butterfly. He saw her flying, decked out all in yellow, bright as the sun – high above the city's rain-swept streets. He saw her twisting and turning, laughing high in the sky. He wished that he could fly with her, away to the distant hills.

But then he woke and there was silence, there in the dark basement room. His mother was gone. And when he looked upon the table, he saw that the butterfly was gone too.

He raced out into the street, hoping to see his mother

returning. Hoping she had been to the Night Butcher to beg him for a fistful of bones to cook up a thin salty stew. But she was nowhere to be seen, and Chilter ran on, down to the corner by the harbour where he stood and he waited for Nipthimble to come.

The wind blew cold and Chilter shivered. The man who sold oranges fresh off the dock threw him one that was half-rotted through, but Chilter bit into it hungrily, the juice leaking damp down his fingers as he spat out the pips and chewed on the pith that clung between his teeth.

And then Nipthimble came.

Chilter clung to his arm, begging the old man for another butterfly that would glitter and shine in the sun.

Nipthimble looked at him sternly.

"I gave you a butterfly yesterday. I cannot give you another one."

"But my mother has taken it... and my mother has gone."

Nipthimble raised an eyebrow.

"No good for me to give butterflies to people who only lose them."

Chilter turned away, his face scowling, his eyes turned down to the ground.

Nipthimble paused, then continued.

"But your mother has gone... You cannot live in that basement all alone. You may come with me tonight and I will teach you to make butterflies all of your own."

Chilter gasped when he saw the room, a tangle of wires and bright-coloured cloth, turquoise and orange and scarlet and gold. Threads and off-cuts littered the floor and hung from the ceiling were rows of half-made butterflies, each waiting for the finishing touch.

"Can they fly?" he asked, reaching out to grab at the fragile wings.

Nipthimble smiled,

"No," he said. "They are there to be pretty, to bring sweet dreams, just as the one that I gave you. The one that your mother took."

Chilter's face crumpled at the memory.

"My mother is gone!" he wailed. "She is gone with the butterfly you gave her."

He stopped a moment and stared around at the shimmering wings which hung from the ceiling, swaying in the breeze from the half-open window.

"Were these mothers too?" he asked. "Have they all left their homes and come to live here?"

Nipthimble looked at him and shook his head kindly, then sat down at his workbench.

"First you take two pieces of wire and twist them together... watch as I do it," he said.

But Chilter was not listening.

He had run down the stairs and back out into the street. There the sky was filled with butterflies, real butterflies, all of them swarming and fluttering and swooping. He reached out his hand to catch them and closed his eyes as he ran, bumping blindly into passers-by, into pillars and posts, until suddenly he stopped as into his hands something dropped. Something soft, made of cloth, bound together with wire.

He opened his eyes. It was the butterfly. The butterfly with yellow wings as bright as the sun on distant hills. The butterfly Nipthimble had given him and which he gave to his mother. He hugged it to his chest as he ran through the shadowy streets and down to the basement room.

"Mother Lundle!" he cried as he burst through the door.

There was nobody there. But the table was piled high with loaves and oranges – and there on the top, a sweet cherry pie.

TSANTOGA ISLAND

Fenya stood in the cool of the doorway as the sun choked the street with heat. The shop behind her was a well of shadows. The old woodcarver looked up.

"Come in," he said.

Fenya glanced around. The woodcarver had never spoken to her before. She edged inside, blinking and staring as her eyes grew used to the gloom. The taste of sawdust and shavings clung to the roof of her mouth. All around lay uncut timber, the bark mottled and dark, while behind the shelves were stacked with carvings: tiny houses and dolls, oxen and carts, butterflies, turtles and even beetles.

The woodcarver's face was creased and wrinkled. He lay down his chisel and dusted off his hands as he peered at Fenya, then lit a lantern hanging at the back of the shop.

Fenya gasped.

In the flickering light she could see a tree carved from the boughs of many trees – the branches, the leaves, even a cluster of creatures all shaped from wood. Beneath the tree sat a great chair with a high back, vines and berries all twined in spirals around its legs and along the arms.

"Can I sit in it?" Fenya pleaded.

The woodcarver smiled and shook his head.

"Even I do not sit in this chair," he said.

"Who is it for?" Fenya asked.

"I don't know." The woodcarver had a far-away look in his eyes. "Thought if I made the chair, someone special might come and sit in it. But no-one's come yet."

Fenya skittered all around the room, picking up carvings from the shelves, holding them in her palm then putting them down again.

"Will you make something for me?" she asked.

The woodcarver scratched his chin.

"I'm busy," he said, gesturing at a stack of timber waiting

in the shadows. "I can't spare any pieces."

"Nobody's come for all the others," Fenya objected.

"But they will, they *will*," the woodcarver insisted.

Fenya's foot caught against a length of wood lying on the floor. She picked it up and weighed it in her hands.

"What about this?" she said. "It feels light and strong, as if it wants to float. Couldn't you make me a boat?"

The woodcarver picked up a mallet and began tapping on a chisel to open the beak of a blackbird.

"Please," Fenya begged, shoving the wood beneath his nose.

The woodcarver snatched it from her.

"Very well," he muttered. "Just to stop you fussing about." Then he winked.

Fenya smiled and stood a while in the doorway, gazing at the haze of heat outside. Even the errand boys moved at a snail's pace, their dark hair plastered to their faces. Behind her she heard the woodcarver grunting and muttering, clattering his chisels and hammer.

"You can look now," he said.

Fenya turned slowly, trying to pretend she wasn't interested any more, then rushing forward when she saw what the old man cradled in his hands. She seized it up and turned it this way and that, gazing at the smooth sheen of the grain and the tiny detail of the single mast and its sail.

"Will it float?" she asked excitedly, then bit her lip. "Yes – of course it will float. *You* made it. You made it for me. Let me take it down to the water!"

The woodcarver brushed his hands down his apron and almost smiled.

"Take it," he shrugged. "Take it and leave me alone."

Fenya was gone, out of the door and into the street, her feet beating quickly through the dust and the heat. On she dashed till she came to the river and there she paused on the quay, gazing down into the cool deep water as it made its way to the sea. She dodged between crates and barrels until she came to a set of weed-covered steps that led down to the rolling current. She clutched the rail carefully with one hand and soon squatted on the bottom step, the water swirling just beneath her. She trailed a hand, feeling the coolness rippling between her fingers. Then she floated the boat, keeping tight hold of its stern as she let it bob gently up and down.

She let it float for a moment before catching it again with the other hand. Back and forth and to and fro, sensing the tug of the current. But Fenya was so intent on her own small boat that she didn't see a cargo ship plunging along in the centre of the river. She didn't see the swell it made until a wave hit the bottom of the steps, nearly knocking her into the water. She gasped and closed her eyes, reaching back to grip the rail with both hands. When she opened her eyes again she saw her own small boat drifting away towards the river's end. Sailing out towards the sea.

Fenya watched it go and then hung her head, gazing down at the lapping water till its drowsy rhythm lulled her and she could feel herself swaying. Could feel creaking timber beneath her feet – and as she looked up there was a mast and a sail and all around her was the widening river. The city was far away.

She clung to a rope and breathed the salt wind as the current swept her on to the sea. But ahead was an island coming into view. Fenya tugged at the line, trying to steer the boat. The gulls swooped about her, beating their wings. Fenya saw the island looming closer. She had no choice but to go where the current took her. The boat landed with a crunch as it beached on a stretch of shingle, the water sucking back and forth, beneath its bows and under.

Fenya leapt onto a shore of dark rocks littered with pale driftwood and a scatter of bleached bones. A line of stunted trees glowered beneath the brooding sky while silent birds circled above. From the woods came the baleful howl of a dog. She shivered in the bitter wind that blew in across the bay and gazed back to the distant city where the dust-filled streets were soaked in heat.

Voices bayed from the depths of the wood where Fenya glimpsed stunted figures hunched between the trees. They crawled towards her, clad in rags, their hair matted, their faces raw with sores.

Fenya looked desperately for the boat but it was gone. Shrunk as small as it had ever been when the woodcarver pressed it into her hands, now lost among the driftwood, trapped by the arrows of grass that thrust up through the sand.

Fenya ran, but as she did, she felt a frail hand catch her arm and turned to find herself staring into the face of an old woman, wild-eyed, a shawl clasped around her shoulders, white hair flying long behind.

Fenya caught her breath.

The old woman gripped her wrist, strong and firm.

"Quickly," she said. "I am Pentille. Come with me."

Pentille placed a finger on her lips then glanced back at the dishevelled group who were lurching across the sand towards them. Fenya stayed close by the old woman as she scurried along like a skittering bird. When they reached a line of trees, Pentille relaxed her grip. Their pursuers had given up and stumbled back to the wood. Fenya stared into Pentille's face, scrutinising every mark and line.

"Don't be afraid." Pentille fixed her with a clear gaze. "This is Tsantoga Island, where they send the Malchancers – the sick and the dying, the outcasts and the children that were born disformed and diseased... but I do not have the sickness. I am old, yes. But I was never sick. My husband had it, long time ago, and when he died they thought he would have passed it on to me. So they sent me here to live with the Malchancers."

"But haven't you caught the sickness from them?"

Pentille shook her head.

"No – sometimes I wish I could. I wash the Malchancers. I hold them in my arms. I tend to their sores. I stroke their hair. I even kiss them. But I never catch their sickness. Every night the sun sets and I sit out under the moon. I think the sickness will take me, the shivering and the pain. But every morning the sun rises and I am still here to begin my work again."

Fenya looked around. The trees were bare, the stream trickling past her feet was dull and black. There were scraps of coloured ribbons tied to twisted boughs while birds squawked harshly from the undergrowth and loud flowers bloomed between bushes sharp with thorns.

Pentille led Fenya until they came to a clearing. A group of Malchancers sat hunched in a circle, their bodies covered in sores. Scattered on the ground were dark husks of Rangore fruit, the golden flesh rotting, flies hovering all around. In a bowl Fenya saw that they had crushed down a mess of Rangore leaves and they passed the vessel from one to the other, pausing to sip and to savour before handing it on.

Fenya turned to Pentille.

"Why do they discard the Rangore fruit? In the city it is so rare that it has become a delicacy. I have only tasted it once."

"They say the leaves help them to sleep."

As Fenya watched, one by one those who had drunk from the bowl closed their eyes and then drifted, swaying and moaning before falling into a crumpled heap on the ground. There they writhed, their limbs shaking in spasms before they lay still, though their faces were twisted.

"They are dreaming," Pentille whispered. "In their dreams the sickness is gone."

"Why do they still look in pain?"

Pentille shook her head.

"The sickness is all that they have. By day it brings them agony. When they drink the leaves they think they are cured. But the sickness is all that they have. Without it they are nothing."

Fenya sat at the top of the squat blistered tree that she climbed every day, staring back to the city across the water. Then she dropped down, running through groves of bright glowing flowers as she searched for a stream that ran clear and pure and was not rancid and blackened. She picked at the Rangore fruit, though the flesh was lurid and rotting. Nowhere could she find the marjoram and cinnamon that would make it taste sweet and warming.

She returned to the tree, and there she found Pentille sitting, gazing across the water. Fenya sat beside her and they stared in silence till the old woman sighed.

"What is it?" asked Fenya.

"I used to live there," Pentille explained. "I remember the markets and the noise. I would go there each day with my husband. He would sell Rangore fruit – that's when they were plentiful. But then one year the fruits were shrivelled and putrid. After that they never came again."

"Maybe Rangore gave him the sickness."

Pentille shook her head.

"Rangore helps keep the sickness away."

Fenya said nothing. She could picture the market. Knew Arrak must be there, searching for food.

"How did you get here?" Pentille asked her. "Why can't you go back?"

"I came in a boat," Fenya explained. "The woodcarver made it. It was so small I could hold it in my hand. But then I dreamt I could sail it."

"Where is it now?"

"Don't know. Soon as I came here, soon as I woke then the boat was gone. Been looking every day, in the streams, in the marshes, down by the water. But it's gone."

"Must be somewhere. Maybe you have to dream again."

"To dream I must sleep," Fenya complained. "I am cold and I am thirsty. My tongue is bruised with hunger. I lie down at night, but when I try to sleep all I hear is the moaning of the Malchancers away in the woods."

Pentille smiled.

"I know what you need."

She led Fenya away to her shelter and there she brewed up a pot of Rangore leaves.

"Take this and drink, like the Malchancers do. You have no sickness but it will help you to sleep."

Fenya nestled in the cradle of a hollow rock. She woke in a dream to run fleet-footed through silvery moonlight. Leaves and shadows brushed her skin as the low trees beckoned until she came to one which stood tall and strong as a boy, bending to seize her up in his arms. She swayed with him a moment, asleep and awake, before walking down to the incoming tide. Waves swept over them, deep and wide, a chaos of rainbow hues, darkness and light. The water was warm as they swam side by side, slippery and sinuous as shimmering fish.

When they stepped out and stood on the shore, the moon was sinking and the stars had grown dim. The boy caught her in his arms and carried her away towards the mouth of a cave where the waters beat with the sound of thunderous waves. He sat beside her on the rock. Fenya reached out to touch him as the water swirled about their feet. The boy smiled, but Fenya pulled back. She looked at his face, and then his hands – blistered with sores. He was a Malchancer, same as all the rest.

She walked away, staring across the bay towards the outline of the city. The din of the waves beat loudly in her ears. She clenched her fists as she heard the boy calling, his voice cracked with loneliness. She stamped her foot then turned around, walking back slowly towards him. She cradled him a moment in her arms then darted away, snatching up ribbons of seaweed, flotsam and shells to twine in his hair.

The boy sat still, his head bowed as she plaited and knotted, running her fingers lightly across his shoulders, down his arms, before leading him away back across the beach, back to the tree where he had come from. He clambered quickly up into its branches, disturbing a bird which fluttered away. He reached into the nest where it had been sitting and lifted out a pale blue egg which he tossed down to Fenya. As it landed in her hand the shell cracked open and the rich yellow yolk trickled between her fingers. She bent to try and pick up the fragments of broken shell, but when she looked back the boy had gone.

She gazed up at the tree which stretched above her and saw that its branches were strung with ribbons of seaweed, flotsam and shells. She felt a warm breeze blowing and reached out to wrap her arms around the trunk.

When she looked down, there where the egg had fallen lay the small boat which the woodcarver had made. Fenya seized it up in her hands and placed it in the stream which ran beside them. The boat floated quickly, bobbing towards the waiting river, growing larger all the while with the flow, its sail unfurling until it flapped in the wind, before coming to rest at the edge of the estuary.

Fenya turned around. Pentille stood beside her. They boarded the boat together. Fenya pushed away from the shore then tugged on the lines to the sail. The vessel pitched and heaved, riding the waves. Fenya glanced at Pentille. Her eyes were closed and she seemed to be crying, muttering –

"I want to go.. No, I don't – take me back... No, don't take me back... I want to go..."

They pitched up back at the steps where Fenya first started. She fastened the craft to a metal ring and helped Pentille as she picked her way carefully up onto the quayside. Pentille gazed all about her then covered her eyes again. Her limbs were shaking as she lurched back towards the steps.

Fenya grabbed her.

"Take me back," Pentille sobbed. "I don't want to be here."

"But you didn't want to be on the island," Fenya reminded her. "You told me you used to live here. This is where you belong – not back there with the Malchancers."

She gently prized Pentille's hands away from her eyes. The old woman blinked and stared about. A man in a leather hood loomed towards her, rolling a barrel. Stacks of crates teetered above them, spilling tangerines and apricots, melons and pomegranates. Bales of cloth unravelled, turquoise and amber, emerald and scarlet. Then out from the sky a seagull came swooping, diving and screaming, flapping at Pentille's face.

Fenya grabbed the old woman and steered her away, down the back alleys where a gang of deckhands staggered towards them, legs still rolling with the swell of the ocean, their bellies awash with ale and cheap wine. From upstairs windows they heard babies wailing and Fenya pushed Pentille into a doorway as a pinch-faced boy sped past quick as a rat.

"He would pick your pockets before you knew it," Fenya explained.

"Ain't got nothing to take anyway," Pentille muttered. "On the island all that you needed grew on the trees. No use for money or trinkets or drinking."

A young mother stood before them, her child on her arm, holding out her hand. Her face was pale, yellowed from the shadows.

Pentille shook her head.

"These people are sicker than the Malchancers... I need to go back."

"You don't know the way," Fenya insisted. "Stay close, you'll be safe. You can't go roaming away by yourself."

Pentille stood, head bowed, tears in her eyes. Her hands were shaking. She reached into her pocket and pulled out a Rangore leaf. The young mother was still staring, still holding out her hand. The child cried into her shoulder.

"Here – give her this," Pentille said. "And tell her to chew. It will calm her colic and then you can rest."

Fenya led Pentille on until they came to the woodcarver's shop. He was sitting inside, mopping his brow, surrounded by sawdust and shavings. He looked up at Fenya.

"Where have you been? And who is this you've brought with you?"

"I've been sailing away, away and away – but now I've come back. This is Pentille. I've brought her to meet you."

The woodcarver looked flustered, though his bright eyes twinkled. He fussed all around, clearing the clutter of discarded off-cuts before ushering Pentille towards the chair that was carved all about with berries and vines.

Pentille paused.

"I cannot sit here," she said. "It is far too fine for the likes of me."

"I made this chair but nobody came," the woodcarver replied. "Then I made a small boat for this girl and now she's brought you here."

Pentille hesitated.

"Didn't she tell you where she found me? I've been living on Tsantoga Island all these years. Aren't you afraid I'm carrying the sickness?"

The woodcarver leaned on his broom.

"Ain't no sickness at all," he said. "Only what folks see."

And for a moment, reflected in a mirror that was hanging on the wall, Fenya glimpsed a young woman sitting tall and proud in the chair, a smile on her face and a long satin dress that swept down to the ground.

The old man saw Fenya watching them and led her to the tree hewn from wood which stood behind the chair. He reached up into the branches and took down the carving of a bird sitting on a nest and handed it to Fenya.

She lifted the bird and found six wooden eggs clustered in the nest. She picked one out and cradled it in her hand, then suddenly dived through the door and ran, still clutching the egg. She ran until she came to the river and there was the small carved boat, lying at the bottom of the weed-covered steps. She leaned down and tucked the egg safe in its belly. Then she floated it on the rocking water and pushed it away, out towards the island where she knew the boy was waiting.

ON THE BRIDGE

"Everywhere there is nothing," Ghresselle skittered down the dim-lit streets that led her to the bridge. "Nothing but rain, nothing but silence, nothing but noise. Nothing but darkness, nothing but walls. Walls to shut out sorrow... walls to shut out pain. Walls to keep me safe, keep me locked away. But then I cannot go out. I cannot touch. I cannot breathe... I cannot breathe......"

She scrambled up onto the parapet of the bridge and stared down at the water below. It was late evening now, dull with cloud. She had walked the streets all day, waiting for the moment when she could come here, where no-one else would see her. She felt a cool breeze on her face, snagging at her tatted hair.

The water was dark, tugging and pulling. She watched as flotsam drifted, rotten fruit, a dead dog, a discarded gown. Stray gulls scudded, squawking and calling before wheeling away. From the other side of the bridge she heard footsteps approaching, the tap of boots. They came closer.

Ghresselle held her breath. As the sound stopped behind her, she turned. A young man stood there. She peered at him closely.

"Who are you?" she demanded.

The young man smiled.

"I am Morrow," he said, reaching out a hand. "What are you doing?"

"I am watching for the twilight to come," Ghresselle replied, turning back to stare at the river.

Morrow gripped her arm gently.

"Come down," he said. "You might slip and fall. The water is deep here. It flows dark and fast."

Ghresselle shrugged, still staring at the water.

"I do not want to drown," she said, almost to herself. "I am drowned already in this city. I do not need to drown again."

"Come down," Morrow repeated, softly but firmly, still

holding her arm.

Ghresselle turned and looked at him, then suddenly lurched forward into his arms. He held her a moment and then let her go. They both stood in silence, staring at each other.

"Are you my brother?" she asked as she reached out and stroked Morrow's cheek with her finger.

She smiled then and giggled.

"I had a brother once," she continued. "I would dance with him wantonly, when the other boys they wanted me. I would flash my eyes and swirl my skirts and then we would run away, me and my brother, out to a place where no-one could find us and lay there under the stars. We'd play a game we taught each other, but nobody knew its name."

She grabbed Morrow suddenly and pulled him to her.

"Are you my brother?" she asked again.

Morrow looked puzzled. The woman smelt of dead water, but her grip was strong.

"I can be your brother if you wish," he said.

The lights of the city were flickering on the river and he could hear the water lapping gently against the hulks of the boats moored below. Then Ghresselle pushed him away and shook her head.

"My brother is dead," she said. "He drowned in a stream, in a bucket, in a thimble."

She stared down again at the waters below.

"I do not want to drown," she cried.

Morrow looked startled and pulled her back.

"Then stay with me," he said. "Walk with me across the bridge till we get to the other side."

She linked his arm and gazed into his face as they set off together. When they reached the shadows away from the river, she gripped him again and kissed him full upon the lips. Then she pushed him away.

"You are not my brother," she said again, then ran into the darkness. As she looked back, her eyes were flashing, her skirts all a-swirl.

The next night Morrow found her again in the middle of the bridge, staring into the water.

"My brother is there," she said. "Look, I can see him. He is swimming."

Morrow looked over. He could see nothing there, only the deep suck and pull of the river. Ghresselle's eyes suddenly flared in alarm.

"He is struggling," she said. "See – I must save him!"

She hitched up her skirt and began to clamber onto the low parapet of the bridge. Morrow gripped her waist tightly and pulled her back. She clung to him, breathing heavily.

"You saved me," she said. "Nobody saved my brother. He is dead. After he drowned he would write to me. The letters were strange. I could not understand the words. I burnt them all. See – I have them here."

Ghresselle plunged her hands into her pockets and pulled out fistfuls of old charred paper. She leaned over the parapet and let them drift down till they floated away on the darkness of the water.

She clutched at Morrow again.

"Now he is gone," she said. "Now you can be my brother. Now you can save me. Don't let me drown."

She held him closer than ever before as pale gulls swirled all around. Morrow caught his breath, then peeled himself away.

"Come," he said, "let us find a place where we can sit and talk."

He led her slowly down a path to sit on a bench in a riverside garden. He noticed that Ghresselle was shaking, her eyes staring wide into the shadows.

"Are you cold?" he asked.

She bowed her head.

"On the warmest nights I am cold," she said. "– but in winter I carry a fever as if my limbs were on fire. I walk and I walk till no-one can find me. Till I cannot even find myself."

Morrow paused, thinking.

"Was it always like this?" he asked.

Ghresselle turned and looked at him, as if suddenly remembering.

"When I was a girl we lived back in the village and my mother always told me not to go to the woods. She said there was an old man who lived there, he had lived there for years, out in a hut by the crossroads. She said he would play such tricks on me and I must never go there."

"What was his name?" asked Morrow.

"Mother said his name was Pickapple and that I should never trust him. But I wanted to go, I wanted to see. So one day I set out when my mother was busy cleaning the sloppens."

"Did you take your brother with you?" Morrow asked. "He would keep you safe."

Ghresselle shook her head. "No, he said he was drowned that day and could not come, and so I set out all alone. I got to the woods. It was dark and it was cold. I was full feared. Leaves rustling and creatures I couldn't see, though I could hear them calling. And I come to the hut by the crossroads, just as mother had told me. The door was open so I looked inside.

"There were spiders crawling everywhere and dust so thick it made me sneeze. Little mice ran in and out the old trinkets on shelves loaded so heavy they near slid to the floor. But nobody could be living there. The chair was all broken and the table was collapsed. And when I moved the rags that were strewn on the bed I found a nest of rats…"

Morrow's eyes lit up and his fingers twitched. He leaned in closer.

"What then?" he said.

Ghresselle stared at him as if she had forgotten he was there.

"A boy came," she said at last.

"Who was he?" Morrow asked.

Ghresselle's voice dropped to a whisper so low he could hardly hear.

"Said his name was Pickapple. We sat together in that hut with rats and mice and spiders crawling all around. He took my hand and kissed me and then he swore he would not trick me. He tied a kerchief round my head and chased the rats from off the bed. He sowed an apple seed inside me. I heard a blackbird singing loud from the top of the tree outside. But when I unknotted the kerchief, Pickapple he was gone."

She rubbed her belly then and stared at Morrow again.

"Now my feet are apple roots, my hands are apple twigs and my eyes, my eyes see only the sky and my ears hear birds a-singing like as if the stars are ringing. After that I was never the same. I bled sweet apple juice when the full moon came. When I woke every morning, I heard Pickapple call my name. And I would go looking for him, out there in the wood."

Ghresselle paused and peered up at Morrow.

"Let me tell you..." she whispered, "I would have stayed with him night and day if I could."

She stared down at the water.

"I do not want to drown... you have to save me again," she said and turned to clutch at Morrow's shirt.

But was not Morrow she saw. It seemed there was a boy, standing there beside her.

"Are you my brother?" she asked, but the boy shook his head and reached into his pocket, then held out an apple. She looked at him and stroked his cheek. The boy smiled once and then he was gone.

Ghresselle turned the apple in her bony fingers, raised it to her lips and kissed it, then took one bite. She swallowed hungrily, but then turned and threw the core into the water. It sank down into the dark eddy of ripples before bobbing back up to the surface. Ghresselle stood on the parapet and watched as it slowly floated away.

LACITURN

Fenya saw the man hunched on a bench, his coat long and shabby, the colour of every weather. A scurry of pigeons swarmed around his feet and a seagull swooped down to perch upon a box which he clutched tightly to his knees. As Fenya approached, the bird flew away. The man's face seemed alarmed as he clung more tightly to his box. Fenya sat down on the bench beside him.

"What do you keep in the box?" she asked, reaching out to touch.

The man flinched away.

"Be careful," he said. "This box is filled with my most precious possessions. I collect ornaments and keepsakes from all over the world."

"Can I see them?" Fenya begged. "I love trinkets and treasures."

The man shook his head and stared into the distance. Across the street a boy sat cross-legged, selling oranges which were brighter than the sun which never reached this dusky corner beneath the looming store houses.

"What's your name?" Fenya asked suddenly.

The man turned and smiled.

"It's Laciturn," he said.

Fenya smiled back at him.

"So can I see the trinkets and treasures?" she pleaded. "Just a little peek..."

"They are fragile," Laciturn replied. "They will break."

"I will only look," Fenya promised. "Let me see – I won't touch them at all."

The man paused, fingering the knots on the cord that bound the box.

"I don't usually show anyone."

"*Please* let me see them," Fenya begged, picking at the first of the knots.

"Don't touch!" Laciturn exclaimed. "Here - if you insist, I will do it myself."

And slowly, reluctantly, he untied the knots till the old frayed cord fell onto the cracked paving stones. Fenya craned forward, eager to find out what was inside. Laciturn waved her back.

"Patience!" he said as he released the catch on the lid, then gazed down, a smile spreading across the lines of his face.

"Let me see, let me see." Fenya craned forward and peered into the box. "It's empty," she said. "There's nothing but dust."

Laciturn shook his head.

"Oh no – it's full to the top."

"But where are the trinkets?" Fenya demanded.

"No-one can see them," Laciturn explained. "That's what makes them so precious."

"But what's the use of a treasure that no-one can see?"

"Some are lost, some are stolen," Laciturn admitted. "Some have crumbled away. Some I've polished so much that all that remains is the memory. But the memories are still there."

Fenya looked puzzled.

"Here - take this one," he said.

Laciturn put his hand in the box and drew it out carefully, as if it were holding something of great value, and placed it in Fenya's outstretched palm.

"What do you feel?"

He studied her face.

Fenya paused, shifting the weight, sensing the surface of something she couldn't see.

"I feel warmth," she said. "The same warmth I feel when I'm with the other girls who catch and run, when we all come together at the end of the day."

"I've seen these girls," said Laciturn. "All they do is cheat and steal."

"We do not cheat," Fenya objected. "We do not rob. All we do is filch those things that others will not miss. How else can we live?"

Laciturn shook his head and sighed, then reached out and took the object. He put it back in the box and handed her another.

"What about this one?"

Fenya shivered.

"I feel cold. The cold that I feel when I cannot sleep, all alone in the city at night."

She pushed the object away. Laciturn grabbed it quickly.

"Be careful," he said. "Do not drop it. If it shatters, anyone who picks up one of the pieces will shiver or burn as if they have a fever. They may call this fever anger or loneliness, fear or happiness – but they will not understand why they feel this way."

Laciturn placed the ornament back in the box which he bound again with the cord.

"I am tired," he said. "I have come a long way."

"Let me carry the box for you," offered Fenya.

Laciturn looked reluctant, but she could tell he was pleased as she took the box under her arm and set off down long narrow streets where the faded paint peeled from the blistered walls, revealing pale grey bricks beneath. They came to a ditch-work of old canals lurking in lost gullies. Rusting bridges rose above them and under the arches, shadows clustered, shuffling and stealthy. Fenya caught her breath. Water slithered down the moss-covered walls which towered all around them.

"Are we there yet?" she asked, but Laciturn seemed not to hear as he strode on ahead. Then he disappeared. Fenya stopped and looked around. "Wait!" she called. "You can't leave me now."

She took one more step then saw Laciturn standing waiting. He seemed taller now, she thought.

"This is where I live," he said, leading her through a doorway.

The building seemed deserted. In the grim light she could smell the stench of the empty rooms as she followed him along the hallway. They climbed the stairs slowly, one step at a time, spiralling around and around in the creaking darkness. At the top stood a heavy door. Laciturn produced a bunch of keys and opened first one lock and then another.

Fenya gasped. The room was filled with boxes, just like the one she had carried all this way. And on top of the boxes stood a clutter of bric-a-brac, covered in cobwebs and dust. She cleared a space next to a broken mirror and sat down, gazing at vases and old chequer boards, blunt knives and dented cooking pots. Through one grimy pane of the window she could see the lights of the city glinting below. She could just make out the figures of the old women who rolled out their mats on the pavement, spreading knick-knacks and trinkets that glittered enticingly in the gathering dark.

"How do you come to have all this?" Fenya gestured around the room.

Laciturn gazed at her with tired grey eyes.

"There was a man who would visit my mother some nights when the moon was full and the stars were bright. He always brought something hidden in his pocket – a necklace, a bracelet, a brooch. Said he made them himself – twisted from bits of metal..."

Laciturn broke off.

"Are you listening?" he asked.

Fenya nodded though she didn't look round. Her eyes had caught sight of a wooden doll perched high on a shelf at the back of the boxes. Its hair was matted with cobwebs, one of its arms was missing, and it seemed a tear of moisture was trickling down its cheek.

Laciturn coughed and continued.

"One night when he knocked, it was me who opened the door. From the depths of his pocket he drew something new. This time it was the figure of an old man carrying a box on his back. He slipped it quickly into my hand. 'This is for you,' he said.

"I used to sit and play with it, taking the hunched old man on journeys through the dust in the gutter in front of the house. I imagined all the places that the old man could go and all the people that he met. I would gather shiny stones and bits of stick and feather and place them in the box on his back till it was full to the brim. Then at the end of the journey I would take them all out again and dream that they were treasures. I would string them together into necklaces for my mother. She would smile and kiss me on the head, but I noticed she never wore them. She would rather wear the trinkets and finery that her visitor brought her..."

Laciturn paused. He watched as Fenya scrambled across the teetering stack of boxes to reach down the broken doll from the shelf. She turned it around and around in her hands, her fingers picking at a piece of frayed string knotted around its neck. As she did so a tangle of tarnished stones and faded feathers scattered across the floor.

Laciturn continued as if he hadn't noticed.

"One long afternoon I was out playing rattle-can with the other boys. We ran wild across the wasteground, scuffed our boots and bruised our knees and when we got home my mother was waiting for me. 'Show me the little metal figure of the man and his box,' she said.

"I plunged my hands in my pockets, but there was nothing but empty shadows. The figure had gone. And the man who brought it had gone too. He never came again, though my mother watched and waited, sitting at the window late into the night. There were no more necklaces and no more bracelets."

Fenya scrabbled desperately, trying to retrieve the feathers and stones from where they had fallen between the boxes. Laciturn seemed not even to see her now as he carried on talking in the gathering darkness.

"My mother kept her trinkets locked up in a casket and some nights I would creep downstairs and see her touching them and counting them and watch as her tears fell glistening, though the sparkle of her treasures had long since gone.

"Ever since then I would find gifts for her, buy them, borrow them, trade them and steal them, so I had something to give her whenever I came home. Soon enough I started twisting bits of metal. Even now I cannot stop. I want to make my mother happy. I want her visitor to come again, even though they both are gone, many years ago..."

Laciturn stopped and looked up. He saw Fenya sitting on top of the boxes, twisting the wooden doll in her hands.

"Will you give *me* a present?" she asked. "Will you give me this doll?" Laciturn shook his head.

"Put it back," he said. "That doll was my mother's. It was once all she had, until I brought her all this." He waved his hand around the room at the boxes filled with trinkets swathed in dust. "All of them are precious, but all of them are worthless, for they have made nobody happy – not her, not even me."

Fenya wiped the tear from the doll's wooden cheek, cradled it a moment in her arms, and then placed it in the old man's hands. He looked up at her and smiled again, as she slowly tiptoed away.

IN THE DARK OF THE STREET

In the dark of the street, a woman lay prone across the cobblestones, her yellow shawl spread beneath her like a pair of silent wings. There was nobody to see her, nobody to know how she came to be there. Every door was locked shut, every curtain drawn closed. The night was nearly over, but the day had not begun.

Ghresselle tiptoed from an alleyway. She circled round the woman and twitched at the yellow shawl. The woman did not stir, her face pressed hard against the cold of the cobbles. Ghresselle prodded her with one boot, then frisked quickly through the woman's pockets.

"Could be the weight of her purse has made her fall…"

But all she found was a hand-mirror, with one crack split across the glass. Ghresselle turned the woman's head and held the mirror to her mouth to see if she was breathing, then peered at it closely. The glass was clear. Not a cloud of mist. Not a droplet of breath.

Ghresselle prodded at the woman again.

"Are you drowned?" she said.

The woman did not move as Ghresselle plucked at her dress.

"Your clothes are drenched…"

She tugged the lank wet hair away from the woman's face.

"Look like someone I knowed once…" Ghresselle muttered.

She paused a moment, trying to remember, rocking to and fro. Then she pulled the hair from her own face and squinted at the mirror.

"Seems you look like me. But this cannot be, for you are drowned and I am breathing."

She blew hot and long on the glass, then shrugged. The glass remained clear. She shook her head and stared hard at the woman. The silence pressed close upon them both. Ghresselle glanced stealthily up and down the street. Still nobody was awake. She frisked quickly through the woman's pockets again. They were empty.

"How come you got nothing?" Ghresselle grumbled. "You're worse as me."

She rolled the woman to lie face up, staring at the last of the stars, then ferreted quickly inside her dress to find a hand-made butterfly: strips of cloth all threaded about a twist of wire. Ghresselle held it in the palm of her hand.

"Tis pretty enough," she said grudgingly. "Wings as yellow as that shawl. But what's it worth? It cannot fly…"

From the broken guttering of a nearby house, a sparrow greeted the first glimmer of dawn with a disgruntled chirrup, then fluttered down to land beside them. It cocked its head then spread its wings to take off again.

"I would like to fly…" Ghresselle sighed, as she tugged the yellow shawl from beneath the woman's body and hurried quickly away.

As the sun rose, Ghresselle walked slower, turning the butterfly in her hands. A tiny bundle of cloth and wire, but she tossed it up and caught it, tossed it up and caught it. Higher each time and higher again.

"But it does not fly," she smiled, as she tugged the shawl about her shoulders and felt its frail gauze tremble in the wind.

Her legs tottered forward, her arms raised high to trail the shawl behind as she ran. Her limbs were light, her eyes blazed bright though her head was filled with swimming cloud.

The butterfly nestled in her pocket, pulsing against her ribcage as she swooped down towards the river. People stopped to watch, but she took no notice, letting out a fevered cry as she looked up towards the sky. Then she stopped and looked around.

"But I'm still on the ground."

The shawl clung limply about her shoulders. She pushed against the door of an empty warehouse. Inside a rattle of pigeons flung themselves upward towards the cage of rafters and out to the sky through the gap where the roof had been.

Ghresselle followed them, climbing a rickety staircase, spiralling up until she stood shivering, out on the guttering, her yellow shawl fluttering in the wind like wings. Below her the river, the cobbles, the wharf-ways. Pigeons circled round her, the starlings, the gulls. She felt her feet sliding as she tottered forward, the morning sun burning her face and her eyes.

She let out a cry, wild as a bird, wanton as a lover, helpless as a child. She clutched the edges of the shawl with each fist. And stepped out. And beat her arms. She felt a rush of air about her. A dream fall. As if she was swooping, floating, drowning. A twisting tumble as the skin of her face stretched back, her lips contorted into a reckless grin. The wind beneath her, wrapped around her, sucked inside her to buoy her up as she twisted into a spin. A glide. A sigh.

To land. Face down. On the cobbles. The shawl draped about her. And still nestled in her pocket, the yellow butterfly.

Old Nipthimble found her there where she lay. He plucked at the yellow shawl, fancying its gauze would make fine wings for the butterflies he stitched in his workshop. Ghresselle stirred and sat up slowly, shaking her head. She gazed at the old man, reaching out to trace his face with her fingers, as if it was a map.

"I'm lost," she said.

Nipthimble nodded.

"You have fallen."

Ghresselle stroked his cheek.

"Are you Morrow?" she asked.

Nipthimble shook his head.

Ghresselle sighed.

"I knew a young man called Morrow once," she continued. "He saved me from drowning… will you save me?"

She lurched forward to embrace the old man, but he stepped away.

"You are not drowning," he informed her. "And I am *not* a young man."

Ghresselle sat back, gathering the yellow shawl about her

shoulders.

"But I have been flying. Flying is like to drowning. Flying is drowning in the wide blue sky. Drowning is flying in the deep dark water... Will you save me? I was flying. I have fallen."

She looked back up at the warehouse behind her. Pigeons flapped in and out of the empty windows while squawking gulls circled all around.

"They are hungry," she said. "We should feed them."

She plunged her hand into her pocket, drew out her fist clenched tight, then slowly uncurled her fingers. There in her palm sat the butterfly.

Nipthimble stared at it, astonished.

He leant forward to straighten its crumpled wings.

Ghresselle pulled away, turning her back to shield it from him.

"Do not touch!" she exclaimed. "The creature protects me. I have fallen... I was drowning... You will not save me... do not steal my butterfly from me!"

She knelt up and glared at him, still clutching the bundle of cloth and wire tightly between her fingers. Old Nipthimble leaned forward. As the yellow shawl slipped from her shoulders, he gathered it and wrapped it around her.

"I made it," he said.

She stared at him.

"I made the butterfly... do not grip it so tight or you will crush it."

Ghresselle loosened her fingers and bent forward to kiss the creature. She lifted her hands then, as if it might fly. Then smiled a mischievous smile.

"Will you show me?" she said, tucking the butterfly back in her pocket and suddenly seizing his hand.

"Will you teach me? Let me help you... I can stitch. I can sew. I can thread a needle quick as quick. I can help you to make butterflies."

She scrambled to her feet, gripping the old man's waist.

"Take me with you..." she said.

They trudged the steps to his workshop, Ghresselle weary now, leaning into the old man, though he scarce had the weight of a butterfly himself. He unlocked the door with a long heavy key. As it swung open, Ghresselle gasped at the dizzying array of bright fabrics and the lines of half-finished butterflies strung along the walls.

Then, without being asked, she slumped down into a chair hung with lengths of cloth. Old Nipthimble winced, then smiled.

"You are tired," he said.

Ghresselle nodded.

"I have fallen…"

Nipthimble busied himself making a cup of comfrey tea, which he pressed into her hands. She blew on it gently as she looked about.

"Do you sleep here?" she asked, casting her eyes around the room, crammed with cuttings and twisted wire.

Nipthimble sipped his own tea.

"I never sleep," he replied.

Ghresselle's eyes widened.

"I like a man who does not sleep. I can be a comfort to you. I can keep you warm through your long, lonely nights."

Nipthimble shook his head.

"These are my only comfort," he said, pointing to the line of butterflies which lay waiting on the bench. "These are my dreams. Every night I sew more to sell in the morning. I have many to complete. You may help me if you wish."

Ghresselle frowned as she stared around. She studied the shapes that Nipthimble had fashioned, then suddenly tugged the yellow shawl from her shoulders, seized up a pair of scissors and began to hack at the cloth.

"It flew once," she said, watching as the fabric frayed between the jaws of the scissors. "It bore me up. It brought me down. Now it will fly again a thousand times."

Nipthimble shook his head as jagged misshapen pieces floated to the floor.

"These are ornaments for ladies. They will be pinned to coats and dresses. They will never fly," he explained. "But they are beautiful things – they will bring happiness in other ways."

Ghresselle placed the scissors on the bench and sighed.

"You cannot buy happiness," she muttered wearily. "You can only find it... have to know the sorrow first, then happiness will come."

"Let us begin!" Nipthimble exclaimed. "Sew your dreams. Stitch what you find behind your eyes."

Ghresselle seized up a strip of the yellow cloth, matched it to a turquoise piece, picked a needle from a box on the table, threaded it clumsily and then began to sew.

Nipthimble watched. Her stitches were crude and uneven. Her hands were shaking, her fingers fumbled. She bit back a shriek and gritted her teeth as the needle pierced her skin. Drops of blood dripped slowly onto the remains of the yellow shawl. Dark red patches which faded into rust-brown stains.

She stitched on as the light faded and the room was lit by the flicker of a single candle. Nipthimble busied himself in the far corner, sorting through bags of cloth, leaving Ghresselle to make butterflies of her own dreams. But as dawn crept through the one high window, he saw that every one she had made was misshapen and grotesque. More like moths that had flitted from nightmares than bright sparkling butterflies to greet the day.

"I cannot sell these," he declared, sweeping them into a basket of stray cuttings and strands of wire.

"What are you doing?" Ghresselle wailed. "I worked all night. These are my dreams..."

"These are nothing that anyone will buy."

Ghresselle reached out and grabbed his arm. Nipthimble glared at her, but then his face softened.

"You are learning," he said. "Once I had to learn too."

He placed her handiwork on a high shelf, the wings bedraggled and mismatched, cut from the blood-stained tatters of the remains of the yellow shawl. Ghresselle watched as he folded a set of completed butterflies carefully into a bag.

"Where are you going?" she asked.

Nipthimble smiled.

"I go out to sell them down by the harbour."

"Shall I come with you?"

Nipthimble peered at her tired eyes, her trembling hands. He shook his head.

"No, you should stay here," he said, "and rest. I will return by sunset. Then we can make butterflies again. I can help you."

Ghresselle nodded and settled down into a chair, watching as he closed the door. As soon as he was gone, she sprang up, stood tiptoe on a stool and reached for the moths she had made. She hid them under her coat and ran quickly down the rickety stairs that led to the street. Then she threw the moths up into the cold swirling mist of the dawn.

She watched them rise, their wings dark against the silver light. She held her breath, giggling as if she was a child. But then they fell and lay silent on the cobblestones.

Ghresselle walked slowly away, back towards Nipthimble's workshop. But then she stopped. Behind her she heard the voices of children, calling and laughing, screeching and beseeching. She turned. The moths had gone. In their place a ragged knot of urchins who ran towards her, surrounding her, tugging at her skirts.

"Come with us!" they seemed to cry. "Come with us!"

Ghresselle followed and soon she noticed that though dawn had broken, where these creatures trod was night. Night of brooding silence. Night of sullen rain. The children ran on, dragging Ghresselle behind them through deserted streets and empty squares.

"Where are we going?" she demanded.

But the children only laughed and gibbered excitedly in words she did not know. They led her down an unlit gulley to a heavy door of rusted metal. As it swung open, Ghresselle saw by the dim light flickering inside, a towering man wearing a bloodied apron. A cleaver dangled from his hand.

He looked towards her, but then turned back to hack at a

carcass laid out on a bench. The cellar was filled with the stench of flesh. Nameless shapes hung on hooks from the ceiling. Ghresselle peered at them. Goats, pigs, dogs, cats, seagulls. Some she could not imagine.

The door opened again, and closed. Shadowy figures came and went, each clutching a cut of meat that oozed blood which dripped as they went scurrying back onto the street.

Ghresselle approached the man.

"Are you the Night Butcher?" she asked. "I know those who speak of you."

The man turned and stared but looked through her. He opened his mouth but did not speak. Ghresselle stared at his teeth which seemed to be welded of metal, glinting in the shadowy light.

Ghresselle peered around.

"Where are the children?" she said suddenly.

The Night Butcher said nothing, returning to his work.

"There were children who brought me here… where have they gone…?"

She could hear laughter, as if from the walls, as if they had scurried like rats into the space where cockroaches crawled, between the plaster and the crumbling bricks. Ghresselle called to them, thinking they might come out, scurrying and spitting and scratching, then laughing again and gibbering, though she did not know their words. She waited, but there was only the rhythm of the butcher's blows, the crack of the blade as it cleaved through the bone, the thud as it bit into the well-worn wound of the bench.

Then she saw them all, not children at all, but dark moths clinging to the damp of the walls. She let out a cry and the Night Butcher turned to where she was standing, but all he saw was a broken butterfly stitched from yellow gauze, lying on the floor.

ONE RED GLOVE

Morrow walked down by the side of the old canal. There was a smell of damp, of dank, of rot. A coat of moss clung to the walls. On the bank, a bundle of discarded rubbish. As Morrow grew closer, it seemed to move, and he saw was a threadbare sack, wrapped around the shoulders of a girl.

She turned when she saw him. The shawl of sacking was all she wore, except for one glove, the colour of blood.

"Where are your clothes?" asked Morrow.

The girl shivered, then smiled.

"Can you not see? This is a dress of finest velvet. My scarves are spun from sheerest silk. On my arms hang charms of polished silver. But I have lost my glove."

Morrow nodded.

"How did you come here?" he enquired.

The girl frowned, as if trying to remember.

"I dropped a pitcher," she said, stepping closer to Morrow. She stared at him, then reached out to touch the pendant which hung around his neck.

"Give this to me," she said. "It will keep me warm."

Morrow shook his head.

"Perhaps you should first find your glove," he said. "Then you will be warm."

"My name is Binnory," she told him. "Once I lived in a cottage all my own, until I dropped the pitcher. It broke on the floor, but I picked it up, placed the pieces side by side and thought I would fix it in the morning. When I woke the next day, it was mended. It sat good as new on the table.

"Next night it was a plate that broke. This time I did not drop it. It flew from my hands and smashed right there on the floor. Again I picked up the pieces and placed them on the table. Again, in the morning when I woke, the plate was mended good as new.

"All night there had been a storm that kept me awake,

tossing and turning in my bed. I opened the door and looked out. The rain had stopped, the wind had dropped, but my fence was smashed to the ground. Then I heard a tapping sound and saw that a man was fixing it with a hammer and a pocket full of nails.

"He was a small man, a wiry man, with clever hands and long quick fingers. He turned to me with the kind of smile that could melt the clouds away. 'You seem to break things,' he said. 'I like to find things to mend. I can help you.'

"I thought about the jug and the plate, and wondered how they came to be fixed. 'Nothing ever broke before,' I told him. The man smiled again. 'That's why I am here.'

"The sun came out from behind the clouds and the ground began to dry. 'I think you *make* them break,' I said, but I was laughing now.

"He told me his mending started when he broke his wifen's chair and she would not let him fix it. She said it had been her grandmother's – and so she sent him away. Ever since then he'd been mending things to try to help other people. I thought he looked sad, standing there with his hammer and his pocket of nails. Just then the rain came down again and I let him stand under the porch. He peered through the door and looked around.

"'I see your clock is broken. I can fix that,' he said. 'Won't you let me in?' The rain was coming down harder now, and so I let him inside. He took the clock from the shelf and quick as quick opened up the back, pulled out all its workings and spread them on the table. I thought that now it would be broke forever. There were so many bits, how could they ever fit back again? But fit they did, in no time at all – and soon the clock was ticking, the hands were turning and it chimed the hours and quarters, same as ever before. The sun came back too, shining through the window.

"I let him stay. What could I do? He said he had nowhere to go, so I let him sleep on the floor. But somehow things went on breaking – a saucer, a teapot, my washing line – worse than ever before. But this man Cuckle, he was there on hand and mended them all again! He was so happy, always charming, with a twinkle in his eye. 'You're so clumsy,' he told me. 'Good job you've got me around.'

"'Good job it is,' I said. But when I found my own best chair broke, that was more than I could take. Even though he fixed it, I said, 'I want nothing more to break. Nothing ever broke before, until you came along.'

"So just like that, the breaking stopped. Nothing slipped, nothing fell, nothing snapped. But Cuckle stayed. He would not go. 'I need to be here, just in case,' he said. And he'd sit around the house all day with nothing to do and nothing to mend, tapping his hammer on the table and counting out his nails.

"One day he sat there staring at me. 'What are you looking at?' I asked. 'Your clothes are shabby,' he said. 'That's no business of yours,' I told him. 'If you do not like what you see, mayhap you can fix them.' Cuckle shook his head. 'I can mend fences,' he said, 'and I can fix pans, but I cannot patch up clothes.'

"But all of a sudden he leapt up, went out the door and down the path and away, off along the road. I thought mayhap I'd seen the last of him, but at sunset he returned with a basket filled with clothes – fine dresses and shawls and trinkets, and a pair of gloves the colour of blood.

"'Where did you get them?' I asked, but Cuckle said nothing and just shook his head. Next day I tried on one of the dresses, chose a scarf and pulled on the gloves. He eyed me with a smile as I turned around, but then he gave a frown. Outside the window, a woman was walking, up and down the lane. She stopped by my gate and stared at the door and then walked on again.

"'Who might that be?' I asked. 'I've never seen her before.' Cuckle was crouching way back in the shadows. 'That is my wifen,' he told me then. 'She must not see me here. If she comes again, tell me you'll send her away.'

"'Why send her away?' I asked him. 'Mayhap she has come to tell you she'll let you fix her grandmother's chair. Mayhap she misses you and wants you to come home.' But Cuckle shook his head and told me, 'I'd much rather stay here and fix things for you.'

"But she did come again, his wifen. Come marching up the path. Come knocking on my door. Soon as I opened it, she burst inside without so much as a glance at me. Cuckle was hiding behind the dresser, but she saw him. 'What are you doing here?' she accused. '– I'm mending things for this girlen,' he told her.

"At that she seized up my broom from the corner to beat Cuckle about the head. 'Why, you good-for-nothing!' she screamed. 'You couldn't even mend my grandmother's chair. I'll show you what needs mending!'

"With that, she swung the broom round and round the room, smashing all my cups, my saucers, my plates, breaking all the ornaments that stood on the shelf.

"'Stop!' I said. 'Stop. You can have your man. He's no good to me.'

"'But who will fix your pots and pans?' Cuckle pleaded.

"'I will fix them myself, now be off with you!' I cried.

"'Don't you speak to my husband like that,' said the wifen, 'after all he has done for you.' She looked at me then properly. She stood and stared and stared.

"'What's that dress you'm a-wearing? What is that fine scarf? You're not content to take my man, you have stolen all my best clothes!'

"She leapt at me then and tore them from me and pushed me out through the door. All I had left was one glove. I stood there all of a-shiver and wrapped this sack around my back. I heard them laughing then inside as they locked the door behind me. I heard them smashing everything the wifen hadn't broke before.

"So there I was, with only this sack, didn't even have no shoes. I walked and I walked until I came here, though now I have hurt my foot."

Her ankle was swollen and bruised. As Morrow bent down to examine it, Binnory stroked the pendant again which dangled from his neck.

"Won't you help me?" she said. "All I need is one glove."

Morrow ran to the glove-maker, a silver-headed woman who sat in her shop, sewing and stitching and patching, her eyes bright and shiny, dreaming of all the hands that her gloves had ever warmed.

"I need just one glove," Morrow told her. "Do you have one to spare?"

The old woman turned and picked up a glove, a blood red glove.

"A woman brought me this, only yesterday. She came in from the country and brought this with her. Said she needed one to match it, for the other was stolen by a wretched girlen who ran off with her husband and all her best clothes."

"That's the one!" cried Morrow, snatching it up. "Let me take it – I will pay you well!"

Before the old woman could object, he stuffed the glove in his pocket and ran out of the door.

He ran all the way to the canal, still clutching the glove, and scrambled down to the towpath.

"Binnory!" he called.

The water lay still and silent. Shadows clung to the bridge. He stopped and listened, but all he heard was the echo of his own voice, then he called again. There was no reply as he walked slowly to the spot where he first found her. A ragged sack was left on the bank, and beside it lay a dog. Morrow approached it cautiously, not sure if the animal was dead. As he came closer, it whimpered and raised its head. Its foot was hurt, he could see that, and bound about with a bloodied rag.

Morrow gently raised the paw and began to unwrap the bandage, to find that when he loosened it, was not a scrap of cloth at all. He was holding one red glove. He slipped the other from his pocket to place it beside the first, then turned back to the dog. But the path was empty. Morrow sat a while and listened. From the other side of the bridge came the sound of Binnory's laughter.

SMOKE CHARMER

Arrak shivered. He could feel the cold bite of winter blowing in from the quayside as he scurried through the gunnels that led from the waterfront. In a dimly-lit street, whole sides of beef hung from corroded hooks while butcher boys wiped their hands down bloodied aprons, their smiles glinting harsh as their knives.

Arrak was hungry. He could almost taste the gutted rabbits, the venison and the fat wood pigeons laid out across the counter. But he knew he would find no scraps here. Better to look for rotting fruit thrown away cheaply than hope for any tit-bits to fall from these stalls.

He thrust his hands in his pockets and hunched up his shoulders, then he noticed a woman, sauntering slowly, her bag half open, with a bright turquoise scarf spilling out.

Arrak moved alongside her. She was busy picking through a bucket of pigs trotters. He seized the end of the scarf and tweaked it quickly. But not quick enough. The woman spun around, grabbing his wrist in one easy move. Arrak struggled, but her grip was strong.

"What d'you think you're doing?" she demanded.

Arrak hung his head.

"I'm hungry," he said.

The woman gazed at him steadily.

"You can't eat a scarf. If you're hungry, come with me."

She led him away down a dingy lane where men squatted on stools, chewing tobacco as they thumbed the tarnished dominoes. They flung them lazily across the low table, grunting in concentration while the smell of thin chicken broth wafted from the slop kitchen next door.

The stench was sour, but still Arrak's hunger dragged him on until they came to the shell of an old warehouse. A winch hung from a trap door above the arched entranceway, but the walls were papered with faded show-bills. Arrak glanced at the woman again. Her face was caked with ashen powder. Her eyes lit up as she saw him staring at the posters.

"You like a show?"

Arrak shrugged.

"Seen them all. They come and go."

She pushed open the door.

"Not this one," she said.

Through a doorway in the darkness, Arrak could make out rows of seats smeared all over with pigeon droppings, and at the end a small stage, its velvet curtain hung askew.

"What d'you think?" she asked.

Arrak blinked as she leapt nimbly onto the stage. A raddle of pigeons flapped their wings as they clattered along the rafters, pecking and cooing. Above them Arrak could make out the grey smoky sky through a gap in the roof. He watched as the woman strode across the stage and flung her arms aloft.

"Are you going to sing?" he asked.

She shook her head and came to sit beside him, dangling her legs over the edge of the stage.

"My mother sang," she explained. "Sang here every night for the sailors and the traders and the errand boys. She looked so fine in her turquoise robe. It's there now. I keep it for her."

She gestured towards a dusty gown hanging in the wings, its creases faded to the colour of straw.

"Everyone loved her. She used to blow them kisses and I'd stand and watch from the side of the stage while she danced in the flickering flame of the gas lamps. Till the Bride Whose Eyes Could Hypnotise came and carried me upstairs. She would dangle a string of buttons and swing it round and round until I went to sleep."

"Did you live here?"

"Still do," the woman nodded. "Still got my room, up in the loft. I am Vesperene. They called me Smoke Charmer. I used to play with an old tinder box that the Fire Eater gave me. I used to like to light fires, till my mother took the tinder box away. But I always found it again. I knew the games that I wanted to play. I would wake up and watch the strings of buttons still swaying in the wind from the skylight. Then I heard the music, the beating of the drum. And some nights I'd creep down and take a peek and sometimes I'd fall asleep right there on the stair until my mother would come to find me and carry me off to tuck me up in my cot."

Vesperene ran her finger along the back of one of the seats.

"This place is dry," she said, "dry as dust. It's held together by cobwebs now. All the dreams are gone..."

"I'm hungry," Arrak reminded her.

Vesperene smiled.

"Ah yes – so am I."

She led him through a low door beneath the stage. There she lit a lantern to reveal a tiny galley kitchen. Matches and flints were scattered everywhere. The snarling shadows of skulking rats scurried across the top of a grease-spattered stove, but she chased them away with a broom. Then she began to busy herself with pots and pans and spices and herbs.

Arrak stared in surprise at an old grizzled fox lying curled in a box of sawdust in the corner.

"That's Roulin," Vesperene explained. "He was born here, like me. His mother used to sit and howl whenever *my* mother was singing. In the end it was part of the act. She used to come on stage and jump through hoops and skip along a wire. But Roulin only hunts for rats and now he's lame in one leg and he's only one eye."

Roulin glared at Arrak silently. Suddenly Vesperene sneezed as a cloud of pepper flew from a cruet. Roulin sniffed the air and stared around the room as if somebody else had entered, but there was nobody there.

Arrak shivered.

"Are you cold, my dear? Here, this will keep you warm."

She lifted down a scarlet jacket that hung on a peg at the back of the door and draped it around Arrak's shoulders. The collar chafed his neck and the cuffs rubbed his wrists but it was warm and Arrak smiled gratefully. His stomach was rumbling now, he could smell the stew that simmered in the pan.

Vesperene sneezed again, and again the fox turned and peered around. The stew was maize and barley and pieces of shank, seasoned with saffron and pepper. Arrak squinted at Vesperene as he slopped it down.

"This is my favourite," he said, scraping the bowl. "How did you know?"

Vesperene said nothing and turned away, sluicing out the pans. Roulin shifted from his box and slunk over towards her.

"Get away with you," she said.

The fox stared up and she relented, dropping a morsel of meat onto the floor which he quickly gobbled before returning to sit in the corner. In the silence, Arrak could hear the rats scratching behind the wall.

"I should go," he said.

The lantern flickered.

Vesperene turned.

"That's no way to say thank-you for a good hot meal. Won't you stay a while? Don't go yet. You'll get cold. Pull up a seat. That jacket suits you well. Here's a game I can teach you to play."

She produced a small black bag and shook out a set of tiny bones.

"Whose bones are these?" Arrak asked. "Dog or rat?"

Vesperene did not reply, only shuffled them around. Roulin stalked slowly across the floor, his coat grey and grizzled, his tail dragging behind.

"See how many you can catch on the back of your hand," she explained.

Arrak tried. He caught four, but Vesperene caught five. They played on, rattling and clattering the bones across the table top. Soon Arrak had the highest pile.

"You've played this before," Vesperene frowned.

"No – I'm just quick," Arrak replied.

"Play again," Vesperene persuaded. "If you win you can go, but if I win you must stay."

Arrak smiled and stretched. It was warm in this kitchen. His belly was full. He liked this game. Roulin snored softly as

Vesperene shook out the bones. They glowed white beneath the lantern's flickering light. But then she yawned. Her hands moved slowly but Arrak caught the bones deftly.

"There," she said. "You have won. My bed is calling. Now you must leave."

Arrak stood, almost reluctantly, and headed towards the door.

"Wait!" Vesperene's voice stopped him.

"Take off the jacket."

Arrak scowled.

"It keeps me warm," he said.

"It's not yours," she reminded him. "Give it here."

He shrugged the jacket from his shoulders and passed it back at arm's length.

"Now you can go," she said. "Run - before I change my mind."

Arrak closed the door, but not before he heard her call –

"Come again! Come any time you like. Next time you're feeling hungry..."

"Can I bring a friend?" Arrak turned and shouted as he picked his way between the broken seats of the empty theatre.

"No," he heard her reply. "No – you must only come alone."

Fenya and Arrak sat by the river watching the reflections of the boats slide by across the rippling water.

"Why don't we just slip on board?" Fenya sighed. "Why don't we just sail away?"

"Where to?" Arrak grunted. "More like spend days and nights hidden in the hold. Nothing to eat. Nothing to drink."

Fenya sighed again

Arrak shivered.

"I'm cold," he said. "It's always cold down here. Why d'you want to spend all day staring at the water?"

He slung a pebble as far as he could. It sank without a trace

"I'm hungry."

He thought of the Smoke Charmer's bubbling stew. Of the

scarlet jacket warm about his shoulders.

"I'm going to get food." He leapt up suddenly, zigzagging away.

Fenya scrambled to her feet.

"Take me with you," she called.

Arrak glanced back.

"You can't come," his words wafted back. "You got to stay here."

Fenya called again, but he sped away.

Arrak rapped hard on the door. His heart was beating quickly but he was shaking, he was shivering. He was hungry.

The door opened.

"Welcome, Ember," Vesperene greeted him.

Arrak looked around.

"I'm not Ember," he said.

Vesperene took his arm and ushered him inside.

"Here, you are Ember," she said.

He followed her between the rows of broken seats to the dust-choked steps that led down to the kitchen.

"Here is your jacket, Ember," she smiled.

Arrak was about to protest, but the warmth of the soft scarlet cloth hugged his shoulders. Already a pan of shank and maize was simmering on the stove.

"How did you know I was coming?" Arrak asked.

"You are always welcome here."

Vesperene sat striking matches, one after the other until they were scattered across the table. Then she clattered about the kitchen, stirring pots and laying out plates. In the corner sat Roulin, his one eye staring. Arrak stroked the top of the fox's head, ran his fingers down its neck and across its back. Roulin twisted suddenly and sneezed.

"Ember, stop playing with that animal," said Vesperene sharply. "Come and sit here, this stew is done."

The fox had slunk back into the corner. It glowered at the two of them as they supped their stew. And then it sneezed again.

206

"Where do you go?" Fenya accused. "I look out for you. Why don't you look out for me?"

Arrak said nothing.

"Why don't you let me come with you?"

He shook his head and stared at the ground, spat slowly into the dust.

"Where do you go?" Fenya asked again.

Arrak stood and paced up and down, the red jacket draped about his shoulders.

"You look so smart now," Fenya murmured. "Where did you get a jacket like that?"

"It's Ember's jacket," he said.

"Who is Ember? Is he your friend?"

"Got no friends," said Arrak and scurried away.

"They would come here every night," Vesperene gestured from the kitchen out into the looming well of the theatre. "Shouting and clapping their hands. Come to see a boy in a scarlet jacket, just like the one you wear. Come to see him climb to the top of the high rope. Come to see him dive. He would spread his arms just like he was flying. Then at the bottom, the other boys would catch him."

She stared in silence at the stage. "Then one night he fell..."

Arrak waited, but she said nothing more.

Next time Arrak came, the door was wide open. He picked his way between the dancing shadows, down to the kitchen, but no-one was there. He sat and waited, playing with the dead matches strewn across the table while Roulin sat and watched him. The room grew chill and the old fox sneezed, then looked around as if someone had just walked in. But there was no-one. Vesperene did not appear. Arrak watched Roulin watching specks of dust float about the room, then stalking to a bowl in the corner as if expecting to be fed.

There was no food in the bowl. Arrak looked around,

searching for something to give him. In the end, in a dish high up on a shelf, he found a fistful of scraps left over from the day before. He lifted it down and scraped half into Roulin's bowl. The fox hunched over, gobbling quickly, glancing this way and that until the bowl was licked clean, then he sat down and peered around, as if he was watching someone else.

Arrak shivered. He looked to see where the fox was staring, as if someone was standing there. He shook his head. There was no-one. Then he noticed a sewing bag hanging on Vesperene's chair. He picked it up and tipped out strips of faded turquoise cloth, hemmed and tatted into smocks and gloves and a scarf. He wrapped the scarf around his neck and strutted up and down, feeling the warmth of it. But Roulin snarled in protest and he put it back.

Arrak rubbed his belly and rattled the lids of the pans on the stove, wondering how long Vesperene would be. Then he sat at the table and tipped out the bag of bones. He tossed them in the air and caught three, then four on the back of his hand.

A cold draft passed through the room. Arrak sat very quietly, not moving – quiet as the fox and quieter still. He heard a door creak and looked around. There was nobody there, but Arrak sensed that someone was watching. Roulin's one eye narrowed, staring and staring.

Arrak turned. He heard a muffled laughing and felt a hand pressed over his mouth. Soft and warm. He sat quite still without struggling. Vesperene laughed again then let him go.

"Been watching you," she said, wagging her finger, but with a twinkle in her eye. "Been watching you. Every move. You like the scarf?"

She draped it around his neck again.

"It will keep you warm. Long nights coming. Dark and cold."

Arrak looked at her.

"I'm hungry," he said.

"You always are."

Vesperene moved towards the stove. Roulin turned his back

disdainfully and scratched at the bare wooden floor.

Next time Arrak came, he looked first of all where he knew Vesperene might be hiding. Not there. He looked again in cupboards and corners. Not there at all. Only Roulin, pacing and stalking. This time he could find no food to offer.

The fox turned its back on him, then sat down and sneezed as if it had been out all night in the rain, though the day was bright and sunny. But here in the kitchen was gloomy and dull. A door banged open, somewhere far off, in the loft at the top of the building. And then a wind blew through, shivering the curtain of cobwebs that clung to the frame of the door.

Roulin sniffed the air and stalked from the kitchen, turning his head to see that Arrak was following. The fox led him to the foot of a darkened staircase, then step by step they began to climb. Arrak edged forward, treading through rat droppings, groping for the handrail which was splintered and broken. Water oozed through gaps in the plaster and high above his head he heard the flurry of pigeons' wings.

Roulin padded on upward until they came to a room filled with dolls stitched of turquoise cloth, stuffed with straw and dust and feathers. Roulin would not come in. He stood in the doorway, his one eye fixed on the strings of buttons hanging from the ceiling. Arrak went over to look at them and realised they were spinning above a cradle. He stepped closer and peered down.

There lay a baby, gazing up at the buttons. But its eyes did not move. Arrak reached out to touch the pale skin of its cheek. It was cold. The baby lay there quite still.

Arrak looked around. Dead flowers were strewn across the floor and a strong sweet smell clung to the air. In the doorway the fox waited, watching the bright spinning buttons.

Arrak turned. Downstairs he heard the door to the kitchen open and close.

He sat at the table, his head slumped on his arms. Vesperene stared at him, as she twisted the tinder box in her hands. Roulin stalked in through the open door.

"What were you doing upstairs?" Vesperene said at last.

Arrak raised his head slowly, then turned away to stare at the fox. He pulled the jacket from his shoulders and slung it over the back of the chair.

"You will be cold without your jacket," Vesperene chided.

Arrak turned to look at her.

"Who is upstairs?" he asked.

Vesperene smiled.

"That is my son. You've met my son. I call him Ember. Isn't he fine?"

"I thought *I* was Ember," Arrak muttered.

Vesperene paused.

"I must go and feed him now. Put on your jacket, you'll be cold."

Arrak sat down.

He put on the jacket.

As Vesperene began to climb the stairs, his eyes darted about the room. A scatter of vegetable peelings strewn across the floor. Unwashed pans stacked on the stove. Arrak stared at Roulin. Roulin stared at him, and then sneezed.

From high in the building, Arrak heard Vesperene singing, her voice soft and low, a lullaby of shadows. And then her footsteps, back down the stairs. Arrak looked up. In one hand she carried a flaming torch, in the other a candle which she placed on the table.

"We must celebrate," she said. "Today is your birthday..."

The flame flickered close to Arrak's face as she stared at him. On the table stood a line of candles, the first a tiny stub, each one taller than the rest.

"One for every year I have fed you. One for every year I have kept you warm."

She lit the last candle, filling the room with an odour as strong as darkness, and then began singing again. But Arrak leapt up and before she could stop him, he opened the door and scrambled away, out through the darkened well of the theatre, out to the shivering brightness of the street.

He found Fenya sleeping down by the river and shook her urgently till she awoke.

"Why?" Fenya demanded. "Why do you want me to come with you?"

"You want to see where I go," Arrak stated flatly. "You want to see where I get food."

Fenya nodded.

"Where is that jacket you had?" she asked.

"It's not mine," Arrak shrugged. "Belongs to Ember."

"Who is Ember? You never tell me."

Arrak looked away then grabbed her arm, pulling her after him.

"I have to show you."

Fenya gaped at the lines of mildewed seats facing the derelict stage, then peered up at the hole in the roof.

"There's a fox," Arrak explained. "You always wanted to see a fox."

Fenya shivered then sneezed. Arrak pushed open the door to the kitchen. Vesperene was sitting at the table.

"I've been waiting for you," she said, her fingers clutched tight around the tinder box. "Who's this?"

"It's Fenya."

"Who is Fenya?"

"She's a friend."

"I told you not to bring friends."

"She's hungry."

Vesperene gestured to the pan on the stove.

"There's plenty for everyone."

Then she walked out.

Fenya lifted the lid of the pan, drinking in the sweet aroma, but Arrak pulled her away.

"No time for that."

"But I'm hungry," Fenya complained. "You said there

would be food."

"There's something I have to show you."

"Is it the fox?" Fenya asked. "You said there was a fox."

"There is," Arrak replied. "Come with me."

Fenya followed him up the stairs to the room in the loft. She gasped at the turquoise dolls, picking up first one and then another and clasping them to her. Then she saw the cradle and clapped her hands.

"Oh! There's a baby!" she cried. "Why didn't you tell me?"

Her voice dropped low.

"Don't want to wake it."

"Won't wake this babe," Arrak said tersely.

Fenya strained forward.

"Why, Arrak – that's no baby," she exclaimed.

"No," said Arrak. "That's what I wanted to show you."

"Ain't no baby, it's…"

Roulin leapt out of the cradle, turned around slowly and sneezed, then hurried away down the stairs. Arrak peered over Fenya's shoulder. The cradle was empty. A swirl of smoke swept through the building. Downstairs, the kitchen door burst open as they heard the crackling of flames and Vesperene, The Smoke Charmer's voice still singing –

"Ember, my child – where are you? Ember, come to me…"

THE MOUTH OF THE WIND

Morrow slipped messages into bottles and left them all about the city, in gutters, behind barrels, on high window ledges. The next day he would return to see if they were still there. Some had gone, some lay unopened. Some of the bottles were broken. Sometimes the messages had been ripped to pieces, sometimes screwed into a crumpled ball.

But once the stopper of the bottle was missing. There was a shred of paper there, but he knew it was not his message. He tipped the bottle and pressed his finger down the neck until at last he prized out the paper and slowly unfolded it.

"Yes," it said in spindly writing.

But which message did that answer? Morrow could not remember. He had written so many. He scribbled a new one every night – but *"Yes"* was never the answer.

Morrow wrote another message on the back of the paper and pushed it into the bottle. He placed it on the windowsill and watched to see if anyone came. He watched as a cat near knocked it over. He watched as a spider span a web from its neck. He watched as the shadows grew longer and longer. And then he knew he should go, because no-one would come while he watched. But soon as he was gone, a girl came scurrying out of an alley, seized up the bottle and riddled out his message.

She read it and smiled, took a stub of charcoal and scrawled something more on the scrap of paper. And then she put it back and slipped away. The cat came again, and the spider, and in the morning Morrow returned.

He read the new message.

He looked all around.

He waited till no-one was watching, and then he did just what the message said. He cut a button from his jacket and pressed it into the bottle. It rattled and clinked as it rolled around the bottom. Morrow stared. It seemed to be watching him, like it was an eye.

And then he felt someone else was watching as the girl stepped out of the alleyway. She looked at Morrow and looked at the bottle.

"Was it *you* read my message?" he asked hopefully.

The girl smiled and seemed about to speak, then she placed a finger on her lips.

"Did you write *'yes'*?" Morrow wanted to know. But still she said nothing, though she was near laughing now.

Morrow shuffled his feet, then glared at the bottle.

"If you read my message," he said, "then tell me – what did it say?"

The girl was laughing loudly now, but then she stopped and looked down at her dress.

"I seem to have lost a button," she said.

Morrow stared at her.

"That is not an answer," he complained.

"And a bottle is not a question," she replied. "But give it to me anyway. Let me see what is inside."

Morrow handed her the bottle.

Inside was his button.

The girl shook it out.

It lay in her hand, staring at them, as if it was an eye.

"This button will suit me well to sew back onto my dress."

"But the colour is wrong," Morrow objected.

"When you have lost a button," she told him, "any colour will do."

He looked at her then. All her buttons were different shapes and sizes. Her dress was patched about with shades that never would match. She wore one red glove, but the other was green. Her hair hung raven black, shot with silver, decked out with a riot of ribbons. And then he looked at her eyes and saw that one was the deepest brown while the other was ice pale blue.

"Do you not know me?" said the girl, holding out her hand. "You gave me this one red glove."

Morrow looked at her again.

"You are Binnory," he said. "I remember – down by the

canal… but where is the other glove? I gave you the red glove to match the one you lost."

Binnory laughed. "I threw it away," she said. "Threw it in the water and watched it float, like it was a drowning hand."

"But now your gloves don't match," Morrow protested. "The other is green."

Binnory laughed again.

"Don't nothing need to match," she said. "Come with me."

Morrow hesitated.

"Where shall we go?"

Binnory grabbed his hand.

"You have too many questions," she said. "Follow me."

Her fingers were the shadows of fingers, flickering silently, unpicking locks as they made their way down to the waterfront, flitting along darkened passages, skittering through rancid kitchens and sunken cellars, down a labyrinth of tunnels, rat-black and dripping with a stench of decaying rain and the filth which poured from the mouths of gaping drains. Then suddenly down an alley so narrow they scarce could press their way through. Morrow lost hold of Binnory's hand and she seemed to be slipping away, further and further into the dark dankness. Until she opened a door. She stood there and waited while Morrow scrambled after her, then she caught him in her arms and pulled him closer.

Morrow gasped then and tried to kiss her, but she turned her head away.

"Not here," she said, "not here."

She led him inside and closed the door.

In the room was a bare wooden table, in the middle of a cold stone floor. The grate in the corner was choked with embers. Morrow sat down on a rickety chair.

"Why have we come here?" he asked.

"So many questions," Binnory replied.

She frowned at him then.

"Why are the nights so cold?" she whispered. "Where should I go from here? What is the mouth of the wind…?"

"Those are *my* questions," Morrow told her. "How do you know them? What are the answers?"

Binnory moved close to him and smiled.

"You know how I know them."

Morrow gazed about the room and saw a shelf all lined with bottles.

"They are mine," he said.

Binnory nodded.

"Yes," she said. "I brought them here."

Morrow seized one up.

"Where are my messages?" he demanded. "What did you do with them?"

Binnory pointed to the fire.

There in the embers, Morrow saw the charred scraps of blackened paper.

"Did you read them?" he asked.

"They kept me warm," she replied.

She drew him to his feet and guided him to her, hard against the flaking wall. Her breath was soft and slow as she murmured his questions again and urged him to search for the answers in the cradle of her thighs.

He gazed into her eyes and in one he saw a green fish swimming to the moon and in the other was a raven, swallowing the sun. Her mouth it held a nest of moss and her tongue a path of rain. Her fingers meshed in twisting roots as she kissed him nettle-sharp, till he was swathed in a foxglove's sway and drowned in its petals' grasp.

Morrow saw beyond the walls, beyond the cellars clustered round them, beyond the vessels rocking gently, lined along the harbour, beyond the oceans that they trawled all the way to lonely islands. And then he saw Binnory once more, close by him still yet far away, smoothing down her skirt.

She reached to the shelf for one of the bottles and emptied it in front of him. Out tumbled a cascade of buttons which stared at them like a forest of eyes, all of them different colours.

A breeze rattled in the chimney and blew a scrap of charred

paper across the cold stone floor.

"I am the mouth of the wind," Binnory whispered, "and the nights need not be cold. Where would you go but here?"

NOW CAN YOU SEE ME?

Now can you see me – here where I've always been?

I lived in this place before its name was ever spoken. I lived here when just my hut stood alone, beside the slope of the ocean.

Now some come here to work, and some come here to die. Some come to be born and some come here to hide. Some come to find love and others come to cry. Some come in fear and some to find freedom. Some come to stay, and some to travel on, over the rim of the horizon.

And then there are some who come never knowing the reason why. But the river runs on, and the sea and the sky. And when all is dust, I will still be here. Let me tell you…

Also by David Greygoose

Brunt Boggart: A Tapestry of Tales
Hawkwood Books: 2015
Pushkin Press: 2018
Mandrake Petals and Scattered Feathers
Hawkwood Books: 2021

A magical, poetic world of tricksters in an ancient village.
THE OBSERVER

*In Brunt Boggart, David Greygoose conjures a rich, primordial
dreamtime from sullen hedgerows and fields... a wonderful
excavation of the story traditions that our ancestors huddled
around for warmth, and highly recommended.*
ALAN MOORE: 'V for Vendetta'

*These are utterly wonderful new-old tales. In his bones, David
Greygoose understands the rhythms of great storytelling, with
its incantations, repetitions, knowing asides and snappy
dialogue, and he has a frankly marvellous ear for the music of
language. This tapestry is inventive and witty, dramatic and
moving, and deeply earthed in the superstitions and folk beliefs
of old England. Now that I've stepped into Brunt Boggart, I
know that part of me will never leave it.*
KEVIN CROSSLEY-HOLLAND: 'The Arthur Trilogy'

*David Greygoose is a master-storyteller, creating the visceral
netherworld that is Brunt Boggart. Greygoose draws deeply on
the riches of Britain's folklore to conjure up dark and
whimsical tales of an imagined village. I found myself lost in
the wildflower meadows, mossy hollows and wolf pits of Brunt
Boggart.*
EMILY PORTMAN: BBC Folk Awards winner

Brunt Boggart is a skilfully crafted collection of timeless tales which connects the reader on a visceral level. Each is as true a tale as ever was told. Just as a great sculptor sees the divine form within the slab of granite, Greygoose has stripped away all that is extraneous exposing the primal folk-tales which lay buried in us all.
JOHN REPPION: Graphic comic writer, 'Wild Girl' and 'Albion'

It tastes fabulously medieval, it smells uncanny, it looks like the roots of half-forgotten herbs, and it sounds like verbs of thunder and earth.
JAY GRIFFITHS: Author of 'Wild'

A fascinating book by a storyteller immersed in the dark folktales of another time.
BRIAN PATTEN: Liverpool Poet: 'The Mersey Sound'

Brunt Boggart is a totally unique and entrancing book... a carnival cavalcade of misfit performers tumbling over and over... troubadour-tellings that take one step beyond imagining... as loaded with dream-stuff as the golden-brown poppy seed... these are stories with the moon in their eyes and the wind in their hair.
ANDREW DARLINGTON: 'Eight Miles Higher'

Real storytelling stuff – a bit like coming across a newly-written Odyssey.
MARY MEDLICOTT: 'Storyworks'

Folklore and nature collide in Brunt Boggart. Greygoose's inventive language makes these tales a joy to read aloud - in true storyteller style.
ANTONIA CHARLESWORTH: 'The Big Issue in The North'

Brunt Boggart is a beautifully written lyrical novel by a master of language. Rich in imagery and poetic in style, it captivates from the first haunting words and never lets go its hold until the last magical lines. Let me tell you, this is a book once read, never forgotten.
THE FAMULUS

[A] many faceted, finely crafted and genuinely enjoyable book... a piece of work that can be enjoyed equally by aficionados of fantasy, of folk horror and of fairy tale and folklore.
GREY MALKIN: 'MOOF' magazine

An exceptional book, truly original and startling. Greygoose's prose is unique, with more than a passing nod to Dylan Thomas' Under Milk Wood. It is a tapestry, heavy woven with rich spangling threads, and embellished with wondrous gee-gaws and trinkets... surreal dreamscapes, wonderful dream snippets and glimpses into a quasi-medieval past.
XPHAIEA: 'Goodreads'

An almost magical realm full of laughter, fun, mischief, dancing, misdirection, villainy and much, much more. Greygoose cleverly juxtaposes the innocence of fairy-tales with the darkness that often undercuts them. If you're a fan of Hans Christian Andersen or Angela Carter – pick this book up. You'll be reading tales full of folklore and mirth, a route to the imagination that we all so need.
PEACH STREET MAGAZINE

Ancient rituals, prophecy and symbolic transformations litter these stories. Like the great myths from around the world, Greygoose uses the fantastical to present and explain ourselves and each other, with the musical syntax and descriptions of untamed nature lending a completely timeless feel, as if Greygoose merely stumbled onto these ancient texts carved into

the bones of an old tree and decided to write them down... Mandrake Petals and Scattered Feathers is a folklorish, abstract elegy that has the capacity to both disturb and delight in equal measure.
LIVERPOOL STUDENT MEDIA

Weird, enthralling, complex dark fantasy folk tales."
Reading Fox LIBRARY THING

...half-remembered dreams and skeins of folktales bound together on gossamer threads into fantastical whimsical stories... Lovers of Irish folklore, magical world-building, lyrical narrative or even the original Grimm's fairytales will surely fall in love with Mandrake Petals and Scattered Feathers.
INDIEBITES REVIEW

Mandrake leaves are poisonous and have hallucinogenic properties and I found this book hypnotic and intriguing from the beginning. Weird characters and beings, names, and totally unexpected and impossible happenings. I liked the way some characters were woven in and out of some of the stories from beginning to end. Grimm-like in some of its more unsettling incidents and the strange bendings of English gave this an ancient folk-lore, fairy-tale feel to it. Read it twice in a short time. Highly enjoyable!
RAY TILLETT Library Thing

Folklore and fable, sinister witchiness and darkly allusive allegory. Read slowly, these tales will haunt your dreams.
SHINDIG

Unlike anything I've read... The invention on display is breathtaking. The characters display the instinct for survival and brute cunning of Ted Hughes's Crow. Take one story a night, just before bedtime. Repeat as necessary.
INTO THE GYRE

A modern-day masterpiece of storytelling... David Greygoose writes with a passion that leaps off the page.
FOLK HORROR REVIVAL

An amazing accomplishment... original fables filled with phantasmagoria – consistently haunting and atmospheric.
DURA MAGAZINE